The Time of the Chrysalis

A Novel

by
Hélène Dworzan

Translation by Lillian Corti

The Time of the Chrysalis

by Hélène Dworzan

translation by Lillian Corti

First Edition

ISBN-13: 978-0615485027
ISBN-10: 0615485022

Published by LZC publications
Cover Design: Evan Hayes
Cover Art: George Dworzan, 1950

Font: Gentium (Open Font License)

Praise for *Le Temps de la chysalide*

"The realism of this story throbbing with truth is softened by emotional immediacy. The characters, etched in acid, command interest by dint of the human context from which they emerge."
                              --*La Tribune de Genève,*
                                        November 23, 1957

"The narration is vivid, often audacious. As for the depiction of recently liberated Paris, it constitutes an authentic historical background that Hélène Dworzan has painted with a vigor and veracity that deserve high praise."
                              --René Bailly, *Les Nouvelles Littéraires*
                                        September 26, 1957

"A novel replete with a toughness rare in women's writing."
                              --*Le Berry Républicain*
                                        Bourges, October 2, 1957

"A violent and authentic novel about two diametrically opposed characters. In this novel, we are also presented with a portrait of Paris in the aftermath of the occupation that could only have been presented by one who no longer lives there."
                              --*La Nouvelle République du Centre-Ouest*
                                        Tours, September 28, 1957

"Now and then, when confronted with a troubling, desperate and strange book, one feels that one would like to know its author. I would like very much to know Hélène Dworzan. What is the face of the author of this astonishing novel, *Le Temps de la chrysalide?*.... As for her history, it has been that of all the young Jewish girls left orphaned and stripped of everything, washed up on the shores of life. Human wrecks stranded on a great empty beach. Condemned never to find peace again, nor stability, nor happiness....

Whatever may be the dimension of truth in this novel (a large one, in my view), it immediately hits you, jostles you, moves you with its toughness, its discreet cynicism, its characters' will to self destruction. This heart-wrenching book leaves a bitter taste in your mouth.

It is, however, unquestionably an important book and Ms. Hélène Dworzan hereby establishes herself as a great novelist whose progenitors are Dostoievsky…. and Kafka.

This brutal book, which is not to be put into just any hands, offers excellent insight into that era and also into a particular experience of youth. Not at all like that of Françoise Sagan. A lot of drinking may take place in *The Time of the Chrysalis,* but those doing the drinking don't have much to eat; and when they dance, it's not to evade some vague melancholia, but to forget authentic misery.

I realize that I haven't summed the book up. Is it not enough to have described the taste and color of the narrative? If not, here, in a few lines, is an outline of the plot.

Mireille and Saul are brother and sister. After the liberation, they find themselves stranded in Paris without a home, without family, without money, devoured by passion one for the other. While attending medical school, Saul stumbles into alcoholism and the sale of counterfeit goods while his love for Mireille—a love that is pure as well as murky, protective as well as intrusive—brings him to the verge of incest. Mireille fights courageously to save her brother and herself.

This novel, whose secondary characters include a prostitute, an American GI, some crooks and a few penniless "hangers-on"; this sorrowful and violent novel, written in down-to-earth language, ranks among the best of the year."

> --Henri Amouroux
> *Sud-Ouest* (Bordeaux, November 19, 1957)

A LA MEMOIRE DE CHARLOTTE

Translator's Note

As a graduate student at the City University of New York, I worked as an editorial assistant for Dr. Donald H. Reiman at the Pforzheimer Library, where he headed the research team engaged in editing the correspondence of Percy Bysshe Shelley for publication in a multi-volume scholarly work entitled *Shelley and His Circle*. After leaving New York for an academic position in Oklahoma, I resigned from my position at the library, but kept in touch with Dr. Reiman, the most supportive and encouraging of mentors. In 2002, while vacationing on the East Coast, I visited him at his home, where I had the pleasure of meeting his wife, Hélène Dworzan, with whom I sensed an immediate rapport.

In reminiscing about her formative years, Ms. Dworzan mentioned that she had written a novel in French that had never been translated into English. In fact, her book and Françoise Sagan's *Dans un mois dans un an* had both been released by Julliard on the same date in 1957. Although *Le temps de la chrysalide* had been critically acclaimed, its reception had been somewhat eclipsed by the eagerly awaited latest work of the already famous Sagan.

Upon volunteering to read Dworzan's book, I was amazed that work of such evident quality had so long remained unavailable to English-speaking readers. A beautifully written and genuinely moving narration, *Le temps de la chrysalide* presents the unadorned portrait of a great metropolis emerging from an excruciating historical ordeal. As soon as I finished it, I determined to translate it into English.

Having produced a first draft of the translation while on sabbatical in Italy during the spring of 2007, I thank the faculty and staff of the American Heritage Association in Macerata for their collegial support during my sojourn there. I am most thankful for the generous assistance of colleagues at the University of Alaska: Sandra Boatwright and Richard Carr read the draft and offered helpful observations on the text; Susan Todd provided generous assistance in technological matters. Finally, I am grateful to Stephen A. Nimis and Evan Hayes of Miami University in Oxford, Ohio, for their invaluable assistance in the preparation of the manuscript.

About the Author

Hélène Dworzan was born in France and fled southward with her family in the exodus prompted by the advancing German army in 1940. During the chaotic flight from the city, her mother and two of her sisters were separated from the rest of the family. Moreover, the slender resources on which they all had to live were quickly exhausted. An armistice having been negotiated with the Germans, many of the fleeing Parisians were persuaded that their government would protect them. Thus encouraged to return, the family was reunited in Paris after an absence a few months. By May of 1942, when the collaboration of the Pétain/Laval regime with the Nazis became manifest, the family abandoned all hope of escaping as a unit, but Hélène managed to make her way to Free France on her own. During the year she was away from Paris, her parents and one of her sisters were deported to Auschwitz, where they were killed.

Under an assumed identity, Hélène returned to Paris, hiding out with friends. In 1947, she married the American painter, George Dworzan, with whom she moved to the United States in 1950. After attending writers' workshops at the New School for Social Research, she worked as a translator and language teacher. She married Donald H. Reiman in 1975.

An active member of the New York literary scene, Hélène Dworzan served as associate editor of *Chelsea*, a literary review, from 1970 to 1981, founding the Continuum series of poetry and fiction readings in 1970 and continuing to direct that program until 1976. In addition to her critically acclaimed novel, *Le Temps de la Chrysalide,* she has written short stories and poems that have appeared in various publications. The Dial Press presented her with an award for fiction in 1953 and she won a Prairie Schooner prize for fiction in 1978. In 1990, she collaborated with Donald H. Reiman on the editing of *Shelley's Last Notebook.*

The Time of the Chrysalis

Chapter 1

On that day, at the Bagneux cemetery on the outskirts of Paris, a funeral with no corpses was about to take place. The chestnut trees in full flower stood out against the blue and gold of the July sky, casting long pointy shadows on the pathways. The blazing heat of the summer sun was so intense that those in attendance, uneasy in their mourning garments, had opened up large old-fashioned umbrellas, as if to shield from unwonted mirth a past replete with tender memories.

Such memories as: images of red and green tops, one-armed dolls draped in mauve velvet, cheeks moist with tears prompted by bad dreams which relaxed the muscles of Mireille's face, taut with present sorrow. It had been a long time since she had thought about all that was past, having carefully buried it in her most secret depths, waiting, to awaken it, for the restoration of peace. As long as the dead were not buried, they were not quite dead, and everything was yet possible, even the past.

Now that it was all about to be brought to a close, she would think about it more often; or maybe, on the contrary, never again. A bitter taste filled her mouth: with no past, what kind of being would she become?

Her eyes turned toward the few blades of grass stubbornly pushing up between the sterile flagstones, the Jewish tombs. What better symbol of the utter uselessness of the dead, of their incapacity to rejoice, even in memory? And as at other moments when she had sensed that death was so close she could smell it, her hands began to perspire. She wiped them on the coarse cloth of her skirt, then slipped one of them into the hand of her older brother Saul, seeking to share the certainty, the strength that enabled him to stand up straight, his face composed if not calm, his limbs so relaxed that but for the gray veil of sadness casting its shadow over his calm face, one might have assumed that what was about to take place had nothing to do with him. She felt proud of him; proud of his manly power, his intelligence, almost pardoning him for the web of espionage he cast about her, his rules which compelled her submission, first by pleading then by threats, which, sometimes, in secrecy and silence, prompted her to hate him. Having pressed their moist hands lightly together, they separated. It seemed to her that a woman waiting in back of her was eyeing them reproachfully. She felt like turning around and shouting: "Can't you see that he's my brother?" But why should she care what that woman thought? She had more serious concerns: if the rabbi didn't show up soon, she would never have time to get back to the studio in time for Sarand's rehearsal and that would mean two hundred francs less at the end of the month. After laying out three thousand francs for this M. Berger (benevolent treasurer of the Temple Quarter's Society for Deportees), she would not even have enough left to pay for her room at the hotel. Old Dufour was not about to wait: "Cash only, Mademoiselle, and in advance; you know very well, I'm only the manager..." No point in turning to Saul, she knew very well what prodigious feats of persuasion he had pulled off in order to get his share of the six thousand francs together. Six thousand francs for a show funeral, to have two prayers said, have the names of their parents engraved on a black marble pyramid, so as to keep them alive after all, if only *in memoriam*. Six thousand francs. Two months' labor; she closed her eyes in shame at the thought of what Saul would think if he knew that in this moment, when she should be rapt in meditation, her head was occupied with gross monetary calculations. Yet she recalled how he argued with this stout M. Berger, who looked at him from under heavy eyelids, like a fat spayed housecat: "This is a swindle, six thousand francs to bury some shadows..." How ugly it had all been! Finally, despite his misgivings, in order to please his sister and dry up her tears, he had said, "Yes," reluctantly.

"It's more than an hour that we've been waiting here," she heard him say. "You'll see, he won't show up. I knew it. I told you so; but it's impossible to get anything through your thick skull..."

The trace of a smile lifted the corner of his lips--she could sense his anger.

"Are you mad at me because I insisted on doing this or because it bothers you to be kept waiting? In any case, it was your idea to get here early."

"Just drop it."

He was getting upset. As always, he could not keep still. His quiet moments were like the calm before the storm. As always, he was in a hurry to get someplace, but once he got there, he was in a hurry to leave; always in a hurry to be somewhere else and nowhere at all. It was as if he could not stand himself, or as if one part of him was always trying to lose the other without ever managing to do so, the two of them always running into each other on the same corner of the future. Then, as if a mirror had suddenly reflected his agitation back to him, he got hold of himself, apologized, and the whole thing would start all over again, more or less the same as before.

The sun seemed to be hanging by a thread over the trees, burning and melting flesh and leaves. Without stockings, her clogs were rubbing blisters into her heels; the blisters had burst and the wounded flesh was sticking to the leather and biting like a burn. She ought not to have sold her shoe coupon to pay... Just what was it? There were so many things to be paid for! On the road to Chartres, six years before, she saw herself again, the burden of a little girl in Saul's arms, close to his heart, while overhead, in the galvanized sky, jets of blinding fire pierced the green sky of the countryside.

"Go sit in the shade," Saul said, as if able to guess that she could not bear up any longer. "Go. I'll keep your place." He wore a bitter expression as he said this, his face creased by a smile that lifted only one corner of his mouth. Mireille noticed large circles of moisture darkening his jacket underneath the armpits.

"No, you go."

"For pity's sake! Stop arguing and just go," he said curtly.

She remembered those evenings without light in that barn where they had taken refuge during the occupation, in particular, the week when, thanks to their stubbornness, what had been the last, blessed piece of bread turned into a moldy crust. It was this burdensome solicitude that had gradually worn down all good intentions, stamped out good will, reduced innocent thoughts to a state of simmering resentment. The die was cast—he would give the orders and she would obey--with rage in her heart. It should have been possible for her to break the repetitive pattern of events, twist it, cast it in some new form so as to alter the course of the future, but Saul was stronger than she.

Under the wide spreading branches of the chestnut tree, the shade was sweet and fresh as twilight. Letting herself down onto the thick lawn, Mireille unfastened her shoes. But beyond the amber glimmerings on the pathway, Saul's silhouette haunted her. Unaware at that moment that she was watching him, he slackened, shoulders hunched over, cutting a poor figure in the grubby hat he had rented from the gatekeeper for this occasion, a hat too small for him, so that it perched on the top of his head like a mitre.

"What are you thinking?" she asked him, limping back to his side.

Startled, he looked up.

"Oh, I don't know. Anyway, you made me lose my train of thought."

"This pyramid, do you think it will be big?"

"What questions you ask! How should I know?"

At this biting response, which she took to mean she was talking too much, Mireille felt chastened.

"See if I ask you anything again soon.... You know, you don't need to talk to me like that, especially at a time like this."

"Precisely."

Saul's long nose had begun to quiver. That and his way of smoothing back his long gray hair was a sign, either of strong emotion or great anger. Mireille moved close to him.

"Now," she said, hoping to please him, "we'll be like the others. We'll have a tomb where we can go to pray."

"An empty tomb," he said, absently.

Then, suddenly going pale, he turned fiercely, grabbed her arm just above the elbow and squeezed until she moaned:

"You're hurting me!"

"We'll never be like the others, understand? Never! And the sooner you get used to it, the better!"

And as he uttered these words, begrudgingly, as if, somehow, trying to convince himself of just the opposite, a childish, almost superstitious fear froze his face. It seemed to Mireille as if the sharpened edge of some invisible blade had just cut into him. How much truer than hers was his sorrow! Once again, she had to bow her head before his superiority. But did he not understand that by dint of being so firmly rooted inside him for so long, his sorrow had become a chronic disease with which he had learned to live quite comfortably?

He had no right to expect, that at the age of twenty, with a war behind her, she should be willing to bury herself in sorrows that she was hardly willing to feel any more; that she did not want to feel at all, and which, nevertheless, would not fade away, and despite her prayers, insisted on waking her up at night.

No. Each and every one of them had to remember forever. Everybody must hear, over and over again, as if pursued by a delirious nightmare, the gun butts of the Germans breaking down doors held back by Jews in nightclothes soaked with the sweat of pure horror. Let them tremble at this memory, as she had trembled four years earlier, hidden with Saul behind a lace curtain, in the apartment of his friend,

Marcel, who lived across the street. The memory of parked trucks filling up with ashen faces, while your heart swells, like a sac ready to burst with the pus that is fear for yourself, compelling the flow of a single, solitary instinct, the instinct of self-preservation. The burning instinct that does not dry up, no matter how bitter the insults endured. The sun of this July morning is a vision of the future, precious, fragile. You watch the ashen faces, fearful of betraying you, carefully turned away from that window. You do not think of risking your life. You tell yourself that God sees everything, knows everything, and in the secret recesses of the heart that is powerless by dint of being human, you turn toward HIM and insult HIM. You tell yourself black lies that make your nerves tremble like an open wound. You feed yourself with empty hopes while following wild-eyed, in devilish detail, the various destinies prescribed by this eternal God whose benevolence you now implore. You admit to yourself that you are not heroic, and it's a truth that hardly wounds you, since the discovery itself seems something of an accomplishment. You tell yourself that life belongs to the young. All the while breaking out in cold sweat, you hold on to a brother who is also looking into his heart, is also transfixed by the hatred and impotence he finds there; a then twenty-year-old brother whose hair, in the heat of a golden July, has suddenly turned gray. Eyes shut with shame as much as with horror, in the night of absurdity into which they are driven, their sharpened imaginations create a blinding snowfall that envelops the world in glimmering silence. Upright and naked, trees burst out of the suffocating earth and a swollen, violet corpse hangs from every branch like the grotesque forms that a sick person discovers on the ceiling in the shadows of delirium. Underneath fingernails, window panes squeak, grating on nerves like the cries of the tortured. Across the way, the windows are open and the panel of the curtain is hanging sideways at the end of its twisted curtain rod.

"If they had gotten us also, that wouldn't have done anybody any good," she said.

Facing out into the street, Saul answered: "No. None at all." Then, softly, with a phantom of hope in his voice: "Maybe they'll come back."

And now, did he remember? With irony and rage in his heart, did he recall the years of religious hope, which, at the end of all the promises, landed them here, in front of an empty tomb?

He seemed calmer now. Sorrow grew dull after four years of waiting and living with hopes that, from the beginning, they knew to be as fragile as a cloud. Sorrow had been refined, transformed into regret. Regrets were not such burdensome things. She searched through the caverns of her memory, trying to retrieve the image of her mother, whom she so resembled, with the same pale freckled skin, the same rust-colored hair, and her sweet, warm lips, which, at night, would chase nightmares away.

And if it was true that death is not the end of everything? She searched anxiously around herself for some sign of certainty in the light of day. She focused on her skin, ready to detect the lightest touch, and to interpret it. But nothing shuddered, either on her skin or in the blue sky. A cry rose in her throat, demonstrating, somewhat reassuringly, the fragility of the shield by which she had assumed she was protected from the flashing of molten rock which beams out from the sun, vigorously projecting its rays outward even as it softens them.

Moving closer to Saul, she sensed a heaviness in the air, the sweetish and slightly sickening odor of the perspiration that was moistening his jacket. The thought suddenly crossed her mind that this was the odor of those flowers that people lay out on the flattened chests of the dead in funeral parlors. That underneath their shrouds of swaddling bands, Egyptian mummies must smell like that. Like the surface of a sarcophagus, Saul's face was expressionless, as if painted, inanimate, a face that she recognized by its name rather than its flesh, its odor, but whose features, frozen into almost absolute calm, did not suggest any familiarity, any hint of the face that he must, like everyone else, be wearing inside. She was stricken with the sight of him. "This is my brother," she said to herself. "He is twenty-four years old, a medical student; he tutors empty-headed schoolboys; he has holes in his shoes; he has a girlfriend named Simone who sells God-knows-what kind of trinkets for guys. He gives me orders and I obey. Who is he? My brother. And what, exactly, does that mean? OK, we have the same mother and father. And beyond that?"

The sound of mumbled words drew her out of the silence into which she had withdrawn. Somebody was putting his conscience in order, and a smothered sob warned her not to look around. Somebody was taking this ceremony seriously. Mireille cast a furtive glance at her large men's style wristwatch. And what if Saul was right? What if the whole thing were nothing but a monstrous swindle? If the rabbi were never to show up, the funeral service never to take place? If there would never be any marble monument gleaming with the names of the immortalized dead. What if they went back to Berger, demanding a refund of their six thousand francs, and found nobody there but a paralytic old woman lying on a cot, who had never heard of Berger, except for voices in a distant fog? And all these people in mourning? Figures on a stage who, at the appointed hour, would perform like puppets. That would explain the odor of flowers.

Sweat trickled down Saul's cheeks like a stream of tears flattened by a man's fist.

"I'm beginning to wonder if you weren't right," said Mireille.

Saul was too weary to respond. He was trying to remember the words and the remote significance of the prayer for the dead. Those words by which their parents had lived, and for which they had died. *Chosen* by God. He guessed at the mute prayer they must have taken with them to their deaths, appealing all the while to a God who punished so harshly, the better to love them. They had invented sins for themselves in order to justify Him, so that the world would not be torn apart by their damning cries, so that one star might still shine out for them in the night of the oven, that the oven itself might become the firmament at night when a god sparkling like the sun reached out to them with one last tender sign of light.

In a little while, far from innocence, with the secret sneer characteristic of blasphemy, which exhausted sorrow can provoke, he would pray. He would pronounce the words of a language long dead, dead as his faith. Soul, an envelope memory gives to a name we no longer pronounce and can only evoke. A slab of powerlessness was weighing down on his chest. Nothing emptier than the void left by evaporated faith. So much so that, in the sunlight fanning out through golden specks of dust, he could see his own death. His death finally giving way beneath the weight of crushing duties, digging little black ditches in his brain at night when, stretched out completely dressed on his unmade bed, he thought: "One ought to have understood, to have been able to choose, before having to promise."

Four years earlier, he had promised, all in a single breath exalted by emotion, to take the place of his father for Mireille if circumstances required. Now the promise was consecrated, and the only one who could have released him from it had been swallowed up by the indifference and simplicity of death.

With shame, he recalled the night before, when, bent over his anatomical diagrams, he determined to consecrate himself entirely to studying for the next exam, sweat pouring off of his face, depositing transparent pearls on his hands. And suddenly, throwing the book against the wall, seeing the plaster dented, crumbling, the book torn in two, while, unrecognizable to himself, he crushed his head between his fists, looking for but unable to find himself. It was as if some impostor, having dealt him a mortal blow, had carried him off behind the walls of a city in ruins.

He opened the eyes he had closed the better to

struggle in the eddying sand. The sun was burning his eyes. Mireille's hair, bathed in the light of the sun, sparkled like burnished copper. How beautiful she was, he thought, with the redheaded pallor she got from her mother, and her fine unalloyed Hebraic features. He had never noticed that, despite its rounded curve, her chin showed signs of obstinate strength. It occurred to him that he would have more trouble getting her to do as she was told than he had imagined. Beneath her faded blue cretonne blouse, which no longer fit since she had lost weight, he sensed her lithe firmness, and the memory of his promise came back to reproach him. Then, like a safety-valve, the sensual face of Simone intervened, her juicy lips covered with the traces of biting kisses, her licorice eyes speaking softly of erotic sojourns, while her shadowy curls spread out in a perfect circle on the pillow. To make her angry, he would threaten to shave her head, and his hand would close over the plump brown breast that he might have liked better if it had been paler, pinker, more fragile. The last time he had seen her, that breast, at the moment of disappearing into her rayon slip, still bore the marks that his fingers, feverish with the urgency of impotence, had left on the surface of her skin. "Are you crazy?" she had cried, pushing him away. "I'm not made out of potter's clay! Are you trying to give me a tumor!" He had answered: "If I can't make you feel good, I'll have to make you feel bad. You can hardly refuse me that!" He had laughed when he said it, nevertheless hiding, behind eyelids closed in laughter, the shame that was turning him inside out. Then, with the self confidence of a sensual being who understands nothing except for her own beauty, she had assured him that the next time he would do better.

Mireille's hair was flaming in the sun. It weighed on the air like perfume, and when she impatiently shook her head, it rippled over her back like a wave.

Suddenly, his long black coat brushing against his calves and the *siddur* wedged under his arm, the rabbi strode forward, regal as a king. Everybody started moving forward with the rabbi leading the procession.

Two gravediggers, sitting on an embankment, smoked while waiting for them. Hidden and demure beneath a gray drape, the pyramid rose up before them. How little and humble it seemed! This is not what Berger promised us, not at all, thought Mireille. In front of the monument, they had dug a sort of a pit. She thought of all those dead who had not had the time to know they were dying, reduced to cinders in an instant on the airfield at Chartres, or riddled with machine gun fire shot from twenty yards up in the air; she recalled other pallid cadavers, completely clean, fallen at the side of the road, lying peacefully beside a disemboweled horse. You saw them now, transformed into crosses in roadside cemeteries. But those others, gnawed away as they were by death, every day a bit more, in these strongholds beyond which nobody ever thought of them except as the already dead, perhaps we should build them an *arc de défaite*, Monument to the Defeated.

The rabbi bowed down with dignity, grabbed a panel of the drape, and with a grandiose, self-important gesture, slowly, in an almost obscene manner, uncovered the vibrant black stone of the pyramid.

A silence as thick as oil spread out over the whispering crowd. A silence that was heavy, unanimous, stupefied. Then the resentment exploded. Not only was the monument far from approaching the dimensions promised by that thief, Berger, but worse yet, the names were hardly legible. Overlapping, suffocated by lack of space, they seemed to jostle each other, fight with each other for the light of day, without dignity, without a face: like cadavers in a common grave.

Quarrelling broke out. People wanted, in the two centimeters of space left, way at the top, an inscription, some inspirational phrase such as: "To those who died for their country." Somebody suggested insistently: "To the martyrs of France."

The rabbi smiled at the gravediggers with a sheepish expression. He really must have felt a bit awkward, this rabbi.

He was doing what he could, with the appearance of not getting to eat every day himself, his little body almost hidden in his great, royal coat. Indulgently, he waited for people to calm down. Most likely, the business of presiding over the burial of corpses had taught him something about patience.

"So, are we going to allow ourselves to be taken in, just like that?" Mireille protested.

Saul shrugged his shoulders. "Well, you know, when it comes to letting ourselves be taken in, it's gotten to be something of a tradition..."

The others were still squabbling. One of them called another a big fathead. But all agreed to register a protest, with words that would wrench the heart with both shame and pity.

"Now have you finished with your idiocies?" A woman with a swollen face had gotten out of line. She allowed her tears to flow without even attempting to wipe them, but her voice was cutting: "Where do you think you are? In the *Carreau du Temple*? Not that you give a damn about the dead. You're just afraid you won't get your money's worth."

"OK. We'll have them put: 'Dedicated to the martyrs of the Nazi war' and let's not talk about it any more."

The last was uttered in a timid voice, and from the silence that followed, it appeared that everyone was in agreement, even those who had heretofore only participated hesitantly in the discussion. They had withdrawn a few paces, intimidated by the clamor. Among the many who would remain frightened and mute for the rest of their lives, they were people for whom neither family nor tribe existed any longer, only strangers who assumed the gigantic proportions of adversity and danger.

"Is that OK with you?" Saul asked Mireille.

"Why should it matter, at this point?"

She would have liked to feel Saul's strong arms around her, feel the fierce male heart beating in his breast, but she didn't budge.

When the rabbi opened his *siddur*, a metro ticket fell

out of its folds and circled slowly down to the bottom of the grave. The first shovelful buried it. It was that sound, hollow as a death-knell, that led Mireille's spirit back toward the dead. The hard wooden handle was placed in her hands. The rabbi pushed her slyly, saying:

"Repeat after me, let's go, the others are waiting, and it's hot."

He had been eating onions and she could smell it. She repeated the meaningless sounds without looking into the grave where one might suddenly have found millions of shattered bodies piled up; in front of her eyes was the face of M. Berger, fat with sin.

One shovelful, two, three. Falling onto nothing, onto the void. And up there, God who sees everything, who understands and knows his job, his work. *Who will pardon God?*

To bury the dead, quickly! Bury them deep, and let's not talk about them anymore. The matter is closed. It was a nice funeral; everybody cried; there were even small children. One could almost have believed it was real.

"Only three shovelfuls," the rabbi whispered in her ear.

He is furious. There she goes, ruining his carefully orchestrated ceremony. Five shovelfuls, seven, nine, and another for good measure.

At the end of the pathway stands the high gate of remembrance.

Six thousand francs down the drain, observed Saul softly, dreamily, passing his arm around Mireille's shoulder.

He stopped for a moment at the gate to return the hat to the gatekeeper and collect his deposit.

Chapter 2

Every evening, Mireille stopped at the corner of la rue d'Anvers and boulevard Rochechouart to look up at the dome of the Sacre Coeur reaching up into the sky like a great cry of sorrow. There, she would reconnect with her fear of the great solitude to come and imagine herself ground down by age, habit, and resignation, extending her empty, worn palms up into an indifferent night.

At the hour when the violet twilight fades into the yellow night of streetlights, she was standing alone with Gérard in the open space in front of the church. The diffuse light illuminated Gérard's face as he leaned over, his elbows on the balustrade. Down below, the garden was quiet. She was quiet; Gérard was quiet. Silence had descended upon the world. No longer any possibility of avoiding explanations. With his savage nostrils and bitter lips, Gérard had what Saul mockingly described as "the perfect face for a *poète maudit*. For the one who loved him, it was a sensitive face revealing as if in stark relief, the imperceptible vibrations, the buried pulsations of his most intimate depths. Hearing him transform old worn-out words into entirely fresh mysteries, she felt herself turning into someone extraordinary. By his side, she was no longer the simple creature that Saul could form to suit himself. She became his inspiration; she was sacred. But this evening, the magician had nothing to say. His penetrating gaze seemed to go right through her, as through a sheet of glass, and extend out toward the infinite. It was suddenly as if she no longer existed.

Finally, she said: "You're cross with me because I couldn't come on Sunday. But I explained all of that over the phone."

"Ah yes,.... the telephone. Just what would become of us without it? And how long will you have this evening before you have to run off like a little thief?"

"Oh, he doesn't know that I'm here."

"And it doesn't bother you to have to lie like that? The things he manages to get you to do."

"They aren't really bad lies. It's as if he were my father."

"Mireille, don't play dumb. I can't stand it. If you have to make excuses, at least take the trouble to think up something intelligent."

"I am not making excuses. And I don't owe you any explanations."

She tried to take the high ground but only succeeded in sounding pathetic.

"If it was just to tell me all these nice things that you begged me to come meet you here, you might at least have had the decency to warn me. Go ahead and shrug your shoulders. At least I know where I stand now. Saul was right: you're all alike, there's only one thing that counts."

"Great. Now you've become his mouthpiece, his echo."

Confronted with this contemptuous tone, she did not know what to say. Speech was beyond her. Only gestures could still talk. To be able to throw herself against him, hug him, make him feel her physical embrace, the intensity of her helplessness. Her arms were ashamed, the trees in the garden already pale with winter's white bloodletting.

"I've never expressed myself any other way," she said defiantly.

"Shut up. For the love of God, shut up. You'll ruin everything, even the memory of everything."

His words ran through her like pointed shards of ice. It was only fair that he should suffer too. "Then spare me. Tell me it's over and let's not talk about it any more," she said, in contradiction to the unspoken clamoring of her entire being.

A cutting response would have brought her back to reason and reality, but his word wizardry had dried up. He looked at her without anger, without reproach, with a sort of pity more humiliating than any insult.

"Gérard... I was hurt. I didn't know what I was saying."

"Would you come to Morocco with me? I'll find work there, in construction, whatever. I wouldn't mind if my hands got tough, Mireille. In fact, making love to you with toughened hands..."

"Morocco. It might as well be at the end of the world."

"Would you be afraid? But the end of the world could be anywhere at all, within easy reach, or as far away as the stars."

Stunned, she clung to his fine hands. He drew her close to him, seeking her lips. Stiffening her back, she struggled free.

"This is madness," she said. "You can't begin to understand. You don't owe anything to anybody. You're free to do whatever you want."

"You could be too. It's entirely up to you. I'm not forcing your hand."

"In any case, I just can't pack my suitcase and take off without telling anybody... Don't look at me like that. You have no right. Nobody has the right. It's not human."

"And your brother? He has the right to watch you fade away? Why are you turning away from me? Are you afraid that I might be right?"

"Gérard, don't be mean."

She placed her hands tenderly on his shoulders. "Be patient. Someday..."

Enraged, he lost patience: "You're cheating. You just close your eyes and lie to yourself."

"You just want to hurt me. Oh. Why else would you say that? To punish me? Everyone wants to punish me. As if there were nobody in the world to punish but me. You talk to me in that sickly sweet tone of voice, all the while sizing me up... as if you were a spider. You wait until I've caught my breath and then you start up again and you keep on until you get me to do just what you want."

"Too bad you don't have the courage to say that to

your brother."

"See. You're doing it on purpose. You trip me up with words. You set them up like a trapper's snares."

"That sounds like something Saul would say. You don't have it in you."

"But it's right on target. Proves he's got a better handle on things than I do."

"Mireille, remember..."

"No. Leave me alone. I can see you coming. You'll start by telling me how much you love me and before I know it you'll be all over me with your needs."

"You're wrong. I ask nothing more of you. Come on. Wish me 'bon voyage'--like a big girl."

She turned away from the hand he offered her. A trickle of shame was burning on her cheeks. The sound of Gérard's footsteps faded away into the night.

"He's going down the steps," she told herself, wheeling around to reach out to him.

It was already too late. In her distress, she found herself wishing he were dead.

For an entire week, every evening, she was to be seen at the Sacre Coeur, the ghost of a memory haunting the open space in front of the church, hoping to catch sight of a man who would not be coming back again.

Every morning, she huddled behind the door of the hotel, waiting for the postman to arrive. The envelope that he finally delivered one day was typewritten and bore the heading of the Criminal Investigation Department. It contained a summons requiring Mlle. M. Goldine to present herself at the Quai des Orfèvres the following day at ten o'clock. Staggering, she fell back against the wall, overwhelmed by the vision of Gérard, chalk white, rigid and stiff in death, waiting for her to come and identify him. It could not have anything to do with Saul. She had seen him just the night before. As for herself, there was no reason why anybody might want to serve her a summons. Yet if... Oh it was just too stupid to be so afraid; we were no longer under the thumb of the Boches. "It must be Gérard," she told herself. He's gone and killed himself." And this *death* was her doing. In a moment of sorrow, she had wished it and death had come running, happy, for once, to be welcomed. But the things we say in a rage of sorrow and humiliation—surely they don't count.

Back up in her room, she leaned against the window, waiting for the relief of tears. Saying good-bye to life, since she was guilty; saying good-bye to sounds and colors, she would live like a widow; Gérard's features would melt into her inner being, would live in her like the eternal sentiment of futility which would be his mark on her. The fog would close in on a world where her fault would render her a prisoner forever. In the evenings, lonely as a widow, she would search through her intimate linens for the pages on which he had confided, like petals preserved in a herbarium, the thoughts and images which had touched her heart. This virgin widowhood would be her mystery. She would wear it like a hair shirt. On her way home from the studio, she would stop off to see Ivan, the door-keeper; she would take comfort and consolation in the broken dreams harbored in the heart of the old man, formerly a dancer with the Russian Ballet, whose leg, broken during his last performance, had remained permanently rigid when the plaster cast came off. He would serve her steaming hot tea from the great simmering samovar, and he would look out at her from his clear Ukrainian pupils, full of sorrow. She would be engulfed in black, and because Gérard had been Christian, she would ask Ivan to light candles in front of the great icon of antique gold. They would keep the door closed so that the draught would not blow out the candles, and Ivan would move about with great dignity, careful to drag his stiff leg as little as possible so as not to make noise. He would put a drop of rum in their tea, partly in honor of the saints, partly to take their minds off sad thoughts.

Saul would understand none of it. She had hit upon

her expiation. She would be a tormenting enigma to him, pale and mute as the death she carried inside her like a coffin. But at the very idea of his long tragic face, at the thought of seeing grief in his ashen eyes, her desire for revenge melted into tenderness. Compared to Saul's suffering, what did Gérard's death mean to her? To tell the truth, she hadn't believed it for a moment. As Gérard would have said, "It was nothing but poetry."

Nevertheless, her old atavistic fear of the police worried her all day, so much so that when she got to Sarand's studio, she found she had forgotten to close the window, thus exposing the contortionist to the danger of getting chills and fever.

In front of the door at the office to which she had been summoned, she hesitated. She imagined a face with vague, hostile features, manifesting the power conferred on it by a uniform, a power multiplied by hundreds of similar leviathans whose cleated boots make such a terrifying racket when pounding on pavement at night. Recalling Saul's dignity, she pulled herself together as he would have done and went on in.

Somber, with the musty odor of closed-up rooms in municipal libraries, the office, its windows covered by rain-streaked dust, was as quiet as a church. Only the bottom row of windows had been cleaned, and the transverse bars of the window frames were encrusted with bird droppings. A rustling of papers, the dry noise of a drawer being closed with impatience transformed the silence that followed into a heavy, oppressive mass. On tiptoe, she moved closer to the desk, behind which sat a man in his forties wearing a dark checked suit, rolling a cigar sticky with saliva around between his lips as he watched her walking toward him. How did he manage to maintain such a tranquil expression when she was so distraught? In an agreeable tone of voice, he invited her to take a seat, but the title of police inspector was sufficient to dig a sort of a moat around him, transforming him into a fortress from which an assailant could rush out at any moment. Full of misgivings, Mireille slipped the summons onto the desk and mumbled that she preferred to remain standing.

Continuing to suck on his cigar, he examined the sheet of paper, then announced:

"Mireille Goldine, twenty years old, single, profession: accompanist. You are a minor and you don't live with your parents."

"They died in the camps. I don't see what is the point..."

"Don't worry, we'll get around to that."

His gaze, resting on her, was direct and penetrating.

"Since when have you been living at the Hotel de la Paix?"

"For a year."

"What's the matter? Do I frighten you?"

"Who me? Why should I be afraid of you?" She heard the trembling in her voice and lowered her eyes.

"It's ten after ten." He laughed. "You know, ever since you came in here, you've been sneaking peeks at your watch. Let's get this straight—we don't summon people for the fun of it."

He threw his cigar onto the floor and crushed it under his shoe. It sounded viscous and sticky like a snail. With a movement of his foot, he tossed it out of sight, under the desk. He smiled with a pleasant expression, but then, she had seen pleasant expressions below many an S.S. helmet.

"Hard times, eh?" he remarked, running a practiced eye over Mireille's clothing.

She felt herself turning pale under his probing gaze which, one by one, examined her mended buttonholes and unmatched buttons, the darned patches at the corners of her pockets.

"Bah! As long as you manage to get by. Speaking of which, your neighbor, Denise Rabaud, she seems to know her way around. You can tell by the way she dresses...no doubt, she must be having one hell of a lucky streak."

He flashed her a conspiratorial smile which shed light on the entire interview. This changed everything. So it was Denise he was so interested in.

"I have to tell you," she observed with studied indifference, "I never notice what other people are wearing."

"Then you're no ordinary woman."

Of the two of them, he was clearly the clever one. She would have to be extra careful. Avoid saying anything whatsoever which might inadvertently hurt Denise, and also avoid enigmatic answers that might suggest she was trying to hide something. Dodge the question and still hit the target.

"What's she done?" she asked with a naïve expression.

"Why, nothing, Mademoiselle. Nothing whatsoever. But we have to get information from all over. Just a matter of knowing what's happening."

He leaned forward in a confidential manner.

"Look here, a woman who is not regularly employed, with no apparent source of revenue, well. At a certain point, you begin to wonder—how, all of a sudden, can she afford such luxury?"

"I have to tell you, I'm not the kind to ask indiscreet questions."

"Look, it would really be best if you didn't try to outsmart me."

The inspector's eyelids had grown heavy and the muscles around his mouth stood out under his pale, clumsily shaved skin. He too, had little patches at the corners of his pockets.

"I wouldn't think of it, Monsieur."

"OK. Then make a little effort. Don't make me worm the answers out of you.

"I am not hiding anything, Monsieur. I don't know anything."

"You'll have to allow me to be the judge of that. In fact, hotel room walls are thin. Without even trying to listen, sometimes you can't help hearing things..."

"If I had known you were going to question me, I would have paid attention..."

"Look, I don't want to have to tell you again—don't play games with me."

And the questions began to rain down like machine gun fire, hardly giving her time to answer. When she hesitated, his fingers drummed on the corner of the desk, and she was terrified by the idea that he might think she was trying to lie. The heat in the office was beginning to make her feel sticky. She wanted to unbutton her coat, but feared that in doing so, she would call his attention to the extent of her uneasiness.

"All the same, I can't make things up just to please you."

"I'm not asking you to do any such thing. I'd be quite happy with the truth."

Another inspector had just come into the room, this one a bit younger. He sat down on the corner of the desk. With both of them staring at her like that, she felt as if they were about to gobble her up.

"But I am telling you the truth." On the verge of crying, she ground her teeth together until her throat hurt.

"Really. And do you know what happens to people who lie to the police?" The younger one spoke with a rude authoritarian tone, as if it gave him pleasure to frighten people.

"Look here," she said, feeling cornered, "I have no part whatever in this story."

"What story?" The question pounced on her like a vulture, claws bared.

"How should I know? "

"Who comes to visit her? And don't try and tell me that you've never seen anybody..."

"A couple of women have been to visit. They met at the orphanage."

"Or maybe at Saint Lazare."

"How should I know? She said they were from the

orphanage."

"You've never seen a man, about my height, olive skin, kinky hair slicked down with pomade?"

"I don't remember seeing any such person. Why don't you just ask the concierge? If it's a matter of who comes and who goes in that building, she's the one to ask. Nothing escapes her."

"Don't worry, I will."

It was beginning to get very dark in the office. The inspectors' features seemed blurry. Then the rain began to beat a steady rhythm on the dust-covered windows. It was hot and dark as in an oven. The policemen, nevertheless, seemed perfectly comfortable. The younger one, sitting on the corner of the desk, leaned over to her, breathing his early morning bad breath in her face. She turned her head away, only to find herself caught in the net of the other fellow's gaze. Staring intently at the window panes, she tried to catch a glimpse of the gray sky through the fat splattering raindrops. The surrounding walls were bolted doors that would never open up again. All she had to do was discredit Denise, say yes to everything, incriminate all those they wished to accuse, and the walls would open right up.

"You understand, of course, that everything you say here will remain between us."

Mireille jumped. The torpor in which the heat and the shadows had plunged her was lifting, disappearing. He was pleading now. The worst was over.

"In any case, I can't tell you I've seen what I haven't seen. That would be false testimony."

"You are not here to testify. But that could happen." Getting up from the desk, the younger guy said to the older one: "You see, Turin, I was right. It didn't do any good."

They whispered for a moment, then seemed to remember that she was there.

"OK, you can go now. We don't need you any more. As for this little interview, it's just between us, understand? So long, now. Maybe we'll meet again, who can say?"

The vague presentiment that their words would prove true followed her all the way to the staircase. She missed the first step, caught hold of the sticky banister, and slowly continued her descent, like a gravely ill person whose destiny lies waiting at the bottom of the steps. Once outside, she began to tremble with the intensity of all her repressed fear. Oh. If only she could go back to the time when all she had to worry about were ogres and ghosts which disappeared as soon as you turned on the light, when, awakened by her moaning, Saul would press his cheek next to hers and cover her face with his warm breath, melting the freezing fear that gripped it. Now he was at the hospital, accompanying the boss on his rounds. "I cannot stand the sight of suffering," he had said, one day. "But I'll get over it. It must be like this for everybody in the beginning."

She would also get over her fear. This fear of an abstraction swelled by memories of horror. If Denise had lots of money, it was because, like so many others, she was dealing in the black market. Mireille felt somewhat reassured. There was also the hosier from Rouen who gave her presents. Maybe he was the one with the olive skin and the kinky pomaded hair? What if he had killed his wife and run off with the cash? Or maybe the hosiery business was nothing but a front and he was really the leader of a dangerous gang of crooks? Good thing she hadn't said anything.

"Thank God I don't know anything," she thought.

Seeing a big puddle in her way, she tried to stop suddenly, but, carried along by inertia, landed right in the middle of it. The water splashed up to her knees and soaked into her shoes.

Chapter 3

Mme. Dufour's big red cat, Titi, was asleep on the table in the lodge. The manager's face was hidden behind the newspaper gripped tenaciously between her yellowish arthritic fingers. At the noise Mireille made when she took her key down from the board, the newspaper rustled and Mme. Dufour lowered it a bit, revealing the black sweater and shawl that she wore all winter long. Blinking her milky eyes, she leaned forward with the honeyed smile she saved for the end-of-year season of giving gifts and tips.

"Finally, you're here, Mademoiselle. I was just saying to myself: How strange that Mlle. Goldine hasn't gotten back yet, since she's usually so punctual. Nothing's the matter, I hope?"

Mireille shook her head.

"Come on in, little one, it would be very bad for you to get caught in a draught." She lowered her voice in a conspiratorial manner. "I have to talk to you."

The lodge smelled of the lung soup she made for her cats.

"There now! Well, I'm sorry to have to tell you this, Mademoiselle, but somebody should let you know, and it might as well be somebody who cares about you. Well, here goes: a couple of police inspectors were here gathering information about you. Really! What they didn't ask me about you!"

She winked as if to insist on the special visionary gifts of the blind, clicking her tongue emphatically. "You haven't got anything to worry about, do you?"

Mireille winced. "Would you mind telling me what they wanted to know?"

"The usual stuff. If you've got a job, whether you keep bad company, things like that. As for me, of course, I didn't know anything much to tell them since you're not very talkative."

"Did they question you about everybody in the hotel?"

"They looked through my receipts and my register, as usual. Maybe somebody has it in for you?"

"That would surprise me. I don't know anybody."

"That doesn't mean a thing, my child, nothing whatsoever. You really have to watch out. You can't imagine how mean people are, so mean that it's a crying shame, for God's sake!"

"It's very kind of you to be so concerned about me. I'm sure it's just some kind of an error. They must have me confused with somebody else."

"Don't be so sure! These guys don't make mistakes. They know very well who they're after and they don't just let things drop. You haven't heard the last of this, I bet."

Mme. Dufour leaned forward a bit more, and her black shawl, slipping off her shoulders, hung off on either side like a couple of decrepit shadows. The old woman was right. They would not let go of her so quickly. Day after day, she would be summoned to other interrogations, ever more intense and severe, always ending with the threat which would start the whole thing over again each time. But she didn't know anything. Therein lay her peace of mind.

"Mme Dufour, I'll tell you this. When they've had enough, they'll just have to stop."

"For my part... After all, it's none of my business."

"Exactly."

From the way the manager got up from her chair, trembling, Mireille realized that she would not soon be pardoned for this "Exactly."

"Well just listen to the brat! The tone of her voice! I was only trying to protect you! Don't you worry! The next time, I'll know what to tell them. And don't worry about whether or not they'll come back, because they will."

As she stood there under the light of the bare bulb

dangling at the end of a cord, the yellow blotches on her face seemed to be gnawing away at her skin.

When, having knocked in vain on Denise's door, Mireille got back to her own room, the odor of mold emanating from the cold humid walls hit her as she opened the door. She took off her shoes in the dark, went into the closet that had been converted into a kitchen and glued her ear to the wall. Over the sound of running water, she heard Denise humming:

> Il était beau lalalala mon légionnaire,
> Il sentait bon le sable chaud
> Lalalala lalalala lalalalère

Mireille could just imagine her on the other side of the wall, standing nude in front of the sink, plump and firm as a berry in her cream-colored skin, her knees round and polished as pebbles and, most remarkable, those fine legs, that seemed to carry her large solid body so effortlessly that you never even heard her footsteps approaching. The water stopped running. There was a gurgling sound in the pipe and then, again, the sound of Denise's voice, more tranquil if not exactly in tune:

> Dans ses yeux caressants...

Surely she did not have a troubled conscience.

Reassured, Mireille lit the overhead light. As she was taking off her beret and her coat, the wardrobe mirror, tarnished and crusty with age, cast back a dreary reflection of the thin silhouette she so much despised. Then, remembering that Saul would soon be showing up for dinner and to take her to the cinema, she took her handkerchief and removed what make-up was left on her face. She looked at herself; pallid, thin, with reddish eyebrows that were hardly even visible and made her face seem inexpressive, a bit too white and freckled. Her eyes wandered over the walls stained with *fly-tox*, up to the yellowing ceiling, the patched curtains, and back down to the shabby bedside rug. How would she ever get out of here? Anyway, if Denise had so much money, she would at least have repaired the walls of her room, which were in just as bad condition as her own. The inspectors' implied threat echoed in her mind: "This little talk is just between us... get it?" Lips sealed or else. A polite, nonchalant phrase with teeth as transparent as the watermark in a sheet of paper. She had better not take the risk of warning Denise.

"Incredible, all the same!" She exclaimed as she leaned over to get some potatoes out of the bagful under the hotplate.

"So now you've taken to talking to yourself!"

Mireille wheeled around. She hadn't heard the door open. Denise was gently closing it again, careful not to make any noise.

"How you frightened me! What's the idea of sneaking up on tip-toe like that? You... you..."

"Don't worry, Toots. It either comes to you naturally or it don't. You know me, I don't stand on ceremony. People are all the same to me. Anyway," she asked, tossing her head so as to show off her long silver blond hair, "How do you like it?"

The week before, she had been ash blond. Both shades were equally becoming. Mireille approved, then began peeling the potatoes.

"So what did you have to tell me that was so urgent? Hearing you drum on my door like that, a person might think you had the cops on your tail."

Mireille had not forgotten the frenzy of her knocking on Denise's door, but for the moment, she preferred to keep quiet about it. She could hear Denise's rough breathing and sensed that her prominent bosom was puffed up with anxiety.

"You're so talkative. That's scary. What was the point anyway?"

"It was nothing. I'm a little short of cash for the manager's Christmas tip, that's all. It was nothing serious."

A long sigh of relief rose from Denise's agitated breast.

"I hope you're pleased with yourself! You really scared the shit out of me! You must be nuts to come banging on my door like a wild woman for crap like that! What the fuck should I care about the concierge's tip? For all I care, she can croak, trap wide open, the filthy old bitch!"

She grabbed Mireille by the chin, staring right into her eyes. "You wouldn't be feeding me a line now, would you?"

Her voice was rough as a cat's tongue, and in her face, which, thanks to skillfully applied make-up, ordinarily seemed so serene, Mireille discerned the alert eyes of an animal which has perceived the silent movement of an enemy in the brush. With a sharp jerk of her head, she broke free.

"No matter. I'll get an advance on my salary."

"Oh don't be silly—no need for that," she said, rummaging in the pocket of her pink and black striped satin peignoir. "So how much do you need? I can easily spare five hundred or a thousand."

She had found her pack of gauloises, took two out and lit them both at the same time.

Accepting one of the cigarettes, Mireille said, "I"ll pay you back, you know."

"Of course, Honey."

In the meantime, Denise had assumed a tranquil expression, the muscles of her face having settled in place. Only the lines between her eyebrows indicated that the chronic headache, which had afflicted her since childhood, was tormenting her again. She insisted that the headaches had begun as a result of blows to her head, but Mireille, who had seen her flat on her back with foam streaming out of the corners of her mouth, suspected that she suffered from a serious affliction likely to be set off by stress. So Denise must have a dangerous secret. Forged food coupons, penicillin, maybe trafficking in illegal drugs. Accomplice to a murder? How ridiculous! And yet... No, no, better not to ask, better not to know. That was the cost of peace, peace and security.

"To think I imagined that you had gotten yourself

knocked up," said Denise, exhaling a long jet of smoke.

Suddenly, her face stiffened with a violent twinge. The lines between her eyebrows got deeper.

"Ah, well. You know, it happens. I was just about your age. Holy shit, I nearly croaked from it. But the concierge's bonus—what a joke! That's a good one."

"Not to worry," said Mireille serenely, putting the potatoes into a pot so as to wash them in the sink.

"No kidding… you still a virgin?" There was a thick hint of mocking incredulity in Denise's voice. As she sat down on the edge of the bed, her peignoir fell open, revealing her beautiful smooth knees. "So it's not an extinct race after all? And still no news of Gérard?"

"You and I are going to sign a pact." Mireille was watching the blue flames of the burner she had just lit jump up around the sides of the pot. "We are going to swear never to talk about Gérard again."

"As you wish, sweetie. Only, if you want my opinion, there's nothing like a man to help you forget the memory of another man. And it so happens that tonight we'll be three: me, Pierrot, and a buddy of his from Marseille, a really swell fellow. You know, three's a crowd. You should come along with us to round things out."

Mireille froze. Wasn't it Gérard who had told her all about Marseille? "Come with me," he had said, "we'll chase the sunshine." No, that was Morocco. On the other side of the curtains, frozen stars trembled in the heavenly solitude.

"No, I won't be able to join you," she said. "I'm waiting for Saul. And besides, I'd get to bed too late. You know, I work. I have to get up early."

"Don't worry about it. I'll reimburse you for the day's pay. For once in your life, you have the opportunity to go out to a nice place… And Pierrot would be so pleased. You know, Pierrot is quite fond of you."

"But we don't even know each other."

"If we had to get to know all the people we like, we'd

wind up not liking anybody very much. Ain't that the truth, sweetie?"

"Pierre is your friend from Rouen?"

"Rouen?... Ah! Yes, of course. My friend from Rouen. And who did you think it might be? Hey, what's the matter with you?" Denise grabbed her by the arm.

"Nothing. Nothing at all. Let go of me!"

She turned around, pretending to check up on the potatoes so as to hide her distraction from Denise. The water was boiling up in big foamy gray bubbles.

"Oh yes! There is too something the matter with you! And don't bother to lie! When you do, it's as easy to see as a virgin's blood on the sheets. Anyway, I'll lend you my black velvet dress. Go on, say you'll come. Nobody's going to rape you." And then, she added, in a teasing tone—"I'll give you your letter."

"Letter? What letter?"

"The letter to 'you-know-who,' you big fool. It came back. The old broad asked me to bring it up to you but then I forgot."

"Give it to me! I insist! She had no right to give my mail to you! And I bet you read it!"

Denise pulled a paper folded in four parts out of her pocket and handed it over, but when Mireille reached out to grab it, she pulled away and hid it behind her back. "Yeah, I opened it. So what? It's not half bad, actually."

She opened her hand and the letter fluttered down to the floor.

"My dearest love!" She exclaimed. "Really, you're off your rocker! After that, you wonder why he got fed up. Maybe if he were an old man, you never know... with old guys that stuff can work... makes them feel all soft inside."

She bent down, picked up the letter and handed it to Mireille. "There it is, your sacred letter. You want me to tell you what? OK. It had already been opened, sweetie, yes, somebody steamed it open. That's why the old lady gave it to me. Not so crazy as she looks, the old bat."

Mireille was horrified. Now they were spying on her, even reading her mail.

"There, there," crooned Denise, taking her gently by the shoulders, "there's no use getting upset over something so silly. Leave it to me, I'll get you a fellow..."

"You leave me the hell alone!"

The violence with which she recoiled from Denise, not to mention the harsh words that escaped her, were a defensive reflex against a woman perceived as clever and crafty. They were all out to get her, even Denise. Every new face was a new trap. *It was a small boat* and she had drawn the short straw; they had made her queen for a day, but they were planning to eat her alive at nightfall.

Denise's laugh shattered the silence. "You'll see," she said, "it's an ill wind that blows no good. I know somebody who'll be overjoyed to hear about this."

"Leave my brother out of this. He only wants what's good for me—he's never wanted anything but that."

"Well excuse me and beg your pardon. I didn't know he was the Holy Father. Dumb broad! You shake like a leaf when he's around. As for me, he doesn't scare me in the least. If you want to come with us, I'll take care of it. I've dealt with my share of loud mouths."

"Then how come you're not so glib when he's around to answer back?"

"Yeah. Your guardian angel. You can have him."

"Is that so? Well, you could do with a guardian angel of your own."

Like a cat whose tail has been stepped on, Denise nearly pounced on Mireille. "So now you're going to give me advice?" She cried. "Maybe even a morality lesson? Well, get this straight--morality and me, we've got a non-aggression pact. We get along fine, but we keep our distance—it's a question of territoriality. So you were raised on mother's milk, were you? Just get a load of this little shit, virgin into the bargain, gearing up to tell me about morality. When you've been through what I have, we'll just see about it. You're all a barrel of laughs."

Mireille hastened to empty the water from the pot into the sink. The wrinkles around Denise's mouth were dug in deeper, all of a sudden making her seem old and cruel.

Frightened, Mireille ventured: "I didn't mean to hurt you."

But Denise was not one to hold a grudge. Already, she was smiling a bit. "It's OK. With your principles, you'll go far. Look at yourself: shoes worn down at the heels, stockings darned and mended—what kind of an existence is that?"

"We don't all have private sources of income," Mireille said softly. "We can't all ride around in fancy cars."

"Yes, we can. And have a warm belly, be able to wash ourselves in a bathroom that doesn't stink of smelly feet. So what are you saying? That some people are cut out to live and others to croak?"

Denise's response was uttered with such self-assurance that it totally disarmed Mireille. In a flash, she saw Denise stretched out, languid and downy, in a pink marble bathtub, enveloped in lavender-scented mist. She shook her head and the vision disappeared.

"Tell me, this friend of yours from Marseille, what does he do?"

"Ah! Glad to see you haven't gotten completely off track. He's in business. Just like everybody else."

"Legal business?"

"How suspicious we are! Some doddering old bureaucrat rubber stamps it and it's as legal as can be."

Mireille nodded. Legal, illegal. She shrugged her shoulders. Laws. They annul some, promulgate others; millions of murders: they just stash them away in files. They become as Christian as can be when it comes to pardoning the wrongs done to other people. She smiled, thinking of Gérard with his need to go off and lose himself in the open sea, when all you had to do was close your eyes and you could easily sink in the middle of a crowd of people. Denise was still singing the praises of the guy from Marseille. Talking about cuff-links, manicures, sleeping cars--about everything and nothing at all.

Chapter 4

The wind was raging in and out among the tall buildings along the boulevard St. Michel. Up against the walls of the lycée St. Louis, painters displayed numerous specimens of copper-colored nudes, fishing villages glimmering in the sun, hurricane-swept waves of biblical proportions where boats foundered in the bluish white foam of the surf.

Saul pulled his coat collar up and shifted the books and dissecting kit that were sliding around under his arm. He turned impatiently toward the urinal Marcel had entered a moment ago, and saw him come out again, the panel of his overcoat thrown back, his legs bowed out, buttoning up his fly.

"It's not my fault if I have a weak bladder," said Marcel piteously as he arranged his overcoat so as to make himself presentable...

"Some weak bladder! Maybe if you drank less, you wouldn't need to piss so often!"

But Marcel was off admiring a candy pink nude. "Just look at that sly smile, that belly, those amethyst eyes. They must not get bored from one day to the next, these painters. A masterpiece! It's a masterpiece!"

"Keep your voice down. If the old guy hears you, we'll never be able to get rid of him. Come on! Let's go! Masterpieces like these are a dime a dozen all along the boulevard."

"All the same," said Marcel, following him regretfully while looking back at the painting, "just think of the fun a guy could have with a belly like that. Once I knew a girl with a belly just like that. But what a puss, what an ugly puss. We had to do it in the dark. But the action was incredible--you could just lie there and let her do all the work.

They waited for the cop to stop traffic at the intersection, then went across the pedestrian passage. Saul's chest felt tight, his throat was on fire. He shivered and his eyes filled with tears. Marcel ambled along, perfectly at ease, with the sturdy constitution of a well-fed native of the Auvergne, toasty warm in his camel's hair overcoat.

At first sight, Marcel Setier gave the impression that all things fleshly were joined together in him. Small and stocky, with thick soft lips that always seemed to be looking for something to eat or drink, thick brown hair with the hairline low on his narrow forehead, he seemed, on the whole, sensual, brutal and not very intelligent. But in his round, small brown eyes, if you took the trouble to allow your own gaze to penetrate so far, you discovered, behind his old-fashioned naïveté, a nostalgic and indulgent tenderness curiously at odds with his external appearance.

"Why, you're shivering," cried Marcel. "As I was saying, let's go have a nice glass of warm wine."

The terrace of the great café was enclosed with panels of glass and heated by large cast-iron brasiers. The patrons were the same, always the same, well dressed, sidling up to one another as if to keep each other warm or tell secrets. This café, even before the Boches issued their official decree, had hastened to post little notices in the window forbidding Jews to enter.

"If you like," said Saul, "but not here. Boularet is not so fancy but their wine is just as good." No point in offering explanations to Marcel. When he became indignant, he could get choking mad and feel the need to smash windows.

"Because of those signs, eh?" he asked, demonstrating uncharacteristic circumspection.

A hundred paces beyond, they got to Boularet's, with its somber, faded shop-front.

"Waiter, two glasses of warm wine," Marcel called out, slipping off the overcoat, folding it neatly and setting it down on the bench where he could keep an eye on it. "Nothing like warm wine to set everything right again."

At the other end of the room, between the billiard table and the phone booth, four men were playing cards. Marcel rubbed his hands together, fiddled with his cufflinks, smoothed his hair. Watching him made Saul feel nervous. He loosened his tie. The heaviness in his head reminded him that he had had another sleepless night. He needed to close his eyes and not think about anything. Most of all, not about the exam he had just failed; also not about Simone, who kept chasing after him; nor about Menard, the fifth form booby who not only needed private lessons, but could also use a new head; nor about Mireille, who was always on his mind, Mireille, who kept her secrets so well; nor about the answers he should have given on the exam; nor about Mireille's secrets; nor about the things she was capable of getting into when he was not around to supervise, nor about the dangers lurking all around her, about her face, the face of a young girl, yet at certain moments, so embittered. Not to think about anything at all.

"With sugar?" asked the waiter, in a sober tone, his dull eyes fixed on the red and white curtains. A soiled apron, wrapped around his waist, enveloped him down to his knees.

"With sugar," said Marcel, absent-mindedly.

At the back of the room, the gamblers were warming up: "Hey, what do you mean I didn't say 'trump'! I said it three times, didn't I Emile?"

"Oh so now you get your partners to stick up for you?"

Saul stirred the tin spoon around in his wine. In the melting sugar, he saw Mme. Menard's indignant face. "Three hundred francs an hour? My dear Monsieur, before the war, for ten francs, you could hire a professor!"

Oh! He had to stop thinking, to throw himself into the kind of peaceful dream from which you never want to wake up. He pulled out his tobacco pouch and rolled himself a cigarette. The warmth of the place had finally gotten to him, the heat of the wine having warmed up his chest and spread out to his extremities. An agreeable laziness penetrated his soul and he had to brace himself against encroaching sleepiness. Noises no longer resonated in his aching head. They were muffled as if by a wall of cotton wadding. His senses were out of joint.

"Shall we have another?" Marcel's jovial voice called him back from the far away place where he had been wandering back and forth, revisiting the events of the irrevocably finished day gone by. The empty glasses. He felt like seeing them full again, enormous and multiple: wineskins full of life surrounding him on all sides, separating him from, also protecting him from, inevitable doom.

Grabbing Marcel by the back of his lapel, he cried: "I flunked!"

Marcel seemed not to understand. Saul's fingers clutched at the cloth.

"You understand? I flunked. But brilliantly."

His meaning dawned on Marcel. It took his breath away. His hazelnut gaze jumped like a frog. "You're joking, right? Just joking?"

"I must have been scared. I must have been very scared. I screwed up royally."

"Not at all, buddy. These things happen. You'll start again. You'll see. It'll work out."

"There isn't any time. That's it for me."

"And how can you be sure you didn't scrape through? Of course, it's a pain in the ass, that's for sure. Bah! You'll come to the party at Sita's tonight and that'll take your mind off it. The truth is, all this drudgery has made you dull. Just look at the results!"

"If you think that by drinking myself into a coma I'm likely to change the results the least bit..."

"There's no law that says you have to get drunk."

"And then, there are always a bunch of stupid dames..."

"Oh! Well, some of them aren't so bad and, what's more, they know what they're there for. You don't give a damn--they swarm around you as if you were made of sugar. You have to let me in on your system."

"I feed them love potions."

"Go on. You jerk."

"Maybe they enjoy being fucked in a scientific manner."

"What a prick you can be when you set your mind to it!"

"Anyway, with all your dough, what do you need with a system?"

Marcel struck the table with his fist. "How long do you plan to bug me about my dough? Is it my fault that my old man got rich during the war?"

"Well don't try and tell me that you have a problem with his money. After all, you may as well enjoy it..."

Saul knew that he was tormenting Marcel, but it was a pleasure he would not, could not refuse himself. "What's the matter with you? You're so touchy all of a sudden!"

Silence settled between them, shutting each one off in his own solitary universe.

Saul saw himself again, in front of the empty grave, torn by tender memories, knowing he had disappointed the phantoms that prowled around him. An elbow in his ribs reminded him of Marcel, who was agitated. A woman of a certain age, heavily made up, bundled up in a red fox jacket, had just come in, and, hoisting herself onto a bar stool, was smiling at Marcel. In the wink of an eye, she had sized him up for what he was worth.

"Well, you're easy to please," said Saul.

"What do you expect? Now if only I had your scientific savoir-faire! How about keeping an eye on my overcoat, old man? See that somebody doesn't make off with it, won't you?"

Saul smiled, picked up the tobacco that had fallen out of his first cigarette onto his knees, and used it to roll himself another, which, this time, he lit.

The phantoms had returned to reproach him for his failure. He should just get back to his room, throw himself onto the bed, and get some sleep. But the reproaches would follow him and slip under the covers so as to haunt him in his sleep. And even if he passed this exam, and all the ones to come, even if he did get the degree? He could always hang his shingle out from the dormer window in his garret, just the thing to attract patients. Or he could do like Rostein: pull a few well placed strings and get a job in a dispensary, or else, become the assistant to some old guy whose bony hands shook too much to hold a syringe. Intravenous—a white arm, a fist, a little blue pulse under the skin where the needle penetrates. In that garret, never to be graced by visits from sick people, there would be a steady stream of women who were full of health, and also full of shame. And if he could not resign himself to any of that, he could always become the sales representative for a drug company, dragging his yellow leather satchel through small provincial towns that were rainy, cold and hostile. Or find a rich man who was just dying to buy his daughter a brand new doctor. She would have soft breasts, a large, gaping umbilicus, a nothingness. From nothingness to life, and in all fairness, from life back to nothingness. A closed circle. Death. Number 18 died during the night. "M. Goldine, what are you dreaming about? Does the patient frighten you? Touch him, sir, feel him. Yes, there, where it hurts him. You need to learn to see with the eyes at the end of your fingers. Let's go, sir, or your patient will have had time to die and get to heaven a hundred times before you're finished." Saul no longer knows anything. The index cards in his head keep getting shuffled around.

Already, M. Sebastien Paul has placed his icy fingers on the patient's pain-wracked stomach and pronounced a diagnosis. M. Paul is four years younger than Saul. But M. Paul's father is a broker at the Halles. For M. Goldine, entrance into medical school was forbidden during the occupation. He has a problem with his memory, this M. Goldine. It seems that there's a little umbilicus in it where everything turns to nothingness. Too many memories. All in disarray. You could forget everything, but not the dead. They don't let go of you, the dead. That's what made everything float around in his memory. And therein lies all the difference between him and M. Paul, between him and Marcel.

A heated discussion was going on at the bar.

"Then keep moving! Skinflint!"

The waiter, wiping the glasses, could not resist a little smile, and Marcel, red in the face, shouting, told him to mind his own business.

Enraged, he grabbed his coat and said, "Come on, let's go. And as for the tip, just forget it!"

As he opened the door, Marcel couldn't help calling back to the woman: "Just wait till the Yanks get the fuck out of here--you'll be lucky to get two bits for your blow jobs!"

At the back of the room, the card game was getting venomous.

In the street, blacked out by nightfall, they walked along, side by side, heads bent against the wind.

"Let's have dinner together, OK, old man?" said Marcel.

"No way. My sister is waiting for me."

"All right. She's invited too. It's been ages since I've seen her. To think we all used to play cops and robbers together! Good God, how time flies! So. We have to keep the wolves away from the sheep, eh! It's not her that I'm after, you know!"

"Mind letting me know who?" asked Saul, remembering the intensity of Marcel's gaze whenever, warm and brown, it came to rest on the nape of Simone's neck.

"You don't know her," Marcel answered quickly.

"Ah!"

It was only a little white lie allowing him to save face. Funny how the self-esteem of little men tended to be inseparable from their reproductive glands. How Marcel must hate him, in spite of himself, when he let down his defenses. "Go after her, old man, go after her, you'll be doing me a favor," thought Saul. He was fed up with Simone's overwhelming passion. Marcel wriggled as if he were covered with vermin.

"So about that surprise party?" Marcel returned to the charge. "Myself, I don't give a hoot. It's because of Simone... I promised her. She sweet-talked me into it, you know. Shit, all she wants out of you is an explanation... Really, that's all, just an explanation."

Did he not realize that no explanation was going to straighten this mess out? That the only valid explanation for a woman is the one she has already decided ahead of time she wants to hear because it suits her just right. To hell with Simone and her explanations!

"Well, OK, I'll try and drop in. And, by the way, thanks for the bag of coal."

With a wave of his hand, Marcel hurriedly slipped away.

In the metro, warm and nauseating as a heated tomb, Saul was once again overwhelmed by the pain that was eating a hole in his chest. On the track across the way, a train filled up with passengers. Red and green cars. Monotonous. They should paint them yellow, pink, blue; midnight blue with silver stars and crescent moons; lunar blue with great suns and flowered curtains on the windows, like the little train he had once painted for Mireille, They had been fighting that day, and so, to make up for being stronger than she was, he told her a story-- "Sleeping Beauty."

"Another story, Saul, tell me another story."

"I failed my exam."

Right away, coming in the door, before kissing her pale forehead, right away, to unburden himself, to be done with it.

One by one, the little cars were swallowed up by the tunnel's big belly. Trailers. Dusty roads bordered by tall spikes. Summer follows bohemians everywhere. A childhood dream come true... They would become Gypsies, he and Mireille, vagabonds. They would get jobs in a traveling circus. "Ladies and gentlemen, come on in, step right up. The terrible secret of death is about to be revealed, the show is about to begin." And that baby, face smeared with jam, whose frightened eyes are clamoring for the secret of life? Ah! A fetus in a jar of formaldehyde. Better yet, a medical museum: wax limbs covered with scrofula, a yellow forehead adorned with the crown of Venus, the birth of a child without arms, admission forbidden for children under sixteen.

Settling down on a bench in the rear of the train, Saul opened his book to a detailed anatomical diagram of the foot. The words sprang up from his memory right away. The problem was somewhere else. He closed his eyes so as not to be influenced by what he already knew, and leafed randomly through the book. Even then, he could find no crack in his memory. He turned the page and closed his eyes again, trying, in the nothingness behind his eyelids, to put what he knew back together again, to get organized, to understand what had happened during that exam. His eyelids shut tight. He no longer knew anything. He closed the book with a slam. Again, he saw himself taking the patient's pulse for the third time, stalling for time. The pulse seemed to quicken under the pressure of his index finger, to run more quickly, jumping, stumbling, just like his thoughts. The inscrutable chief's pencil beat an accelerated rhythm, devouring the short seconds accorded to him for rummaging about in his head so as to extract a single answer, clear and luminous with intelligence...."It's not what you know that counts, M. Goldine, but what you don't know."

Next to Saul on the bench, a man who had just sat down opened up a newspaper that smelled like printer's ink. The man himself smelled of nicotine and pine tar. Saul's mouth filled up with viscous, bitter saliva. Nausea, a sickness that one day takes hold of you, making you choke on everything you breathe in, making everything in sight seem repulsive. Across the way from him, a woman was picking the bloody enamel off of her nails. Her fur coat was nothing but a patchwork of rats' skins. And tomorrow, he would have to go back to the hospital, lift the lid of a dying man's spittoon so as to examine his phlegm, pry into the infected womb of a woman who would never have any more children, and who would be made to pay dearly for it. Make sure that all things putrified would once again feel as warm and dry as a kitten's fur; that desperate faces would light up as they lifted toward you. But where the images of hope and purity once were, his memory is blank, stiff, like the fist of a dying man consumed with hatred before his own impotence in the face of death. Death who--she too-- forgives nothing.

The glimpse of a poster displaying a smile bursting with health. Now let's show off all thirty-two beautiful teeth, sweetheart, your soft shiny hair, your empty eyes clearly remembering nothing: the secret of endurance.

Two American soldiers are circling around the white enamel pole. Anxious about the flasks of anti-boredom potion stashed in their rear pockets, they slip their hands back to check if they're still there. Their smiles bursting with health, their eyes empty: endurance. Yoo-hoo! Standing up against the doors, a young girl folds her arms across her young breasts, very much the object of admiration. She fixes her gaze on her own reflected image, suffocating with shame. The soldiers ogle her. A tiny flame lights up in the depths of their dead pupils. They are young and the flasks of forgetfulness in their back pockets contain lovely mirages. The young girl keeps still, her fingers clasping the lapels of her coat. Awkward compliments, obscene propositions fluttering all around her. She has become deaf and dumb; but her wandering eyes meet those of the soldiers, then retreat, fix themselves on the pane of glass, heavy with shame for what has just been revealed to her. In the tunnel, a series of posters go by: DUBON, DUBONNET. Stealthily, the soldiers push each other toward her, playing like a couple of young dogs trying out their fangs. The taller one has a scar on his neck that's still red. A taunting thrust and he stumbles against the young girl, crushing her against the doors.

Saul leaps up and pulls him back by the collar. His fist is ready to strike. He orders the guy to leave the girl alone. The soldier backs off, breaks free and pushes him away with a casual gesture. His companion moves in stealthily, a good brawl wouldn't bother him at all. He's so bored. The other passengers have all become deaf and blind, their heads buried in their newspapers, focusing on their shoes or the movement of their knitting needles. Then the soldier with the wound breaks into an awkward laugh. He smoothes his hair, readjusts his cap, all the while continuing to laugh, a laugh thin as a dribble of water, a bored laugh, an oblivious laugh which goes right to his heart and anaesthetizes it. Then he directs a volley of insults at his companion, the one who started it all. He apologizes, stammers a few words, all red in the face. His wound turns violet under pressure. Liberated nation, conquered nation, soldiers and whores in the alleys. He no longer knows what's what. He's babbling; he pulls out his package of cigarettes and offers them all around. There are indulgent smiles all around; a man gives him a little military salute, raising two fingers to his right temple, sticking his cigarette behind his ear. The young girl smiles also. Everybody is in a good mood. Now she is no longer frightened, no longer ashamed. The peace pipe smoothed everything over. She avoids Saul's gaze.

At the next station, Saul will get out. He'll walk the rest of the way home. The icy wind in the streets whips across his face.

Chapter 5

"Well, hi there, come on in," said Denise. "What are you afraid of?"

Saul ignored her, as always. He waited in the corridor, refusing to enter Mireille's room until Denise cleared out.

"Saul, don't be so sulky. We were just chatting. There's no harm in that."

Sensing the weakness of her position, Mireille avoided his eyes and bustled about setting the table.

Saul remained stubbornly silent. He stared at Denise, sensing her body stiffen in response to his contemptuous gaze.

"OK. No need to dot the "i"s," she threw out, unable to stand it any longer. "Anyway, I was about to leave. No problem." she added, resisting Mireille's gesture of sympathy. "It's sort of obvious that I'm one too many in here."

At the door, she stumbled skillfully, in such a way as to bump into Saul.

"It's OK," she grumbled. "I don't have the plague, you know."

She clicked her nails against his books.

"So, still spending all your time with your head stuck in the books, Mister Know-It-All?"

"Tell me, would it bother you so much to leave my sister and me alone?"

"Oh! But these things are just amazing! Look, it even talks!"

"Denise," Mireille whined pitifully.

"What can I tell you! Guys like him make me sick."

She left, went back to her own place and slammed the door.

"Good riddance," said Saul, leaning over to kiss Mireille, who was reaching up on tiptoes.

"What do you get out of taunting her like that?" she

asked.

"What the hell does it matter?"

"I can't stand to see people taunted like that."

"Tell me, is it Denise you feel you need to defend here? Or yourself?"

She shrugged her shoulders. He ran his finger across her lips and, satisfied that she wasn't wearing any make-up, gave her an affectionate pinch on the cheek. If only he could get her out of this place, away from the nefarious influence of that woman. Money. The books that Mireille had just taken away from him and set down on the bed reminded him of his failure. Maybe this would be a good time to tell her everything. She was bent over the books

"Mireille?"

In the face she turned toward him, he recognized an incipient sense of self. In those piercing eyes, the light of anger and revolt was beginning to shine. She straightened up, and the books tumbled out on the bedspread. Never again would he be able to think about telling her. She had to believe in him.

"This better be the last time I find that woman in here. I don't want to have to tell you a second time. Understand?"

"I'm sorry, Saul, but from now on, I will continue to do what seems best to me. Now, let's try and avoid an argument. For once, Saul, just try. I have no more fat; this will be a little dry."

She sat down in the armchair and seemed so small, in spite of the two cushions she used to prop herself up.

"You're mad at me, eh?" he said, seeing that she wasn't eating. "Yes, you're mad at me. You're pouting."

She shook her head, smiling, and he thought maybe, after all, there might be a way to deal with reality.

"By the way," he said, "I had an exam today."

Although she remained impassive, he felt her tensing up, her attention sharpening. "She doesn't know," he thought, "but she can guess."

"You're not going to ask me how I did?"

"Well of course. Tell me."

He dallied a bit before answering, enjoying the pleasure of sensing her breathless anticipation, her eyes riveted on his lips as if both their destinies were also suspended there. They stood holding onto each other. He managed to smile, despite the wretched truth, perhaps because of some perverse mysterious pleasure which, at that moment, turned him into a god. She clapped her hands and cried out:

"You did well—I knew it! Was it very hard?"

"I thought I'd never get through it. That shouldn't stop you from eating."

But she wasn't listening. She was smiling happily. No way to ever get back to the truth now.

"Great! When we get out of the movie, let's treat ourselves to some fries."

"It'll be too late. You'll be too tired."

"That's what you think!" she exclaimed joyfully, raising the glass of wine to her lips. "Well, here's to the future chief of staff at the hospital! Drink! By the way, I didn't do a thing today. First of all, practically nobody comes to the studio any more. Even Sarand told me that he's going to practice somewhere else if we don't manage to get some coal in there soon."

"Don't worry, you won't get rid of him that easily."

Mireille laughed softly. Goose that she was, it flattered her to be courted by that boneless wonder, Sarand.

"Idiot. Can't you see that he's circling around you?"

"Sarand? He does circles around everybody. He can't help it. Really. Even the old cleaning lady isn't safe. Anyway, what's the harm in that?"

"You never see the harm in anything. Such innocence is beyond me. Like for instance with your neighbor... Or, look, a woman gives birth at the hospital, the kid is jaundiced. And there she is, falling all over herself, ooing and ahing: 'An apricot complexion, really it's just like apricots,' as if she had just given birth to some kind of prodigy."

"I see no connection," she observed, ingenuously.

"The connection is that your neighbor is a whore, and if you don't watch out..."

"That's not so." she cried, casting an anxious glance at the wall."

"Oh no? Well maybe she's a nun? A saint?" He shouted even louder, hoping that Denise could hear.

"That's not fair. You don't even know her. And anyway, what business is it of yours?"

Saul pushed his chair away, making a screeching noise that unnerved them both.

"Whatever concerns me is my business," he yelled. "Our parents entrusted you to me and I have no intention of letting them down. What do you think? I bring this stuff up for fun, because I have nothing better to do?"

He was struggling to calm down, to lower his voice. There was no point in frightening her and humiliating her. Not if he had any hope of persuading her to be reasonable.

"One day, you'll understand, but then it will be too late. The damage will have been done. I have nothing against her. It's just that she's dangerous. At times, I even feel sorry for her. But it's not out of cruelty that people with contagious diseases are put into quarantine: just try and understand."

"But I'm the one you're putting in quarantine! I'm not exaggerating! I don't have a single girlfriend. Nothing. If I did it your way, I'd bury myself alive."

"Well, you still have your friend Gérard," he said in a mocking voice.

"Oh, just shut up!"

She got up so abruptly that her weight nearly pulled her right back down into the armchair. She picked up a glass of wine that was spilling out over the table, set it down neatly, then went to sit on the foot of the bed. In that moment, knowing she was slipping away from him, Saul sensed her cruel loathing.

"Some loss," he said, following after her. "A failure

who plays the wretched outcast--*le poète maudit avec des filles naïves*. Come back and finish your supper. Stop sulking. I'm not the one you punish by not eating."

But when he took her hand, it slipped through his fingers like the leaf on a slender branch you think you've bent down to your level, that gets away, snapping back up with renewed energy. He wanted to let himself sink down beside her, give up this ongoing fight against his fever and let it carry him off into a sickness that would allow him to run away from everything, especially this new consciousness of Mireille's, that blinded her.

"God damn it! he cried out desperately, I'm doing everything I can. Nobody has the right to ask any more of me."

"Nobody is asking all that much of you," said Mireille, in a dull voice.

"But my conscience, that's what I have to deal with. My conscience is clear."

In the silence that followed, Mireille broke out into a forced, dramatic laugh that quickly stifled itself.

"Your conscience! Do you hear yourself? It's my life that's at stake and you hold forth about your conscience. Too bad about your conscience! As for me, I intend to run the risk of living my life."

Defeated and tired, he lost himself in thought. If only he could figure out what he needed to say to break through the wall of stubbornness behind which she was retreating. The thoughts swimming around in his mind were so fluid that he could not trap them into words. He sensed Mireille's gaze upon him, calm and distant, but did not dare to meet it. He had to make an effort and do it soon, but he was not really up to it. She had already slipped out of his hold over her. He wanted to bend over her, to fondle her, to kiss her forehead, but her expression, like a barbed wire fence, made him keep his distance.

"There, you're tired, I knew it," he said with forced playfulness. "We'll go to the movies tomorrow. Go to bed. We'll talk, quietly, without arguing, just like we used to."

"I don't think so! Go to bed yourself if you want to. Me, I'm going out. I've been invited out."

It was at that moment that he understood. She was playing the cruel game of no longer including him in her life.

"What do you mean by that?" he asked.

"I'm going out. I've been invited out. It's not really so complicated."

"You liar, you're only trying to get even. Not twenty minutes ago, you were the one who wanted to go to the movies."

"Suit yourself."

Enraged, pushed beyond the limit by her detached and mocking tone, he pounced on her. Grabbing her under her armpits, he pulled her up by sheer force, demanding that she acknowledge his presence. For a second, he felt the swelling of her chest, but she held herself at a distance from him, pulling at her pullover, which, in the struggle, had slipped up under her breasts, exposing her bare midriff.

"What's gotten into you?" She demanded angrily.

"Who are you going out with?"

"That's certainly none of your business."

"I'm warning you, Mireille, don't push me too far!"

She shrugged her shoulders and turned on the radio. The sound of a cello filled the room. Mireille stood there defiantly next to the radio, but from the stiffness of her posture, he realized in that moment, how much he frightened her. Never had she seemed more fragile, more lonely, more vulnerable. He wanted to take her in his arms, hold her tightly so that nothing would ever be able to bruise her. She took her coat down off the hook with slow, deliberate gestures, but beneath these apparently calm gestures, Saul sensed her fear looking out at him.

"Mireille," he cried, "listen to me. Don't go. You'll only regret it. All they want is to get you into bed. They're all swine! For God's sake, listen to me!"

He could hear himself yelling desperately. Mireille was looking at him blankly, not understanding, terrified, and he was the one who was terrifying her! This was not what he had wanted. He was soaked in sweat. His head ached so badly, he couldn't even see straight. It was the fever, rising in a wave and submerging him, twisting his features, making him stumble and bump into the furniture as he moved toward her. She had no way of knowing that the fever was the root of it all; eyes wide open, she watched him come closer. She let out a prolonged yell and Saul's hand swung out. Mireille uttered the moan of a newborn, and her gaze, full of resentment, tightened around him like a snare, holding him prisoner to his own shame. Didn't she understand that it was the fever, the failure, and that she had pushed him beyond endurance? Falling from her long eyelashes, the tears made the imprint of his five fingers gleam on the surface of her pale cheek.

Saul crumpled onto the bed. Nothing was going to erase that slap, no gesture, no word. The wardrobe mirror reflected Mireille in tears, leaning against the wall, weary and dejected.

In years past, he would have said: "Come on now, don't cry, I'll tell you a story." But how to tell the story of this fever, of the exam, of the poor old man who twisted and turned his tormented belly away from the skilled, cold fingers investigating him. The books were pressing into his side. A curious little stairway that would never get him anywhere, anymore.

"Mireille," he called timidly.

In the mirror, he met her indifferent gaze. Her silence was an embrace reaching out to pardon him. Painfully, he got up, picked up a little comb that had fallen on the floor, and put it in her hair.

"My little, oh so little one," he murmured, drawing her to him.

For a moment their hearts beat against each other, but Mireille's face soon clouded up with embarrassment and she turned away. Like a child allowing himself to drift off into dreams, Saul rested his head on his sister's slender shoulder and they both drowned in the silence engulfing his soul.

The black velvet sheath would look good on Mireille, who had narrow hips. The guy from Marseille would be happy, and if Pierre didn't manage to bring the deal off, at least he wouldn't be able to blame her for not doing everything she could to help. But the Marseillais would have to handle the kid properly. Look, sniff, lick your chops, but don't touch. Denise dismissed the vague sense of betrayal that held her back outside of Mireille's door and went on in. Mireille was in bed, her eyes still red from crying. The table had not been cleared off.

"He hit you, didn't he? Bastard!" said Denise as she sat down on the edge of the bed.

With the tips of her fingers, she stroked Mireille's face, which was still moist.

"Don't say no. They could hear you yelling all the way to the Samaritaine."

"It's my fault. I pushed him beyond endurance."

"If you insist on making excuses for him, it serves you right. In any case, you have five nice sausage-shaped marks on your face. It'll take a bit of powder to hide that. I wouldn't have believed he was that mean. It drives him nuts just to know you have friends."

"Leave me alone," said Mireille, turning her head away.

Everybody was always finding fault with everybody else. How was she to make sense of it all? Where was the real danger? She was nothing but a balloon being bounced from hand to hand, and the danger seemed to have a new face every time she landed.

"Mustn't get upset, Sweetie. What I was saying was for your sake. When you're young, you need to let people guide you. Now get up, throw some water on your face and slip into this dress. If it bothers you for me to see you undressed, I can turn around. Come on, are you going to get up or not? We're going to be late. Pierre will grumble. As a favor to me, OK? You can do me a little favor, can't you? Especially since it won't cost you a thing, right? You'll see, Sweetie we'll have lots of fun!"

Denise's face was pale under her make-up. She whined like a puppy who has soiled the carpet and fears he will be beaten. Mireille sat up. The question that both frightened and obsessed her was on the tip of her tongue. Then, as if responding to the prick of a spur, she plunged into the abyss of the unknown.

"The police are investigating you," she said. "Why?"

Denise remained impassive, but her hand stiffened on the sheath, and when she let go of it, the pattern of reflected light on the velvet was broken up. She emitted a strident laugh.

"What the hell are you talking about? Well, answer me! Oh, no, my little chickadee," she said fiercely, "you can't stop there! You have to go on. You have to tell me everything you know!"

In a menacing tone, she kept on asking questions, Mireille told her about the fancy outfits that had prompted suspicion, the tall skinny guy with the dark complexion, the friend from Rouen. But there was no way to tell her about the rain on the windowpanes, the suffocating heat, the inspector's bad breath, even though that was what she remembered most vividly.

"And now they're investigating me; they came to talk to Mme Dufour; they asked her a bunch of questions about me and..."

"Don't you see," cried Denise—"they're investigating everybody! They get paid to sit on their asses all day so they have to find some way to keep busy. So what? You don't believe me? Go ahead and tell me I'm a liar! That's right! call me a liar! And to think, I was trying to help you improve your situation! Ah! You won't have to reproach me again for inviting you out for a good time!"

"Denise, I assure you..."

"Too late. You should have said something earlier."

In a bound, she was up, but her legs were wobbly.

"In any case, you had no intention of joining us," she added as she closed the door.

Her high heels echoed in the corridor. Mireille felt fear creeping up on her. It was the first time she had ever heard the sound of Denise's footsteps.

Chapter 6

Inside the phone booth, Denise was getting anxious. That guy outside who would not shove off made her nervous. And that blockhead Antoine was taking his time picking up the phone. Listening to the phone ringing at the other end of the line, she thought: "You're wasting your time, old man, I'm on to you cops." She was just about to give up and leave the booth when the ringing stopped.

"Well, it's not a minute too soon, what the hell're you up to in that dive that you can't hear the phone ring any more? It's me, Mlle. Denise. Yes, yes, hello, I don't have time. Go get Pierrot for me and tell him to get a move on."

Breathing hard, she watched the guy outside, who seemed not in the least bit anxious. As if she didn't have enough trouble already with Pierre, who was going to bawl her out for not bringing the kid along. Tears welled up in her eyes. "If he lays a hand on me, I'll kill him," she promised herself. Hang up, run away, slip into the station and jump onto the first train that came along. Yeah. No harm in dreaming. She was done for and there was nothing to be done about it.

"Tell me, do you take me for a jerk?" said the voice at the end of the line.

A cloud of cold air moved in and froze her up. She heard herself whining.

"Pierrot, don't give me a hard time. Not now. I'm in a real jam. I can't come."

"What the hell are you saying?"

"I can't come."

"You trying to fuck with me, you bitch? What am I going to tell the guy from Marseille? I promised him. You don't just get away with stuff like that."

"Listen, Pierrot, please listen to me." Her voice was

stuck in her throat.

"Speak up. It's noisy as hell in here."

The guy walked over to the phone booth and seemed to be leaning closer so he could listen.

"Listen," said Denise, cupping her hand on the receiver, "I'm at the bistro downstairs from my room. Oh please! Stop yelling at me! I'm not made out of iron, you know. Get into a taxi and come get me. Tell him to keep the flag up."

"Have you lost your marbles or something?"

"There's a guy outside who won't go away. Maybe I'm being trailed. It has to look like I'm the only one in the car."

But in leaving the phone booth, she noticed, to her relief, that the guy was rushing in to make his own call. The street seemed quiet, but you could never take anything for granted. Very shortly, a taxi with its flag up slowed down in front of her, quite naturally, as if to pick up a fare. Crouched in a corner so that he could not be seen from the outside, Pierre was waiting for her, a small shapeless lump, a bundle of fear on the back seat. And it was this that had terrorized her, this little thing here?

"You can relax," she said. "The coast is clear."

"What's this monkey business all about? I'm warning you…"

"Monkey business? The cops are on my ass!"

"Shit! For sure?"

"Look, I wasn't born yesterday."

"I'm warning you, if you're trying to pull a fast one…"

"Just put on the light and look at my face, you'll see. And instead of hollering at me like that, give me a smoke. I've got the heebie-jeebies."

He lit a cigarette and handed it to her. She took advantage of the fact that it was dark to wipe it before she put it in her mouth.

"And as for your bright idea of bringing the kid along, she's been summoned to the precinct for questioning. How about that?"

Pierre was quiet. Denise savored the shock she had just delivered, but her pleasure was short-lived, because, when all was said and done, she was the one most at risk.

"Do they have a description of the Marseillais?" He asked after a while.

"Seems so."

"And the kid?" He asked, lighting another cigarette.

"She said she never saw him before. No reason not to believe her."

She placed her hand on Pierrot's arm. "Look, Pierrot, you've got to move the stuff out of my place, OK? It's not safe now."

"Yeah? And where do you want me to move it? To my place?"

"All you have to do is let the Marseillais have it back. We'll get along without him, just as we did before. You had everything you needed."

"No dice! Anyway, the Marseillais won't go for it."

"In any case, I don't want it in my place."

She stiffened but didn't budge when he smacked her, so as to avoid getting another one.

"You just keep your trap shut and do what you're told," he said calmly, knowing she would obey him."

"And if they search my place?"

"Just be careful and see that that doesn't happen. All you have to do is hide it well."

"If it were up to me, I know just what I'd do. It just so happens, it's cold at my place."

She clutched his sleeve.

"Just kidding, Pierrot. Come on, Pierrot, you know it was only a joke. You didn't think I was serious, did you? You know that I'll do everything you ask, right, Pierrot? Say something. Hey, what do you say?"

"Shut your trap."

She kept quiet and sank back into the seat, looking out blindly at the night speeding by outside the windows. She was very cold. She closed her eyes and dreamed she was stabbing Pierrot with a dagger. But when she opened her eyes again, he was there by her side, smoking peacefully, while the taxi drove down one dark street after another.

Chapter 7

Thoroughly familiar with the local terrain, Marcel ended up at the Palais Montmartre. Among the regulars were the little maids from the neighborhood, the divorcees and widows looking for the balm of forgetfulness. With an expert eye, Marcel looked them over as they sat there, meekly nursing their eighty-franc orangeades, sipping slowly so as to make one drink last all evening. He knew from experience that, in order to be sure of achieving his goal, he would have to move in on the homeliest of the lot, that she, grateful to be singled out, would not play hard to get. Tonight, by chance, the homeliest one, only about forty years old, was still quite appetizing, despite her plumpness. She had nice smooth skin and was provided with a monumental bosom. Just looking at that pair of breasts, Marcel felt chock full of virility. *"Amor... Amor... Amor..."* Glimmering in his red satin tunic, the singer waddled around, his arms crossed in front of him, his eyelids half closed. On the dance floor, a leg sheathed in rayon caught the glare of a spotlight and rippled in the violet light. The tip of a polished shoe shone with the brilliance of a mirror. Marcel got up and went over to ask the lady of his choice for a dance.

She danced stiffly, tugging at her corset, audibly keeping time under her breath. When she missed a beat, she would bump into him and her enormous chest would be crushed softly against the delighted Marcel, who found a certain way of turning that never failed to make her lose her balance.

"Good God," he said to himself, slyly pressing up against her, "What knockers! A guy could bury his face in there, breathe in the good sweet warmth of her tits and just nestle up!"

In vain might she waddle around like a trained bear,

Marcel knew: that which caused her awkwardness now, would later be a source of pleasure, when she would gather him to her in the nightwarmth of the bed, protective as a mountain with her abundance of flesh. A wave of desire swept over him. She lived close by, at the top of the hill. Her name was Mme. Marinette. The name was nice and fresh. She probably sold eggs and cheese in the open market.

"I bet you live alone," he said.

"Well, yes and no. After all, I have two little ones. You see, I'm a war widow."

Uncomfortable, she fidgeted as she spoke.

"And don't you get cold at night, all alone in your little bed?"

"Oh!" she said, lowering her eyes, "I warm it up with a heated brick."

With some difficulty, Marcel managed to crane his neck over her enormous bosom and rest his cheek against hers. Growing bolder, he licked her earlobe.

"Oh! You mustn't do that here!" she said with a gasp.

"There! Right you are! Then may I take you home?"

"I wouldn't want you to get ideas."

"Absolutely not. But with the streets as dark and dangerous as they are, it makes perfect sense that I should accompany you home."

In his ear, she whispered: "Only one thing—you have to leave early in the morning because my oldest leaves early to go to work in the factory."

It was only eleven thirty when Marcel, unable to take any more, left Mme. Marinette's apartment. Upon emerging from her carapace, she was monstrous. No question of taking refuge inside her, you could drown and be annihilated. What was worse, she scratched at him and smelled rancid.

Marcel set out in search of an open café, where a good glass of brandy would counteract the rancid taste. But the streets were silent and dark. No light anywhere. Yet, let it not be said that Marcel Setier couldn't manage to get himself something to drink. It was a point of honor. He directed his feet towards the great boulevards.

On the first floor of a building, finally, he saw a neon sign: "Hotel de la Paix," hospitable and engaging, despite the fact that the "L" was burned out. Hote de la Paix. Sort of made you want to go on in. Rent a room and be able to tell yourself as you climbed up the stairs, bouncing the key up and down in the palm of your hand—finally: peace. But the door was closed and, in any case, he knew well enough that he'd wind up going back to his room in his father's house, holding on to the wall so he wouldn't stumble and make noise.

Across from the hotel, there was another light, that of a café, "Chez Gaston." It was still open.

Not a single customer. The proprietor, sweeping up, leaned over to check if a cigarette wrapper was really empty. There was a newspaper lying on one of the tables.

Leaning on his broom, the proprietor warned: "I close at midnight."

"Not a whole lot of fun around here," muttered Marcel. "Maybe something going on in the back room?" he asked. Propelled by a last glimmer of hope, he walked back to take a look.

"Hey, you! Don't go tracking back there! I don't want to have to sweep the whole place up again. There's nothing back there for you," he added in response to the skeptical look Marcel gave him. "It's some guy. I don't know him. He comes in every evening and stares out the window until closing time. You know, it takes all kinds to make a world. As long as he keeps buying drinks, I don't ask questions. So, what can I serve you? Maybe a little calvados?"

"OK. I could go for a little calva. I'm not fussy."

While Gaston busied himself behind the counter, Marcel leaned over and looked at the little soccer players in their case, stock still under the glass cover. Pushing on a spring, he set one of them in motion, enjoying the little vibration at the tips of his fingers. He soon had enough of that.

Above the counter, the large pendulum clock was missing the big hand, so that time stood still from one hour to the next. The hole where the minute hand had been looked like a big black beetle, and as Marcel stared at it, he seemed to see the big velvety black tuft of the minute hand moving slowly. Swallowing the calvados in one gulp, he ordered another.

"This will have to be the last," said Gaston as he closed the bottle. "In five minutes, I close. No ifs ands or buts."

They should break all the watches, pendulums, clocks, church bells, alarm clocks, hour glasses, sundials, clock watchers, stop people's skin from turning yellow, growing loose and hanging from their bones like a turkey's gullet, like Gaston's gullet and Papa Setier's. How time flies, they told themselves, as they devoured birthday cakes as tall as temples. Nevertheless, the black beetle stood stock still.

"Three more minutes," warned Gaston. "Hurry up and swallow that calva."

Three minutes, two, one, like watching the fuse on a bundle of dynamite; like Papa Setier counting out his hundred steps, arms crossed on that sacrosanct belly, murmuring: three, two, one, midnight. The loafer. In the end, he'll just have to come home.

"Hey, you back there," shouted Gaston in the direction of the back room, "I'm closing up... Did you hear me? I'm closing." He finished with a rap of the dish-mop on the edge of the counter.

"You'd think he'd get a move on. He better not think he can spend the night here. The cops don't fool around these days... Hey! You back there, it's midnight and we're closing up!"

"He wouldn't be dead, now, would he?" quipped Marcel.

"For goodness sakes, bite your tongue and try not to jinx me. That's all I need. You'll see. He's just fallen asleep; I'll have to go get him. You could lend a hand by going back there and giving him a shake. In the meantime, I'll lower the shutter. At least that'll be done."

As he pushed the swinging door, Marcel immediately, and with considerable surprise, recognized the man looking out the window.

"Hey old buddy," he cried out, rushing over to him, "and here I've been, wandering around for an hour like a lost soul!"

Saul did not turn around.

"Say, old buddy, are you traveling incognito, or what?"

Gray in the face, red around the eyes, his clothes all wrinkled up, Saul finally turned around, looked at him without saying a word, then went back to staring out the window. Marcel leaned over Saul's shoulder to see what he found so fascinating. An entrance with closed double doors, and above, an illuminated sign with a broken bulb. Had Saul gone nuts? Suddenly, it hit Marcel.

"So that's it, is it? You come here every evening to spy on your sister. Shame on you!"

Turning around swiftly, Saul roared: "Leave me the hell alone. Fuck off. Do you not understand--I'm telling you to leave me the hell alone?"

"Boy, are you soused," said Marcel. "At the very least, we might have gotten plastered together."

"I am not drunk. Now you run along and go bug somebody else."

Saul was right. He wasn't drunk. Maybe not far from it, but he was holding his own.

"Come on old buddy, let's both get out of here. They're closing up, and anyway, I'm bored with my own company."

"Get yourself a nursemaid."

"Oh, shut up!"

Grabbing hold of him by the lapels of his coat, Marcel forced Saul to his feet.

"Whoa! Watch it, you're not going to pass out, are

you?"

In trying to dodge Saul's punch, Marcel lost his balance and caught hold of the bench. Woefully, he followed after Saul, who, having glanced out the window one last time, without uttering the least hint of an apology, walked out toward the door.

"You know this guy?" asked Gaston, as he held the shutter up for them.

"He's my brother."

"What a coincidence!"

Gaston disappeared behind the shutter.

Saul would not step down off the sidewalk. He couldn't take his eyes off the entrance with the double doors.

"Are you going to stand there until sunrise?" asked Marcel, dragging him along by the sleeve. "Here you are, gawking at that hotel entrance while Simone... Well, fortune favors the innocent. If you could see the walrus I just made it with, you'd be flying over to la Motte-Piquet."

Saul turned around. His gaze was drowned in the beam of light from the streetlamp, but his mouth was set in an expression of cruel rigidity.

"You're just chock full of good ideas," he said. "For once, you're right. You can drop me off at her place. It's on your way."

Marcel was sorry he had said anything. To think that he was pushing Simone into Saul's arms. He had to be nuts.

"How about I drop you off right at your own place? You have to admit, this is no time to be dropping in on people..."

Too late. He was hailing a cab.

So as not to frighten Simone, Saul opened the door as quietly as possible and then, softly, closed it again. Automatically, he put the key back in his pocket.

"Don't be afraid," he said. "It's only me."

"I'm not afraid. I knew very well it was you. What

name did you give them downstairs? Leblanc?"

"Well, I thought of telling them I was Charlemagne, but then I figured they wouldn't go for that."

Simone burst out laughing.

"What a nut you are," she said, reaching up to kiss him.

Her brown skin was visible beneath the lapels of her pajama top.

"It's not a bit too warm in here," he said, bending down to plug the heater in.

"Well, you know, it's expensive. It's crazy how that thing eats up electricity. I don't want to get stuck paying a fine. Are you getting in?" she asked, throwing back the covers. "You know you're welcome, even if you're like a bedbug. You know, you never see them until they get hungry."

"Look, I can leave. It's not as if I had nowhere else to sleep."

"We can't even kid around anymore."

She lay her head back down on the pillow; her jet black eyes sparkling between eyelids heavy with laziness and desire.

"Come closer. You didn't show up at this late hour just to have a chat."

"Well, how can you be sure?"

"Why, you're shaking," she cried, putting her hand on his forehead. "You're burning up. That's it! You have the flu. Get into bed. I'll make you a hot toddy. I had no idea! And I'll bet you're not even wearing a sweater!"

All the while chattering away, she slipped out of bed and stood before him, her smooth, strong brown thighs within reach of his lips.

"There, you see," she said as she spread his gabardine open, "I knew it! No sweater! If your head weren't attached to your neck..."

He put his arms around her and pressed his face against her warm belly. She rumpled up his hair.

"First, I have to go make the hot toddy," she said, with an air of authority.

While preparing the drink, she shivered. Her thighs were covered with goose bumps and the muscles of her heavy buttocks were tightening up.

"Come back to bed! I'll make the drink myself! So far as I know, I don't have a broken arm!"

In a single bound, she was back in bed. Saul made the hot toddy, drank it down and rinsed the glass.

"You haven't even kissed me," said Simone.

"Well, I don't want you to catch the flu."

"I could care less about the flu. Kiss me."

"Simone, I've come to talk things over with you, once and for all."

"Come to bed. We can talk later. Come hold me in your arms."

"Simone, I'm not joking. I won't be coming around any more."

"Sure. This must be the thousandth time I've heard that story. Come to bed. I'm cold here all by myself. But I'm warning you, if you crush my breast again like that, I'll bite you so hard I'll draw blood!"

The sharp taste of the rum still in his mouth, he took his shoes off, got undressed and slipped in beside her, drawn to the warmth of her thighs and belly.

"Try as you may, you have a hard time doing without your little Simone," she cooed, nestling her head under Saul's armpit and tickling him with her curly hair.

"Cut it out, you get on my nerves with all this nuzzling. I have to talk to you!"

Simone dropped the game immediately. Resting her weight on her elbow, her face suddenly pale, her nose puckered up, she said: "Mister President, the floor is open for comment."

She was so much the plucky urchin that Saul would have smiled, if he had not felt as if his head were about to explode.

"You wouldn't happen to have an aspirin, would you? I have a headache that would kill an ox."

"Poor lamb!"

Already having forgiven him, she got up to bring him the tablets, which he proceeded to swallow dry.

"Turn out the light," he said, resting his head on the pillow.

"In a minute. You see... you did wind up coming back here."

"Don't fool yourself," he said, shading his eyes with his hand. "You can thank Marcel for that."

"Ah!" she sighed, looking embarassed. "He told you. I should think he might have been a bit more discreet."

"Don't hold it against him. He did his best."

"Some help he is! Saul, you don't find me sexy any more?"

"It's not that. I don't have time any more. I have too much work, too much on my mind."

He recalled Mireille's poor face, wet with tears, and his chest stiffened cruelly. He opened his eyes, as if he wanted to blind himself, drown the intrusive memory in this other face so eager for affection. Why did Simone have this dark skin, the greedy eyes of an animal in heat, this ample body, powerfully given to pleasure, which squeezed him as if to drain him and fill him back up with her own passion, without ever quite succeeding in doing so. A woman should know how to turn herself into calyx, silence, mercy.

"All the same, you aren't going to fall asleep on me," Simone said suddenly.

"I'm not sleeping. I just have my eyes closed."

The light was burning into his head with long needles of white gold.

"What are you thinking about?"

"About you."

"Ah!" She pounced on him and held his mouth

prisoner in her own. "I don't hold a grudge, you know."

She did her best to draw out of him a quivering that no longer existed.

"Good. Good. I'm delighted. But do turn out the light."

"You don't feel any better?"

"Yes, yes. But good God, turn out the light."

The flip of a switch and the room was flooded with darkness and rest. Poor Simone, she who prided herself on being a lover who could not be resisted; how he would have liked to be able to offer her, as a reward for her efforts, some proof of her power, but his flesh was weary.

"Ah! Damn!" she muttered, rolling away from him. "I give up. If I'm so repellent to you, you could just say so."

She did not understand that the sweat in which he was bathed had more to do with his erotic efforts than with his fever.

"I don't understand it myself," he said languidly. "But when all is said and done, it's your fault. If you had chosen Marcel, you'd have no complaints."

"That's it. Blame it all on me. I guess the fact that you've become impotent is also my fault."

Saul did not answer. He was thinking of Marcel, who, regretting his own advice, had probably gone back home, seeking on his cold pillow, the warmth he must imagine the two of them were basking in now, in this bedroom full of rage and impotent passion. "So, just like that, you're spying on your sister." What could he possibly have imagined, that idiot?

Mireille's face surged up in front of him in the dark, like a magician's flower. Through the suddenly visible hotel entryway, passed the shadow of a furtive male figure. A mute cry rumbled up from his chest and Mireille's name escaped from his lips.

"Well, if that doesn't take the cake!" cried Simone. "At three o'clock in the morning, in my bed yet, Monsieur is thinking of his sister. I'll guarantee she has better things to do with herself."

"Shut your trap, you dirty bitch!"

The words shot out of him with the force of a torrent. He wanted to take them back, crush them in his fists, but already, they had hit Simone, and were sinking in. He wanted to seal her lips with a kiss. As he closed his eyes, a warm bitter taste filled his mouth, and he felt her nails digging into his back to make him let go of her. He fell, listlessly onto the pillow, the light blinding him with pain.

"Sadist, brute! You bit me! I'm bleeding!" she cried, raining a shower of vengeful punches down on his upper body. "What better souvenir could you leave me! Tomorrow at the shop, there I'll be with a swollen lip... the ribbing I'll get! And besides, it hurts!"

He wished he could pass through the wall without making a move and just disappear. Overcome by shame and sorrow, he could find nothing to say.

"Put cold compresses on it. That'll make the swelling go down."

In a shrill tone, Simone echoed his words, an octave higher: "Put cold compresses on it. That'll make the swelling go down. Is that all you have to say to me? 'Put cold compresses on it'!"

The blood had begun to bead up on her lip. With a grimace, she licked it off.

"Simone, I'm truly sorry. You can bite me back if it'll make you feel better."

She took his face in her cool hands and looked into his eyes.

"But what is the matter with you?" she asked, her voice at once harsh and tender. What's eating at you to make you hurt me like that? You been pushing too hard? It's true, it can drive you crazy when you just can't make it."

From where did she draw this strength, disregarding her own violence and rancor, to extend this simple charity? Maybe it was another manipulative ploy.

"We have to stop seeing each other," he said. "Don't

you agree?"

She nodded; the sheet she had pressed to her lip was soaking up the blood. She looked at him sadly, with pity. He got out of bed, leaning on the iron bars long enough to get over his dizziness, and pulled on his trousers. Simone watched him get dressed. When he had put on his shoes, she kneeled down, casually, and did the laces for him, knowing he suffered from vertigo, and if he leaned over too far, he could lose his balance and topple forward; she tied the laces as if it were the most natural thing in the world for her to do so, as if nothing much had just happened between them.

"All the same," she said, "men are weird. I don't get it. Just my luck, I suppose. Too bad. We would have gotten on so well together."

Saul began to laugh; softly, hoarsely, his chest full of sickness. The irony of the situation had just hit him in all its drollery: Simone all alone in this big double bed, and Marcel, also alone, charging around like a bull, hardly able to contain his erotic power. And in between the two of them, Saul, the inept lover, the bungler of opportunities, spoiler of good fortune... the incompetent. How fucked up it all was!

"Why are you laughing," she asked. "I forbid you. Why don't you just say that I jump into bed with the first guy that comes along? You see, I liked you..."

"And why not Marcel?" said Saul dully. "He would fall all over himself in his eagerness to please you; you would make him happy. Everybody would be happy. He might even marry you; you know, the guy loves you..."

"Shut up. Get out. You! I can't believe how mean, how vicious you can be..."

"You're right about that," he admitted mournfully. "I can't understand. I don't do it on purpose... It's like those two princesses in the fairy tale; fine pearls from the lips of the first, and from the other... toads and snakes... I don't remember exactly how it went... it's incredible how I'm losing my memory."

Simone wrapped her arms around his neck. Her voice filled with deafening pity, she murmured: "My poor little fellow..."

He pushed her gently away, rummaged around in his pocket, and threw the key on the sheet.

"You should always have a spare key," he said. "A master key, an open sesame. Or else don't have any mysteries in your past, or better yet, no past at all, no master key; otherwise, not knowing where you are, you find yourself, one fine morning, stone cold, the fingers of mystery tight around your throat, and no key..."

Her eyes overflowing in disbelief, Simone looked at him without saying a word.

"All the same, think about what I've told you," he said, smiling. "He's really not so bad as all that, I mean, Marcel. And then, with him, you always know where you stand."

Simone kept on looking at him with the same kind of terror in the depths of her pupils that he had already seen in Mireille's eyes. He went out and closed the door behind him, without making any noise, so as to avoid the malicious gossip of neighborhood busybodies.

Chapter 8

When, surrounded by medical students and interns, the chief physician makes his entrance into a hospital ward, he is generally greeted by widespread last-minute scrambling about. The nurses hurry to remove bedpans from the patients, record temperature readings on their charts, and quickly bury in the large pockets of their aprons the little bribes that patients may have slipped them in hopeful moments. As for the patients, they hoist themselves up on their pillows so they can see and hear better; their lips move silently. An apprehensive silence descends over all.

Those who are getting well assume expressions of vaguely cool superiority. With the nod of the juror who has weighed all the pros and cons, they approve the verdicts and punishments inflicted on the others. The one for whom the doctors have already signed a release form can be recognized by his fresh shave and the crisply starched shirt that his wife brought in the evening before. All night, he's been telling himself that he's cured, but he still feels a bit weak and anxious. He's somewhat encouraged by the sight of those who will only leave the confines of this place to be carried out to the cemetery or the operating theater. They lie on their backs, their eyes set somberly in their yellow faces, and if their fingers fidget weakly with the sheets, if they toss and turn and groan a bit, people hardly notice. It's only out of respect for the principle of equality that they aren't altogether forgotten. But their hearts aren't in it; they're wearing down quickly; in their dull eyes, no glint of hope is to be seen. With disabused ears, they listen as the chorus of complainers gets going; it's their only distraction. One fellow protests that the nurse twice refused to bring him the bedpan even though she brought it to his neighbor four times during the same interval because the latter, being on a strict dairy diet, slips the nurse the oranges his wife brings him from home. And the guy whose bed is closest to the door reminds the doctor that, in his condition, he's not supposed to be exposed to drafts.

"The guy in the bed next to me smokes under the covers at night. You wait and see, one of these days, he'll set us all on fire."

"Liar. He's bellyaching because I sleep at night, and he can't."

Retracing his steps, Doctor Leret stopped at number thirteen. "My friend, if you can't keep from smoking, just go home. You know very well you're not supposed to smoke. If you want to croak, there's no sense taking up space in one of our much needed beds. Unfortunately, we have no shortage of sick people around here."

Running his tongue over his lips, number thirteen turned as white as a sheet. When the doctor moved away, he turned around to number twelve and hissed: "Bastard!"

Number twelve smiled sanctimoniously up at the ceiling.

Files in hand, spectacles on his nose, Leret seemed even slighter when he got to the bedside of number fourteen, who was sitting up anxiously. Enormous, with a head like a cannon ball, number fourteen was a war amputee. He was also the darling of the nurses, since he had a way of amusing and flattering them.

"Still!" he exclaimed, upon being told that they are not ready to disconnect him from the intravenous tube. "No fair! My arms are already like a couple of sieves!"

At the look Leret shot his way, he turned red as a beet, and the corners of his fleshy lips, stained with brown, began to tremble.

"It's not that I'm ungrateful, only, could you please have M. Goldine do it? He only sticks the needle in once, and you don't even feel it. With all due respect, M. Paul, I really feel it when you miss your mark."

When the doctor and his entourage had moved on, he turned to number thirteen and whispered in a disgusted voice: "Did you hear? They're gonna keep on boring holes in me. Talk about bad luck."

But thirteen didn't hear a word. Eyes wide open, flat on his back, one hand over his heart, he was listening to himself breathe.

Saul has put in an appearance. He followed the others from bed to bed, but his gaze was wandering beyond the bars, beyond the night lights, to rest on the outside wall, so gray, so sad. Through the closed window, you could see the naked branches of the big oak tree in the courtyard. That lugubrious courtyard, surrounded by great rigid, cold pavilions, in front of which, a hearse was parked. Fortunately, the patients were too absorbed in the doctor making his rounds to notice it.

All noises reached him through a steady barrage of humming: the tinkling of pitchers, the rustling of curtains, a throat clearing itself, somebody spitting.

"M. Goldine, go over and see your protégé; he's asking for you."

Doctor Leret's voice cut through the isolating wall of humming and reconnected Saul with the suffering that hovered over these naked bellies and limbs spread out before his indifferent eyes.

His protégé--Saul was the only one who could communicate with him in their ancient common language--was a young Polish Jew, who had, only a few months ago, gotten out of a camp for displaced persons. He suffered atrociously from pain in his large colon, but the most exhaustive exams had shed no light on the sickness that was slowly consuming his flesh. Hospitalized upon his arrival in France, he had only managed to learn enough of the new language to express his most immediate physical needs. For hours on end, he would writhe silently on his bed. Others turned away so as not to have to see him, nevertheless glancing at him in fascination out of the corners of their eyes. At night, he would suddenly wake them up with a great agonized cry, pouring nightmares into their ears.

"Moishe," Saul said to him, sitting down on the edge of his bed, "Moishe, you seem to be feeling better today."

"It hurts so bad."

"Yes, I know."

"Here."

Moishe grabbed his hand and guided it over to his stomach; under the light pressure of Saul's hand, his face twisted up with pain. Saul tore his hand away as if it were, itself, the source of sickness and pain, sensing the contortion of his own face, as if, in the contact between his skin and that of the sick man, the pain had penetrated his own body.

"I leave you the task of explaining to him the significance of this surgical operation."

Leret had walked over and was looking down at Moishe with a somber expression.

"We'll begin to prep him this evening, the sooner the better. There's no point in waiting any longer. Oh, and then, come by and see me this afternoon. I have to tell you, I don't care too much for the way you've been moping around here lately."

Saul knew he would not be showing up for this talk; Leret was good at what he did, but he was not a sympathetic fellow. Saul looked at the chair reserved for visitors the young man never received, except for the fat bourgeoise who volunteered out of pity and dozed away while the young man watched her with expressionless eyes. Now, Moishe's gaze was resting on him, anxious, breathless, penetrating, painful. How he wanted to take off running, to get away from those eyes that plumbed his soul. Other faces of tortured souls rose up before him. To forget, forget the unforgettable wounds of the past and begin to live. Although he had promised himself not to set foot in the hospital any more, here he was, back again. It was for Moishe that he had come back. He bent over towards him.

"Listen to me," he said.

Moishe was listening with every fiber of his distressed being, and Saul sensed the great anguish that his altered voice inspired in him.

"You have nothing to lose and everything to gain. If you agree, they will operate on you tomorrow, and maybe after that, the pain will go away. You have to agree. It's your only chance."

Saul reproached himself for blurting it out so brutally, but the fellow had to be realistic. An old man at the age of seventeen, Moishe had to understand. You have to be realistic. Moreover, Saul had no idea how else to handle this. These subtleties required too much composure, too much detachment; you had to feel in control of yourself and also in control of the destinies of others. Somehow, their destinies did seem curiously linked together, his and Moishe's. And what if the operation only succeeded in delaying the onset of death by prolonging his suffering for a while? If there was no longer any hope for anybody, and it was Moishe's sorry lot simply to prove it? Nobody knew; not even that god of sick people hiding, ashamed of his ignorance, in the corners of hospital wards, waiting confidently for mankind to correct his bored little bad boy jokes. Moishe said nothing.

"Do you want to think it over for a while? Until this afternoon? No? Then you agree?"

Moishe made an effort to sit up and then fell back again, exhausted, murmuring in the affirmative. Saul watched him for a long time, his heart aching, and finally, with a shock, he realized that this sudden animation was not an expression of terror, but one of hope. He would have to be encouraging, tell him what an excellent man the surgeon is, that he need have no fear... Even so, Saul knew that the next day, when, rolled up in blankets, white wool booties on his feet, Moishe was rolled into the operating room, that glimmering ray of hope would vanish and the terror of the unknown, lying in wait on the operating table, would grip his heart.

"I'll come back tomorrow," he said. "Everything will

be fine."

That lie was his farewell. He ran to the door, knocking into Paul, who uttered a curse, fumbling with the syringe he was carrying. He caught it just in time to continue on his way over to number fourteen.

In the corridor, Saul lit a cigarette, smoking it stubbornly despite the pain in his chest, despite the fact that his throat was on fire. From the maternity ward, a howl pierced the wall. He tried to imagine Moishe as a newborn; but in his mind's eye, he could only come up with the face of an old man disappearing into the swaddling clothes. They had said of him: "Look, he's smiling at the angels." At the angel of death, which any odor of new life summons from the cemeteries, eagle wings outspread. How many times had he felt them, those black wings, slipping furtively into the wards, in back of the nurses, and, in their shadow, bringing on the night? And peace? Moishe told them no, agitated with a single thought, eloquently audible in his eyes: to live. Say yes to life with a passion that scares memories away and keeps them at bay. The power of the past is something we can determine. A man who could overcome his memories without having to destroy them, that man could calmly welcome all the days to come. Tomorrow, Moishe would bring this proof back from the unknown. But Saul would not be there, he would not know. He would never know. It was not enough to see bodies fall, in surprise, at the side of the road without ever having had time to know why. It was not enough to have seen, in the morning, the emptiness of beds that were occupied the evening before. You have to have been on familiar terms with death for a long time, to have known her intimately, like Moishe; to have struggled with her, in order to be able to talk to her, come to terms with her. You have to be able to sit up in the coffin before they finish hammering in the nails, and, stretching out cheerfully, push it far away with your two arms outstretched.

Back in the cloak room, Saul tore off his surgical jacket, rolled it up in a ball and put it in a paper bag. He also threw his instrument case and his fingernail brush in, checked to see that the locker was empty, and leaving the door ajar, went out into the street, his gabardine thrown hastily over his shoulders.

Chapter 9

Sita had a luxurious apartment in Passy and from time to time, she gave parties. Whoever heard about them was welcome to show up. A bagful of petits-fours for the young women, a bottle of something alcoholic for the young men, served as the requisite admission pass. Saul had always refused to take Mireille. But on this occasion, she had been so insistent that he relented.

Mireille stood with her back to the blood-red velvet window drapes and, for the tenth time, having nothing else to do, admired the pleasant living room decorated in tones of burgundy accented with antique Chinese jade. She didn't know a soul among all these young people, except, of course, for Saul and Marcel, who were engrossed in a conversation she didn't want to interrupt. There was nothing for her to do except get absorbed in the contemplation of prints and porcelains, doing her best not to seem bored. Impressed by all this luxury, she was glad she had borrowed a new dress from Denise. She was just beginning to be frankly sorry she had come, when, sensing the mute appeal of an insistent gaze, she turned her head. She was startled to realize that she had guessed correctly. Two eyes were staring at her, smiling and amused, through honey-colored irises. The fellow was sitting on the ground, back to the wall, knees brought up to his chin, his thumb stuck in the pages of a little pocket dictionary. Ill at ease, she returned his smile. With an astonished expression, he buried himself back in his dictionary, leaving Mireille with the disagreeable impression that she had been mistaken, that she had been too forward, that she had made a fool of herself.

It was consistent with Saul's character that he would have agreed to bring her along only to leave her by herself in a corner, so as to make her regret having accepted the invitation.

She would manage without him. A bunch of young people gathered around the grand piano: all she had to do was join them. Circling around so as to avoid a tall gangly fellow with a long neck who was demonstrating a dance step, she slowly approached the group. A man whose face was red with a skier's sunburn was using his left hand to dabble with the keys, while wrapping his right arm around the waist of a blonde who was openly laughing and making fun of him.

"Are you going to stop making this racket any time soon?"

Throaty and mysterious, a woman's voice spoke out behind Mireille, startling her.

"Good grief, are you going to stop? *Ou faut-il que je vous vide?* Do I have to throw you out? Still, if only you knew how to play. At this rate, you'll wreck the piano."

The skier stopped fingering the keys, pursed his lips and said: "See here, old girl, if you throw us out, I'm taking my bottle with me."

Sita had green eyes and high oriental cheek-bones. She rested her eyes on Mireille and stared unapologetically.

"What's your name?" she asked in her throaty voice.

"Mireille. I'm here with Saul. I'm his sister."

"Very good. I love seeing new faces. That joker! He never even told me he had a sister! Mireille, eh? It's a name for shy people. You are shy, right? Just wait. By dawn you'll be over it. A kiss to seal our friendship."

Sita had lifted herself onto the tips of her bare feet and brushed Mireille's lips with her own before Mireille had a chance to turn her head and present her cheek for a kiss.

Then she walked off, slipping her hands in the pockets of her tight-fitting black velvet tights.

"Pamela," she cried, resting her hand on the arm of a tall young woman with straight, drabby-looking hair, "would you be so good as to explain to your compatriot that he's not here to do his homework?"

Pamela was chattering away. She interrupted herself

long enough to turn toward the man with the honey-colored eyes, and say, in a weary tone: "*Frank, please put the book away.*"

"Just a minute, Sita, I'm looking up the word '*vider*,'" said Frank, with a troubled expression.

Sita burst out laughing. "You won't find it in there," she said, walking over to Frank and mussing up his hair. "'*vider quelqu'un*' means to throw him out, make him *clear out*. Get it?

Frank's face lit up. Breaking into a grin that showed all of his teeth, he set the dictionary down on the floor.

When Mireille looked around to see if she could find Saul, he had disappeared.

"Did my brother leave?" she asked Marcel, sitting down next to him on the couch.

"He'll be back. He went out to see somebody. A friend. Tell me, have you noticed that the *Amerlo* can't take his eyes off you?"

"Oh!" she said, shrugging her shoulders, but she could feel herself blushing. "My brother is incredible. Do you think he could at least have introduced me to the hostess? By the way, is she Chinese?"

"You'd swear she was, huh? No, she's Indochinese, and only on her father's side, at that. Her mother is Russian. You may have noticed her green eyes? That's the real Sita. It's best not to be taken in by her smiles. You wouldn't think so just to look at her, but she can be remarkably cruel... you see that tall gawky girl, the American... you should see the two of them together, a veritable game of cat and mouse. Just watch."

Mireille watched. Among the dancing couples, Sita's tights were a flash of light moving in and out. She danced with Pamela, holding her very close.

"I would have expected her to dance with her American friend," observed Mireille in a tone of studied detachment.

"You're adorable," answered Marcel.

He not only had a glass in his hand, but also a spare bottle, and he drank incessantly. Mireille was just about to tell him he was getting drunk when, all of a sudden, she caught Frank staring at her. Instantly, he turned his eyes away and settled his gaze on Pamela, a strange look of pity glimmering in his eyes. The young women were hardly moving, squeezed up so close against one another that they hampered each other's steps. Mireille suddenly felt ill at ease. Sita's hand wandered up and down Pamela's back and stopped at the nape of her neck, which she proceeded to knead gently. Except for Mireille, this spectacle did not seem to surprise anybody, not even Frank, whose expression of pity seemed frozen on his face.

"I kept telling myself that you'd figure it out," said Marcel. "Look, part of me shares your opinion. Some things are just not attractive. They should be indulged in private, like all other human weaknesses. But wait for daybreak. Then you'll see the trick she is going to play on her. I wonder how Pamela will hold up."

"Well, now that you mention it, just what happens at daybreak? Everybody here seems to talk about nothing else."

"The magic will be over. It's that simple."

Magic. She had succeeded in meeting Frank's gaze once again. All the while filling his pipe, he did not take his eyes off of her, and was spilling tobacco all over. The desire to speak was visible on the tips of his eyelids. Soon, Saul would be back and that would be the end of the magic; it would be daybreak. Incapable of making any effort, mustering any courage, she felt only desperation and rage. And what about the others?

The heavy clay of their faces in the filtered light of the lampshade, the sickening pervasive odor of alcoholic drinks and overflowing ashtrays. A tunnel of thickening silence was building up around each one of them, sealed up at both ends, shutting them off from the light, locking them up in solitude; a chrysalis from which no butterfly would ever break free, a worm condemned to feed on itself eternally, in the dark, with no dream of possible escape. It was the time of the chrysalis, of the strangled voice, of unseeing heavens and this thing that was herself beginning to twist and turn, to suffocate in the lethargy overwhelming her and dragging her down into nothingness.

They passed by, talked, touched each other, made love, and it meant nothing. Boredom and apathy had softened their muscles; they dragged each other along in the snare of the dance like shipwrecked people afraid of drowning all alone.

Mireille threw herself back among the cushions on the couch and closed her eyes. The faces passed by like figures in a curious Mardi Gras parade. A strangely syncopated music, sensual, irresistible, rose from the record player. It spoke of unfamiliar, primitive lands where boredom was unknown, of warm eddying wind and sand, of grass breaking into flame, of scarlet cloth draped on bronze-colored bodies imprisoning the violet reflections of a sky that was too blue. All around Mireille, everything faded off into the madness of instinctive cravings awakened by the music, flowing the length of her legs, her thighs, her belly and breast like the lips of a man with a honeyed gaze. The rhythm, accelerating into rage, arched her back, made her breasts swell, squeezed her waist with its liquid hands, nestling, trembling in the depths of her flesh. Tensing up, Mireille was open to everything: palpitations hitherto unknown to her body, guts knotted and drowning in the overwhelming fluidity of her belly, the cruel hunger invading her and the tall grasses, still far away, where she could throw her face down on the earth, there to stifle the trembling of an exhausted body.

At the grinding of the needle on the record as it finished, she held back a great cry of distress as her field of vision shattered into a thousand splinters of light.

She opened her eyes. The living room was plunged in darkness. A sound of flushing water burst forth indiscreetly. A door slammed. A phantom on the wall disappeared. Somebody was snoring peacefully, sated.

"Twenty to four," Marcel said suddenly.

"And Saul hasn't come back yet. I hope nothing has

happened to him."

"Don't trouble yourself. If what's happening to him at the moment should happen to me, I wouldn't complain about it."

There was such bitterness in Marcel's voice that she was prompted to ask: "Have you two quarreled?"

"You don't quarrel with Saul. The worst of it is that he would rather destroy something when he's finished with it than let somebody else enjoy it. I don't understand."

"That's Saul for you," she admitted. "That's the way he is. There's nothing to be done about it."

"He must really run you through the mill."

"Oh, it's not the same for me. I'm his sister. Anyway, he hasn't always been like that, as you well know. But these days he's getting worse, he's getting to be bitter. He doesn't have an easy life."

"Oh really! And you do?"

It was a challenge. Mireille shrugged her shoulders.

In the midst of much grumbling, yawning and stretching, the lights came back on. Garments in various stages of disarray were hastily tidied up. Blinking his eyes, Frank seemed to wake up. The sound of shattered glass and Sita roaring: "If that's another glass, I... I don't know what I'll do."

Her face was smeared with lipstick. Clumsily buttoned up, her bodice pulled under one arm. Pamela was also smeared with lipstick.

"Marcel, put some music on," cried Sita. "What's the point of installing yourself next to the turn-table? Next time, we need to get a warm body in there. Put on a rhumba. Armand, come over here. We're going to do the rhumba."

Pressing close up against the man with the long neck, Sita shook her hips, and wiggled about, defiantly gauging the effect she was having on Pamela, who, with her lips set in a bitter smile, never turned her eyes away from her.

"There! Now it begins," said Marcel. "Poor Pamela!"

Mireille made no comment. She was not at all sure

that Pamela was the one most to be pitied. Dark circles forming beneath her green eyes as she clung to Armand despite her evident lack of feeling for him, Sita seemed utterly exasperated, and her exhausting effort seemed much more pathetic than Pamela's frank jealousy. Sita was only an exhausted soul, trying to forget her limitations, trying to escape in a whirlwind of pleasure that continued to elude her. A little Narcissus lost between two flowers: the troubled stream and the reflection of his own face, his water-green eyes. Pamela's lustreless eyes sparkled now, shining with silent hatred, her ashen face rigid with it.

"They simply detest each other!" murmured Mireille.

"Who?" asked Marcel, sitting back up.

"Who do you think?"

"Sita and Pamela? Perhaps." Then, after a pause: "You are kind of a romantic. Well, look here," he announced, suddenly, pointing at the doorway, "It's the return of the prodigal son."

Saul was bent over the doorsill, tying his shoe laces. His hair was wet.

"It's snowing," he announced as he stood up.

"Did you succeed?"

Marcel's voice was bursting with restrained impatience.

"At the Rotunda, tomorrow at three o'clock. Don't keep her waiting. I know Simone, she's quite punctual."

"No problem. Say, you don't think she's going to stand me up, do you?"

"That would surprise me."

"Thanks, old buddy. How much do I owe you for the taxis?'

"You didn't hear me say it was snowing?"

"No kidding, you walked all the way?"

"No, I hopped an angel. Anyway, I would have gone straight home only I had to come back to get this one here. And how are you?"

Suddenly, he was overcome by a coughing fit. He flopped down onto the couch, bent over, soaked with perspiration, quite pale, his body shaken with spasms. He quickly pulled out his handkerchief and put it over his mouth.

"He must have swallowed the wrong way," said Marcel, slapping him loudly on the back. "Here, have something to drink, that'll help you get over it."

"You stupid ass!" said Saul, when his cough died down. "You nearly did me in with your slapping!"

He nevertheless accepted the glass of alcohol Marcel offered him and emptied it in a single gulp.

"I thought it would help, I thought you had swallowed the wrong way. I shouldn't have asked you to go there in this weather."

"Don't worry about it. This is chronic. I caught it during the Occupation. In April, it goes away."

Marcel turned toward Mireille testily. "You could at least see to it that he takes care of himself."

"If you think he'd listen to me..."

She recalled the terrible winter of 1943. The snow had piled up against the walls of the barn and, in spite of the cold coming in through the cracks, Saul would pile all the blankets on her every night, insisting that men don't feel the cold.

"Don't listen to him, Mireille, he means well. But he... It's crazy. You have no idea how tired I am," said Saul.

How frail he seemed, all of a sudden, fragile, as if the least blow could reduce him to a pile of dust. In the amber light of the lamp shade, his eyes seemed to sink into his face, in the hollows of his cheeks. They focused desperately on Mireille's, enveloping her in their gray solitude.

"She's a good girl," he said wearily.

"Who's a good girl, Saul?"

"Simone, of course. You see..." It was a mystery he was trying to explain, some old medieval mystery. "That girl... it's a pity..."

His distant gaze became piercing, almost mean. His

mood changed suddenly. "Anyway, I don't see why I'm telling you all of this. After all, it's none of your business."

"Go on, I get it. You both disgust me with your manipulations. If I were in her shoes, I'd tell you both to get lost."

"You're wrong, Mireille. We're not manipulating anything. We're doing our best. We don't always do brilliantly, but what do you want from us? Come, I'm going to get you to dance. It's nearly daylight."

He was light on his feet and danced well, sober and dignified, holding her firmly in his arms. But the natural movement of their bodies made their thighs and their bellies brush against each other. A troubling warmth ran over her. She stiffened and stopped.

"I can't dance so close," she said, "my feet get tangled up."

"Sure you can!" Saul's gaze cut into her while he drew her closer. "When we were celebrating the Liberation, as I recall, your feet didn't get tangled up. I was watching you."

Abruptly, she disengaged herself. "With others, it's normal, but..."

Then, Saul did what only he, in all the world, could have done. Stepping out into the middle of the room, he announced: "Hear ye, hear ye, good people. My sister is dying to dance. Any volunteers?"

Then, turning to Mireille, he added: "You won't be able to say that I haven't done everything I can to make this a pleasant evening for you." Having said this much, he turned on his heels and went to get himself something to drink.

Mireille was aghast. Tears of shame and anger rose to her eyes; her throat choked up: she could hardly say a word. And then, as if to put the finishing touch on her humiliation, Frank had gotten up, choosing this, of all moments, to approach her.

"I'm volunteering," he announced, cheerfully.

"Oh, please, I beg you. This is not the right moment.

Don't pay any attention to my brother. Sometimes I wonder if he's crazy."

She turned around to wipe away a tear that she had not been able to hold back. It was not supposed to be happening like this. He would have come over to ask her to dance. He would have held her close, awkwardly, pretending not to be aware of what he was doing. In order to break the ice, he would have murmured something silly in her ear... Their cheeks would have brushed up against each other. And then he would have asked if he could see her again and Saul would never have known anything about it. He had waited too long to make his move. Saul had come back and was already constraining her.

"I don't feel like dancing," she said with the tips of her lips. "Let's sit down."

"Yes."

He seemed relieved.

"I dance awkwardly."

She led him over to the back of the piano where Saul could not see them so easily. He offered her a cigarette and played with the empty pipe between his lips. When he extended a light, the match lit up a pair of thick, stocky, powerful hands, with strong, squarish fingertips, nails cut short with no concern for elegance. He lit another match, lighting his strange eyes up with ironic glints of blue, green, gold as the flame, evasive as the flame, and rather openly checking her out.

Prompted by questions, he responded casually, in an evasive manner, which revealed a taciturn nature; but Mireille conducted her interrogation skillfully, and little by little managed to glean sufficient information for a first encounter.

"Well, America is OK," she said with admiration. "So, just like that, all veterans can go to school for four years at government expense? Even those whose parents are rich?"

"My parents are not rich. They aren't poor either. In America you have to have lots of money to qualify as rich."

"Here too," she said, and they both laughed.

Now, he was talking more easily. He loved France and the French. He found them sympathetic. He had been in the battle of Normandy. Already, at that time, he had promised himself he would come back after the war. He was studying etymology.

"Why?" she asked.

He didn't know why; he loved languages, it must be that.

"Ah!" she said, "so that's why you carry your dictionary around with you."

A bit embarrassed, he smiled. "There are lots of words I don't know. And the grammar! French grammar is terrible!"

He pronounced "grammar" like "*grand-mère*," which made Mireille laugh.

He was pleased to be able to make her laugh. His blue-green eyes gleamed with glints of gold. A summer day glimmering in his eyes.

"And Pamela?" she asked, point blank.

"Oh, Pamela is very rich."

This remark shocked Mireille, but she didn't let it show.

Frank went on. He had known Pamela for as long as he could remember. For years, they had lived on the same street, gone to the same school, played in the same great park in New York City. Then she had gone away to a boarding school for young girls. When she returned, she had changed. She had found herself.

"I'm Frank Karson," he said, suddenly remembering that he hadn't introduced himself. "And you're Mireille Goldine. I know that because I asked Sita." He took her hand and shook it.

"Charming custom, getting to know each other through the hands. Friends?"

"Friends," she repeated, nimbly pulling her hand back.

Saul was walking over, and the way he was nibbling

his lip presaged no good. Her hands falling into her lap, the bitterness of dejection filled her mouth. She began to smile at him, a weak, needy little smile, all the while reproaching herself for her weakness, all the while hating herself, she invited him to join them.

"Do you realize what time it is?" Saul asked, thrusting his wrist in her face.

"Have a seat, Saul. M. Karson is telling me all kinds of interesting things about America. It's an extraordinary country. Tell him about this business of scholarships for veterans."

At Saul's approach, Frank had stood up, and since, despite Mireille's invitation, Saul did not sit down, Frank also remained standing.

Somewhat diffident, Frank said little to Saul, who, by ignoring him, humiliated Mireille much more than her companion. As for him, he seemed to know all about family quarrels, and to have had his fill of them.

"It's getting late," he said to Mireille, resolutely turning his back to Saul. "I'll say good night to Sita, and then, if you'd like, I can accompany you to your place."

Before Mireille had the time to realize what was happening, Saul grabbed Frank's arm and asked him rather belligerently what he meant by that. Frank responded that Saul was mistaken about his intentions. He spoke in the dry, biting tone of a man who will not be able to contain his anger much longer. With a rather violent movement, he had pushed Saul back and stood there, his body on the alert. Alarmed, Mireille looked around for Marcel, hoping he would separate them, but he had already left. She recalled Frank's powerful, muscular hands, made for heavy labor, and Saul's delicate, slender hands, shaped like leaves, made to bring children into the world. She didn't know what bothered her more, the fear of seeing them come to blows, or the humiliation and ridicule to which Saul was exposing her in Frank's presence.

Her aversion to violence won out. She grabbed Frank's

fist and pulled it back before he could land a punch in Saul's face.

"Don't pay him any attention," she breathed, "you can tell he's crazy."

At that moment, Saul began to insult him, shouting that he could pack up his friendly intentions and take the next steamer home, that his friendship was one thing a Frenchman was not obliged to buy from America, Marshall Plan or no. Frank looked at them both with compassion, shook his head and walked off, striking the flat of his hand against the little dictionary that made a lump in his pocket. Maybe he would never come back. She wanted to run after him and ask him to wait, but Saul wasn't budging and she was afraid to start the whole thing up again.

"Don't touch me!" she hissed. The effort of keeping her tears back stiffened her lips. "Are you happy now? Are you satisfied? This time you were lucky. But don't rub him the wrong way. You think you frightened him? Did you see those hands? They could break you in two like a piece of dry wood. Like a piece of dry wood, do you hear!"

Saul looked at her, smiling indulgently: "Go get your coat," he said, "we're leaving."

"You're so sure of yourself. If you think I'm going to leave here with you..."

He began to laugh, and suddenly his fingers, like steel hooks, bit into Mireille's arm. She moaned: "Stop, you're hurting me," trying with no success to make him let go.

"You come along, without making a fuss, or I'll drag you."

"Leave me alone. My arm will be all black and blue... OK, I'm coming."

He loosened his fingers.

"I'll say good-bye to the others and then I'll come back," she said, rubbing her aching arm.

"Mireille, I'm warning you, I'm not taking my eyes off you. I know these Americans. They think that all French women are whores and all they have to do is flash their dollar bills to make them fall on their knees."

Stricken by the cruelty of his words, she responded defiantly: "You're beside yourself with jealousy. You think nobody sees it... it's not his affluence that bothers you, it's your poverty!"

Saul turned white as a sheet, his lips moving soundlessly.

"Stop following me around like that," she said, turning around, "it's insufferable to have you all the time in back of me like a watch dog. I think I'll ask Frank to take me home."

"Oh, so now we're nice and familiar!" Saul's tone seemed less confident. His voice trembled.

"And so? Does that bother you?"

"And while you're at it, why don't you just leap into to bed with him?"

She did an about face. "Is that a suggestion?"

She watched him blanch and turned on her heels. He did not follow her. What could he be cooking up? Had she finally gotten the better of him? The cruelty, the defiance, the physical confrontation: was this the only way you could defend yourself?

Down on all fours, Armand was crawling on the carpet, looking for his tie, pure silk, imported from Italy, and with the aid of his long neck, thrusting his head quite comfortably underneath the furniture.

Not in the least subdued, Sita was hanging onto Frank's neck, reaching her lips out to him. At Mireille's approach, she disengaged herself from Frank and, staggering a bit, set her hands down on Mireille's shoulders, greedily sizing her up through the fog of alcohol that clouded her vision.

"Sister loves sister," she chanted, "but sister loves brother, and brother loves sister."

She repeated these words several times, with a sullen air, a pouting expression, hitting Frank and Mireille, each in turn, on the chest. Then she wandered off, very sad, and none too steady on her feet.

"Where's your coat?" asked Frank.

Secretly, instinctively, they had both understood they would slip out together.

"In the bedroom. It's brown, with big buttons on the sleeves."

Leaning on the doorframe, Saul smoked as he watched her. He allowed Frank to pass quietly by. Mireille's guts were all in a knot. How could she have been so naïve as to imagine, even for a moment, that she had finally gotten him to see the light?

"And where do you think you're going?" he asked, quite pleasantly.

"Where do you think I'm going? To look for my coat."

He looked at her with a mocking expression, not saying anything, continuing to smoke. At that moment she noticed, showing beneath Saul's gabardine, thrown casually on the chair nearby, a panel of brown fabric.

"Saul, give me my coat."

"Your coat?"

"You know very well that you've got my coat. OK. Sita will lend me one."

"I doubt that."

Frank appeared in the doorway. He had put on a blue-gray overcoat with long straight lines that made him seem even taller than he had before. "I've looked everywhere. No brown coat."

Saul was smiling with a smug expression that made her feel like smacking him. With his left foot, he kept time to some silent tune. With all of her senses alert, Mireille kept her eyes on him. Only by means of a stratagem would she ever get out of here; but she would have to be very skillful, because if she muffed it and Saul hit her in front of Frank, she would die of shame. She took a step forward and Saul, alerted, tensed up with a look that hit her like a smack in the face.

"I was just going to pick up the pen that you gave me.

It must have fallen out of my pocket, there, behind the chair."

Taking advantage of the split second when he bent down to look under the chair, Mireille leaped over, grabbed the coat by one corner, and pulled with all her might. The chair tipped over and fell on Saul. She had already fled out into the corridor, dragging the coat on the ground behind her. The heavy, loud footsteps of a man followed her down the stairway. Her heart stopped. Then, blessedly, Frank's voice called out, urging her to be careful not to fall.

In the street, panting, out of breath, she let herself fall into his arms. He helped her get into her coat. Then they walked in silence to the Metro station.

"Was it you who stopped him from following me?" she finally asked, when they had sat down on a bench to wait for the first train to come along.

He nodded his head.

"You hit him?"

This time, he didn't answer right away, even with a gesture. Instinctively, she moved away from him. Those giant hands had hit Saul. She wanted to run to him quickly, caress him, cradle him, love him, make him forget all the trouble she had just caused him, forget that Frank had hit him because of her.

"I just gave him a tap," Frank finally said. "He was the one who started it. I didn't hurt him much."

He smiled.

"You would never have forgiven me. Brothers and sisters are like that. They detest each other and they adore each other."

"I cannot tolerate brutality," she said.

They were alone in the car at that early Sunday morning hour. The warmth and the rhythmic rumbling of the train cradled them softly. Once on the way, Frank said: "Your brother is a strange man."

She replied: "Yes."

After that, they remained silent.

At the Jules-Joffrin station, he insisted on getting out with her.

"But Rue Cujas is on the other side of Paris," she protested. "Don't get off the train. You'll just have to pay another fare."

She was thinking: "If I let him walk me home, I'll have to invite him in to warm up and drink a cup of coffee. Out of the question."

As close as they had felt a while ago, a long hallway of shadows now separated them from each other. The sense of the impending unknown had slipped in between them. They looked at each other awkwardly and Mireille sensed that if it had not been for their concern for conventions, they would have turned their backs on each other and each one would have run away from the other. In his eyes, the blue layer resting on the green suggested a ferocious winter night. Suddenly, he took her in his arms and crushed her mouth against his.

Suffocating in the arms of that colossus, against that mouth that took her breath away, she struggled.

"*Don't tease me, Baby,*" he murmured in her ear.

Her only answer was to close her eyes and reach for him with her lips.

Chapter 10

Denise sniffled and sucked her abdomen in, the better to slide her dress down over her hips. "Bunch of bastards," she thought, crouching down and running her hand along the slit of the skirt, "degenerate, stingy bastards. To listen to them talk, you'd get the idea that we should pay them."

She unfolded the thousand-franc bill, smoothed it out and slipped it into the wad that she stashed away in a crack under the sink.

"One more that bastard Pierre won't get hold of. Not so dumb. In a world crawling with the likes of Mme. Dufour and Pierre, it took a magician not to starve to death or have to walk around bare-assed."

She lifted the moss in the wicker basket of artificial flowers on the bedside table, peeked under it, and then put it back in its place. Up to now, all was well. "If only it lasts!" she said to herself, knocking wood. Her short silk slip displayed her pale thighs sheathed in transparent black stockings. Pretty well stacked, for a thirty-year-old. If only she could manage to get out while there was still time... She undid her stockings carefully and rinsed them out. She was down to the last of three pairs that handsome captain Marty had given her. Rotten luck that he had had to go back to America. Such a nice fellow, not at all tiresome, not demanding. All he asked was to lick the soles of your shoes; that was all it took to make him happy. A pity that guys like that didn't grow on trees. So much money, he didn't know what the fuck to do with it all. It was enough to make her scream to think of all the cash that passed through her hands before winding up in Pierre's pocket. Pierre, for one, was a guy who could never get enough money, not ever. The bills slipped through his fingers so fast that it made you wonder if he was gobbling them up or wiping his ass with them. "You're getting lazy, you slut, you're letting yourself go." For Christ's sake, it was her business to let herself go flat on her back with her legs spread open. "Don't you be getting any ideas, Sweetheart." And a smack in the mouth just in case. He was all bluster with her, but let a man, a real man show up, and you want to see him skedaddle. Problem was that men, real men, a one-armed cripple could count them on his fingers.

Denise sniffed and pulled out the bidet. While the water was warming up, she stood in front of the mirror on the wardrobe door and submitted her body to the ritual examination to which she exposed herself every evening. Her skin, after all, was her meal ticket. She caressed her shoulder, her neck; not a pimple, a blemish, a spot. Proof that she had no disease.

Straddling the bidet, the bottom part of her slip bunched up under her chin, she shivered, hummed, and to make herself forget that she was cold, amused herself by popping soap bubbles. She raised the water in her cupped hands and poured it over her belly, eager to feel the way she had long ago, clean and fresh and pure as when she was eight years old and no man had stuffed his filthy hand into her little girl panties.

Once again in front of the wardrobe with the mirror on the door, she contemplated herself from behind, the towel stuffed between her thighs, spreading out on her ass like a big white tail.

"Rally to my white panache," she commanded the mirror, "I'm a bird of paradise; a regal bird of paradise with a panache for a tail."

And she took to walking back and forth, prancing like certain nude dancers all decked out in ostrich plumes.

"Good grief, what an idiot I am!" she said to herself, hanging the towel up and slipping into her peignoir to go out to the toilet.

The corner of a *France-Soir* was sticking out between the wall and the pipe running down from the water tank. She tore off two pieces and covered the seat with them before she sat down. Elbows on her knees, she started to read what was left of the newspaper. The Corsicans were having a jolly time killing each other left and right. The cops didn't have to lift a finger, since their work was done for them. Just last year, she had gotten to know a guy from Corsica. When he was just out of the slammer, still shorn like a sheep. Ten years for chopping the head off one of his women and throwing it into the Seine after sewing it up in a potato sack. "Why are you telling me all of this?" she had asked, feeling kind of uneasy. He had a swell kind of half smile. "We have to get to know each other," he had answered. At least he was a guy who did things properly; not one of these pimps who would ruin your cheeks with two swipes of a razor just so as to avoid being picked up for murder. But all her efforts had been for nothing, because he had had his fill of the slammer and had no interest in bumping Pierre off. She shivered. "Shit! Maybe someday it'll be my head they'll fish out of the Seine! Say what you like, things like that didn't seem to happen to men. She looked for the feuilleton so as to distract herself from the bad news, and then let out a curse: she was sitting on top of it.

The violet-gray dawn was slipping in through the little bathroom window. There was a furtive noise in the corridor. Startled, she sat up. Maybe it was that disgusting old man in room 21 who spied on her from behind his half-open door, as she had often seen him doing, grimacing with his rotten teeth. To have to put out for a monstrosity like that! She'd rather croak. Fortunately, she was still young and beautiful; but later, when she wasn't any more? She hadn't forgotten the old whores along Toulouse Canal Street, half eaten away with disease and filth, crouching in corridors crawling with vermin, all their dreams of escape boiling down to this: the water in the market gutters carrying away their leftover rotten vegetables, the ordure from the latrines, the debris of fetuses. Sooner than that, no doubt about it, she would rather croak.

Stealthily, she went over to the door and brusquely

opened it. There was nothing but a woman's shadow at the other end. Mireille, coming home.

"You know, that's how people fall into debauchery," grumbled Denise as she sneaked up on Mireille, slipping her hands over her eyes.

Mireille let out a cry.

"Hey! I didn't mean to frighten you all that much! I only wanted to surprise you."

"Well, big surprise--you did surprise me. I could have done without it."

"But I'm telling you it was just for a laugh. And what about that surprise party? How did it go? Come in and tell me all about it. Just for two minutes! Surely you can spare two minutes. I did lend you my dress!'

She cajoled and pleaded until Mireille finally gave in.

"OK. Quick. Tell me everything," said Denise, taking a bottle of Armagnac out of the bedside table, along with a couple of glasses, which she proceeded to fill up.

You had to admit, some people had all the luck. To go to a surprise party and meet a guy who didn't right away slip his hand up your skirt. Mireille had met a man, a real man. It was as if she had won first prize in the lottery. Denise's eyes wandered over to the photos pinned up on the wall over her bed. Robert Taylor, Clark Gable and a boxer with a Turkish towel thrown over his well-oiled shoulder. For the past few minutes, she had stopped thinking about Pierre, about the Marseillais, about the stuff parked in her room. Suddenly it all came back to her. If only she could at least get rid of the stuff. But Pierre would kill her, probably roast her over a slow flame! Even if she could get away from him, the Marseillais wouldn't let her get far. Then, after all, there was the old creep in number 21 at the end of the corridor. There was nobody for her... nobody...

"I hope for your sake he's tough... someone who'll hold his own... because some of them, whew!"

"He's an American."

Talk about luck. This girl had it all.

"Maybe he'll take you back to America with him. Nothing like that would ever happen to me. Do you think he'll take you back with him?"

"He has eyes that keep changing color. When he's happy, they're all golden."

"I don't mean right now, but maybe later, when ya know each other better. As for me, I sure would know how to handle it."

They were talking at cross purposes, like a couple of flies on opposite sides of a window.

"He's a student," Mireille continued. "That's why he speaks such good French. He kissed me."

This admission of tenderness startled Denise. Was it possible that a simple kiss, the contact between two mouths could light up somebody's face with so much happiness? She watched Mireille stretch out with pleasure at this simple memory, her eyes shining despite the fact that she was sleepy. Denise wanted to rush over to the mirror to see if she too could once again become so alive, if she could make the bad luck lines around the corners of her mouth disappear. Mireille had taken off the dress and handed it back to her with a grateful smile.

Denise threw it angrily on the bed. Not that she was envious, but the cruel pain of jealousy seized upon her heart at the sight of this skinny slip of a girl in front of her, smoothing back her tousled hair. With her shoulder blades sticking out from under her freckled skin, her small arms, and her breasts the size of your fist, she looked like a plucked chicken. Yet happiness had come calling on her, fallen out of the sky on her head like a blob of pigeon shit, dumb and ugly as she was.

"Go on, go on," she said, pushing Mireille towards the door. "You're about to fall over, you're so sleepy. I'll call for you tomorrow."

Denise buried her head in the pillow she had rolled up in a ball, but she couldn't get to sleep. The room was cold and damp as a crypt. She had never felt so cold. She slipped farther down under the covers, rolled herself up in a ball, and stuck her icy hands between her thighs. Through the yellow curtains, the light, pale as a memory, was beginning to dawn. Denise closed her eyes, stiffening her eyelids to keep other gray days from surging up out of the past. But they pushed through the door, and made themselves at home in her mind, settling over her spirits like a layer of lard on the tongue. The dawn forcing its gray light through the tender flesh of her eyelids was as gray as the Metchnikoff ward, where the walls hadn't been whitewashed for an eternity. A special ward for special women. Heels imprisoned in metal stirrups, and underneath her back, the cold damp rubber sheet. And the doctor with the lips of a priest and the eyes of a vulture who was rummaging around in her insides, as, powerless, her eyes wet with shame, she lay there like a dead one, counting her teeth with the tip of her tongue, wondering, terrified, if they would be able to tell from the number of teeth she had that she was only seventeen.

"The Lord's love washes our sins away like rain flooding a field of fertile soil, flushing out the sand that would ruin it," said Sister Mary Joseph, smoothing a wrinkle in the top sheet.

Her short, square nails were translucent as the scales of a fish. Her plump cheeks, protruding from the folds of her coif, made her look like a fat rabbit.

Denise agreed with a pious nod. Perhaps this would entitle her to marmalade on her bread, as it had at the orphanage.

Sister Mary Joseph's impeccable hands joined together, like a couple of twins, in the ample folds of her black skirt.

"You're not a bad girl," she said, prolonging the visit so as not to be skimpy with her good deeds.

Little did she understand that she ought to have left right away, that she had gone into the wrong door by mistake. If only she would leave right away, and take with her the cold dampness of church pews that followed in her wake like the stink of a tomb.

The little book with the golden pictures had not lasted long after Pierre got hold of it. "Give me a break! What's with this fucking St. Theresa shit!" Actually, they had been quite pretty, those pictures. Talk about watching her step, he made her toe the line. If she didn't watch out, he could put her back out to work on the street. After all the trouble she had taken to build up a clientele of businessmen and government employees, with an extra on the side here and there. Lucky for him she had her principles, that she wasn't a squealer, or else, long ago... a phone call to the cops on a day when he was walking around with the junk. They'd send him up for twenty years, maybe even life. "But what can I do," she'd say to herself, "I'm just a dumb broad with a belly full of principles, as if you could live on that."

When she realized what she had been thinking, she began to tremble. If Pierre knew, he'd slit her open, from her belly button to her meal ticket, like the Marseillais had done to one of his women who'd tried working on her own. She clutched her belly with both hands. You'd have to be crazy to mess up a piece of merchandise like that. How smooth the skin on her belly was, soft and warm as a butterfly's wing, warm and velvety, fond of caresses, caressing, made for pretty hands with long, pale, delicate fingers, hands like Saul's, for example. "Hey," she thought, "if you didn't think you knew everything, I could teach you a few little things that you won't find in your books." Then she sighed, squeezing the sheet which had slipped in between her thighs. Outside, a horse-drawn carriage clattered over the paving stones.

Mireille finished lacing up her shoes and sat back up. She smiled happily, at nothing in particular, at everything, at the walls stained with *fly-tox*, at the courtyard, at the sky showing through the window where she had forgotten to draw the curtain yesterday evening before going to bed. But especially at the sky, wishing that spring had come, as, overnight, it had in the depths of her soul. Noontime Sunday. How calm everything was! The snow had finished melting and the paving stones in the courtyard were drying in the sun. Soon the pigeons would come back and settle down on the drainpipes, on the window sills, murmuring and cooing, then emboldened by hunger, darting in through the open window to pilfer a crumb of bread right off the table. It was a happy vision which was suddenly spoiled by the image of Saul, stretched out on his bed, eyes filled with rancor and hate, staring at the handkerchief-sized patch of sky framed by the dormer window on the roof. She would go see him, she would explain, they would be friends again.

Denise was knocking impatiently at the door. Mireille let her in. Denise, without make-up, wearing low-heeled shoes, hair pulled back in a chignon, was hardly recognizable.

"Don't I look like a boarding school girl?" she asked with a laugh in response to Mireille's look of astonishment. "See, it's true. Clothes don't make the man. Look, I'm not pretending to be the May Queen... well yes, you know, Queen of the May. Oh, true, you were brought up here in town. I'll bet you didn't know that I know how to make cheese and preserves, or how to milk a cow. It's just a matter of knowing how. Crazy, how sexy I already was at that age. Guys used to slip me sugar afterwards."

"As they would a dog," thought Mireille, and she had an atrocious vision of a child being tumbled on the manure in a barn, a child who was howling."

Denise watched her peacefully as she smoked a cigarette. For Denise, everything had a certain immediacy. The past no longer existed and the future not yet, so why worry? Even if somebody showed her her own death in a distant mirror, she would probably shake her head, without recoiling or complaining: "tsk, tsk, to die like that, what rotten luck."

"Got a date?" she asked.

Mireille shook her head. "I have to go see my brother. I don't want him to stay mad at me." She said it testily, expecting Denise to mock her.

"Are you out of your mind? It's like you're not happy unless somebody is giving you a hard time!"

"What good does it do to hold a grudge?"

"You! A person could shit on your head and you'd say thank you!"

"He's all alone. You of all people should understand what it is to be all alone in the world."

Denise crushed the cigarette butt out on the sink and threw it on the floor.

"And whose fault is that?" she shouted in a rage. "It serves him right!"

"You don't know what you're talking about."

"Oh come on. Don't go getting sentimental on me. It goes without saying family is a beautiful thing. You call each other every name in the book, squabble with each other so bad that if nobody pulled you apart, you'd scratch each others' eyes out, and then all of a sudden, out of the blue, there you are, licking each others' wounds and wiping each other off, like a litter of kittens. Yeah, well if that's what you call family, I haven't missed a thing!"

Mireille grabbed her brush and started brushing her hair with long furious strokes. Their eyes met in the mirror, Denise's sparkling with mischief.

"All right, my little chickadee, don't worry about it. We're not market women and there's no reason to be squabbling as if we were in the middle of the square. It's just that you're not very clever. If I were you, I'd wait for things to settle down. If you think he'll open the door and welcome you with open arms, you better think again."

Mireille kept on brushing her hair. She wasn't about to admit she had lost the argument. For once, Denise seemed to be demonstrating that she had better sense than Mireille. There was no doubt about it. If she made the first move, Saul would feel encouraged to keep on treating her the same way...

"You should come take a stroll with me," continued

Denise. "It's so beautiful out. I get the blues walking around by myself. The two of us would have fun, don't you think? We could walk up the hill to the Sacre Coeur, nice and leisurely."

"No, I tell you! I'm not about to play your 'Who-do-you-take-me-for' game again. It's just nuts. Besides, one of these days, we'll probably wind up getting into trouble."

Denise made a face and stood there pouting.

"That makes it much harder. We'll just walk around the block twice. Mimi, don't you remember how we laughed last time?"

"Yes. But now it's no fun any more. What's more it's not really all that amusing to sit on a bench counting points while you prance around."

On her own, Denise was not above inventing such games as getting a man to follow her, then when he felt sufficiently encouraged to say something to her, wheeling around indignantly to snarl: "Do you want me to call the cops?"

Denise's face grew somber. Suddenly, she snapped her fingers. "I've got it!" she exclaimed. "We'll go to the street fair. You must like street fairs, tents, merry-go-rounds, beignets?"

Smiling, Mireille conceded defeat. She loved street fairs. "Well, OK, but you have to promise..."

"Anything, sweetie, everything you like, I promise. It'll be just you and me. No kidding, I swear it."

She thrust her head forward and scrupulously spat on the floor.

"We'll go on all the rides. We'll stuff ourselves with marshmallows, we'll go see the crocodile man and we'll have our fortunes told. We'll laugh like a couple of kids! OK, Honey?"

Laughing, Mireille said yes to everything. It had been years since she had been to a street fair.

"Be careful not to catch a chill, young ladies," said Mme Dufour, out in the hallway.

"The old bitch is priceless," said Denise, as they walked out onto the street. "As if she lost sleep at night worrying about our health. She can smell the thousand-franc bills in my pocket. I tell you, she can see them! It's as if my pockets were made out of glass!"

"Now, now," said Mireille, "old people are always worried about questions of health, even other people's health."

"My eye! She can't stand us. She's sneaky, just like all these old biddies. They resent us because they're out of the running, and we're not. Me, I'm not gonna hang around until I'm rancid and envious. I'll die while I'm still young and desirable like *La Dame aux camélias*. You know, it's no joke to die of TB. Did you see the film? It was enough to make your hair stand on end. I wish I could stay young forever and never die. That's what I'd like. I wish they could find a magic medicine. But just for me, only me... and you too.

"And why not for everyone else?" asked Mireille.

"Oh no. Not them. If nobody ever died, everything would go on just the way it is forever. What an existence! You've got to be kidding! It would be like being thrown in the clinker for eternity."

Denise was right. A perpetual reprieve for everybody? What a preposterous idea! They had built underground trains, and airplanes, and pumps that drew water up from out of the earth and into their apartments, they had squelched epidemics, then built infernal machines capable of sowing more destruction than a thousand epidemics, and, with the flick of a finger, they ordained, like God, that there should be light. They had a penal code, archives, midwives, and they trembled in fear; an eye for an eye, but be sure to get the first strike. Another chance? What for?

Children, all dressed up in their Sunday best, were playing in the gutter, navigating little boats made out of newspaper along the artificial stream.

An urchin, too thin for his big brother's sailor suit, his cap falling down over his ears, was standing with his nose smashed up against the window of a pastry shop, ogling fluffy meringue pastries and little cherry tarts.

"Just for good luck, " said Denise, giving the pom-pom

on his sailor hat a flick of her finger, "tell me, are you gonna give me a kiss?"

The child looked at her with a disdainfully gloomy expression.

"Since I touched your pom-pom, you know you have the right to kiss me, don't you?"

The child shrugged his shoulders and went back to looking in the window.

"Just for that, you're not getting any goodies," she said, going on into the pastry shop. "You know, it dawned on me that the war was over for good," she said to Mireille, sinking her teeth into a meringue, "when I could smell real butter and vanilla in the pastries again. Have a meringue. They melt in your mouth."

Then, noticing the child again, she burst out laughing. "He's about to have a conniption!"

Picking out a cream puff and an éclair, she ducked out of the shop.

"Here, little bunny, little guy. You really thought I wasn't going to give you any, didn't you?"

Without a word of thanks, the child gobbled up the cakes and went back to staring at the window with the same hungry look. A troubling reality surged up in front of Mireille: the children of the war would never again have enough of anything. They would devour the world. The thought took her appetite away. She leaned back against the counter and waited until Denise had eaten her fill.

Sated and smiling, Denise was humming as they walked down the street. Already, they could make out the gray canvas roof of the Marine Monster's tent, they could hear the racket of the wheels vibrating on the rails in the canyons between tall buildings, the clamor of paper trumpets, the loud speakers, the accordions, all of it punctuated by the occasional shot of a rifle. The boat-shaped giant swing flashed its green hull as it rose up into the sky with a bound; skirts filled up like sails and flapped out in the wind, revealing legs, garters, underwear. From the warming pans full of fries emanated odors of smoking lard and horse-meat sausages. A chestnut peddler with a potato sack on his head, pushed his portable stove along ahead of himself. The lottery wheels were grinding, and fortune, in the form of rag dolls dressed up in bejewelled paper dresses, gleamed beneath garlands of Chinese lanterns.

"Hurry up, you slow-poke!"

Denise was tapping her feet with impatience. Her face was glowing as, eyes open wide, she gaped at everything. She dragged Mireille first to the right and then to the left, pushing ahead, weaving in and out among the rubberneckers, pulling Mireille behind her. Ecstatic, she emitted little cries of joy, admiration, incredulity.

"Just get a load of those biceps," she said, pushing Mireille with her elbow.

A man wearing nothing but a leopard skin, was lifting barbells. The effort made his enormous muscles stand out and roll. Denise couldn't take her eyes off of him. In a low voice, she offered him encouragement: "Go for it, man, don't give up... easy does it... there you go."

"Now that's a real man!" She exclaimed proudly.

It wasn't easy to get her away. Behind the Beignet Emperor, bumper cars rode around in circles, racing each other, running into each other, making sparks shoot out on the track and tracing arabesques of flame on the grillwork ceiling with their long iron rods.

Denise was not about to be outdone by anybody. In a few light bounds on her rubber soled shoes, she had leaped over the enclosing barrier and jumped behind the wheel of one of the bumper cars. She made desperate signals to Mireille, urging her to come and join in the fun, but already, the mechanism had started up. Lips set together and hair flying out of her chignon, Denise handled the steering wheel with violent glee. Nobody got away from her. She backed cars into corners, ground into them, turned and rushed out to catch those she had missed. She was radiant, her entire body bent over the steering wheel, her eyes lit up with piercing intensity.

"Me, I just love the excitement," she said, redoing her chignon when her turn was over. I could spend hours in those things. OK. Now let's go have our fortunes told. It'll calm us down."

"No, it's too stupid," Mireille protested. "You know very well that it's impossible to predict the future. These women will even go so far as to tell you the winning number in the lottery. It's a racket, pure and simple."

"That's not so. They've predicted bunches of stuff that came true for me."

"Coincidence."

"Oh yeah, sure. Coincidences like that, I'm telling you, I'd rather know about them ahead of time."

For better or worse, Mireille found herself following Denise into the caravan of a certain Madame Carmen, who, for two hundred francs, not only predicted the future, but gave you a prize when you left, a fetish to protect you from bad luck.

Her head wrapped up in a scarf, large gold hoops hanging from her ears, Mme. Carmen invited them into an artificial darkness maintained by heavy drapery on the one tiny window. An oil lamp lit up the Spanish shawl covering the table, and also the tarot cards.

"What is it that you would like to know?" she said, addressing Denise directly, as if a real gift of clairvoyance had enabled her to guess, not only that Denise was the more credulous of the two, but also that she was the one in charge of the purse strings.

"Everything."

The gold hoops shook.

"It's better not to want to know everything, since there's nothing you can do about it anyway."

"Me, I prefer to know everything, even if I can't do anything about it."

"So, a complete reading? Two hundred francs?"

"Go for the complete reading while you're at it."

Denise shuffled the cards, cut them with her left hand, and counted out thirteen.

"For you," said Mme. Carmen, spreading out the cards. "There, you lead out with your husband, or fiancé. Watch out, he's up to something. Put another card down on this one... It's a matter of money. Put another card down... Uh, oh. Not a good sign. He's going to hurt you."

Denise shrank back in her seat as if to parry a blow. Mme. Carmen gave her a compassionate look and counted out a few more cards.

"Let's look at those who are close to you. Oh, that's better; here's the queen of hearts. Some minor irritations with the men, but nothing serious."

"See how amazing this is!" Denise exclaimed when she got her voice back. "See, the queen of hearts is you--it goes without saying."

"Somebody close to the queen of hearts. Let's see... the cards show a young man, yet his hair's all gray."

Unable to contain herself any longer, Denise clapped her hands together.

"See that? Do you see that! She even sees your brother! This will be good. We'll find out all kinds of stuff, just wait..."

A wave of uneasiness swept over Mireille. She wanted to get up and run away; she wanted to throw the cards down on the ground and slap her hand over the fortune teller's mouth. "It's all smoke and mirrors," she told herself, "only a coincidence."

"Quick, what do you see!" asked Denise.

"Be patient," said Mme. Carmen. "You never ask the cards a direct question. It brings bad luck."

She counted out a few more cards, and, in turning the last one over, let out a cry of surprise and said nothing, looking terrified. Mireille found herself standing up, leaning over the last card dealt. Denise, her hand over her open mouth, didn't make a sound.

"Let me see your left hand," said Mme. Carmen.

Timidly, almost with repugnance, Denise held out her hand.

"Well, there it is," said Mme. Carmen in a barely audible voice. "Are you sure, do you really want to know everything?"

With a grave expression, Denise nodded her head.

"Even the worst?"

Denise and Mireille said nothing. Terror was about to emerge from the unknown.

"Make up your mind. Once a thing is said, there's no going back."

"It's in the cards, eh?" mused Denise.

"Look, I don't make things up."

The silence closed back in on them, infusing the shadows with secrets.

"All right, say it," Denise blurted out suddenly, as if she were afraid she might change her mind. "Say it and let's be done with it."

"No!" The prolonged cry that escaped from Mireille's lips rose up from her guts. It came out all covered with blood, like the howl of someone being tortured. Her legs were shaking; she held on to the table.

"All right, Sweetheart, for somebody who isn't superstitious! Maybe it's good news. Even death can be good news. It all depends on who's marked for it."

Mireille did not answer. She could not take her eyes off the card that the tarot reader had just turned over.

"If it bothers the little lady," said Mme. Carmen in an obliging tone, "I can always whisper it in your ear."

She leaned over to Denise, and poured the awful oracle into her ear. Dumbfounded for a few seconds, Denise leaned against the back of her chair and began to laugh softly. At the sound of this laugh, so low, so soft, Mireille guessed that she too had been very frightened.

"That's a good one," she said. "Really good. Wait 'til I

tell you."

Then she pulled out a hundred-franc bill, threw it on the table and walked out, despite the protests of the tarot reader, shouting back that if everybody always gave her the negotiated fee, she'd be a millionaire by now.

"Were you ever right," said Denise when they got far enough away from the caravan. "It's just a lot of bullshit, the whole thing! Would you believe, your brother'd do me in? Him with the hands of a holy sister! He who avoids me like the plague! Give me a break!"

Her face grew dark. She slipped her arm into Mireille's and pressed up close to her.

"If somebody's going to settle my hash, I don't have to look all that far to figure out who it'll be. Anyhow, it's just for laughs. I never really believed in it."

Mireille thought about it. You really couldn't attach any importance to the mutterings of a fortune teller, or else, why not take the horoscopes in the newspaper seriously too? Besides, it was so ridiculous. Saul who wouldn't hurt a fly, Saul for whom Denise didn't even exist. But what if it was a sign, a warning, a chance for her to redeem herself, to undo all the pain she had caused him last night?

"Now don't tell me you're going to take all that stuff seriously!" Denise exclaimed.

"No," said Mireille, smiling. "All the same, it would have been better if we had never gone in there."

Chapter 11

M. Sarand was a contortionist. Dressed in a black leotard that came all the way up to his chin, he performed as a featured attraction in suburban movie theaters and small provincial circuses. Three times a week, when he was in Paris, he came to the studio to do his stretching exercises. He pomaded his hair with a preparation redolent of jasmine and considered himself irresistible.

Rolled up on himself like a strange black snake, his feet sticking out from his ears, his hands from his hips and his head from between his thighs, he seemed perfectly at ease. He remained in this position for a few minutes as if he were relaxing, and Mireille took advantage of the opportunity to slip her cold hands under her armpits.

Mireille paid him compliments, knowing how much that pleased him, though he invariably did his best to dismiss them.

"The public is always satisfied, but then, what does the public know?"

Slowly, he got back up on his feet and made a sweeping bow to his reflection in the mirror.

"But the artist, Mademoiselle, the artist who knows the nude body under the glitzy tights, and is aware of every imperfection, he is not satisfied; the artist is not at all satisfied. All right. Let's take it from the top."

He went and stamped on the resin and then stepped back in front of the mirror.

While she started the introduction up for the third time, he admired himself, wiped his teeth with a big sweep of the tongue, and lovingly smoothed out his heavy black hair. It was fascinating to watch them, the man and his reflection, so identical in form and movement, each one the perfect image of the other's foolishness and vanity. He rolled himself up, rolled back out, tied his legs behind his neck, rocked back and forth on his belly, did somersaults. Thus, he went through his entire repertoire, never seeming to tire of it.

"I've got it just right now," he said, landing on his feet again. "but we're no longer in style, we contortionists. Years ago, I used to tap dance, then, before I knew it, thousands of others were tap dancing. It's pretty simple. Everyone was doing it. We were a dime a dozen! But you don't get to be a contortionist just like that. No way! You wouldn't think so, but it takes muscles of steel. All the same, maybe I should try tap dancing again."

Automatically, Mireille said "yes." Frank was five minutes late and she was beginning to wonder if he would show up. The sound of castanettes and heels came from the next studio over. Sarand's confidences were annoying her.

"I need to find a sensational gimmick," he said. "You know, something that would make a splash. That's all anybody understands these days: Something that will make a splash, attract the public. You have to make people notice you. It isn't easy. As for talent, it's been a while since that made any difference. The proof..."

He stood back up, puffed his chest out. "If I could commit suicide on stage every night, they'd like that. That's what we've come to. The perilous triple somersault, motorcyclists of death, demon trapeze artists, the springboard of death, the plunge into the dark... nobody is interested in Art anymore."

He raised his leg slowly and passed it around his neck without seeming to move a single muscle in his body.

"That, you see, doesn't count for anything anymore."

He remained like that for a few minutes, looking at her out of half-closed eyes, all of which made him look like a stork perched on one leg.

Mireille nodded her head. "He isn't going to show up," she said to herself, caressing the keyboard with a distracted expression.

M. Sarand did a few more exercises, always the same, then went in to change. Frank had still not arrived. The sound of the castanettes stopped. Sarand, in street clothes, stuck his head in through the wide open door to say good night to her.

When Frank finally got there, he was three quarters of an hour late. He smiled as if he had nothing to be sorry for. Mireille turned her back to him, not that she wasn't glad to see him at whatever hour, but you had to have a bit of pride. Taking her by the shoulders, he made her turn around, and raising her chin, looked her right in the eyes.

"You're angry because I got here late," he said.

She shook her head. Furtively, she patted her hair, adjusted a barrette, wiped the corners of her mouth where her lipstick was perhaps a bit smudged. What if, all of a sudden, he didn't like her anymore? She looked up. He was still smiling, with that warmth flowing from his eyes.

"You're forty-five minutes late," she said reproachfully, and then, seeing his eyes narrow, the cold blue of his irises eclipsing the liquid gold, she immediately regretted it.

"I know," he said, stiffly. "I got lost in the metro."

It really didn't matter if it was true or not. What mattered more was his reaction. He didn't acknowledge her right to reproach him or suspect that he was speaking in bad faith. They were already looking at each other with rancor. However, he did make an effort. Timidly, he moved closer to her and said:

"I get grouchy when I'm hungry."

Then she just let herself go, all too happy to accept this excuse, and nestled her head into the hollow of his shoulder. Then, not sensing the same impetus in him, she was stricken with anguish. He was looking at her, checking her out from head to toe as if he were seeing her for the first time as she really was, no longer embellished by the black velvet sheath she had borrowed from Denise, but as she was, in her faded sweater, the skirt which had been turned inside out and sewn back together again and still showed the traces of the old stitches. He held her in his arms like a package just delivered that he didn't know what to do with. Since the pullover she had washed yesterday evening had not dried out during the night, she had been obliged to put on the one she had worn last week. Maybe she even smelled of sweat? She had heard so many stories about the odor of redheads. She made a point of maneuvering, without his noticing, so as to sniff her underarms, and felt somewhat reassured. She smelled clean. No, it was the magic of Sita's living room, the rays of light reflected in the black velvet sheath, the drop of perfume that Denise had put behind her ear, that had bewitched Frank. Now he saw her as she was, and there was no magic in that. He had expected this; that's why he was so late. He must have forced himself to show up, wondering now if he could get out of it, and, having thought of no way out, resigned himself to coming after all.

"Come on," she said, taking her coat off the hook. "Ivan is waiting for us to leave so he can lock up."

"Who is Ivan?" asked Frank as he followed her.

"The concierge, the manager, everything. Whatever you do, don't comment on his handicap. He limps."

With both hands crossed on the copper knob and head raised up, Ivan watched them come down the stairway.

"Mademoiselle Mireille," he grumbled affectionately, "because you have a soft heart, I wind up working overtime. That Sarand is a crook. Pays for one hour and stays for two."

All the while grumbling, he was checking Frank out with a sharp eye. Mireille introduced them to each other. Balancing himself on his good leg, Ivan bowed with all the dignity of the best years he had known. Then he gave Mireille a newspaper clipping: in the margin, he had scribbled the phone number of the Menards, where, twice a week, Saul gave private lessons in algebra and geometry.

"He phoned while you were working. You know, that's

against rules," he explained in an irritated tone, avoiding her eyes.

At any other time, she would have teased him, threatened to drink up all his tea, which he guarded jealousy. But this evening, she was not in the mood.

"I have to make a phone call," she told Frank. "I hope you won't die of hunger while you're waiting."

"No," he said. "Go ahead."

"I won't be long," she said, furious with herself for feeling she needed to tell him so.

She watched him sit down on the last step and light his pipe, then went into the lodge where Ivan lived and managed the studio, amusing himself by playing old records on his gramophone. She didn't want Frank to hear her conversation yet didn't dare openly close the door in his face. At that moment, Ivan shouted at Frank: "Pardon, too drafty in here," and slammed the door. Mireille gave him a thankful glance and took the phone off the hook.

First, there would be the shrill voice of Mme. Menard, then the dry crack of the receiver being plunked down on the table, then the shrill voice of Mme. Menard muffled by distance: "M. Goldine, for you *again*" then steps, and his voice: "Hello?" a clearing of the throat and then again: "Hello?"

"It's me," she said. "Ivan just told me that you called. You know you shouldn't call me at work. It's against the rules."

"I didn't realize that. I, I went to your place yesterday. You were out."

"Yesterday? Oh yes, that's true. I went to the street fair."

"Oh. Did you have a good time?"

Everything was trembling, her voice, the line, and her hand on the receiver.

"It was OK."

He had not asked with whom. He was quiet. She listened to the silence, waiting. Even the silence was trembling.

"Saul, you haven't said why you called. Is it

important?"

"What?"

"How would I know? You're the one who called me."

"Oh, no. Not really important. I wanted to say... I'll be in your neighborhood tonight... I thought maybe..."

"Ah. Bad timing. I'm going out tonight."

"What do you mean? Yes, Mme. Menard, yes, I know, I'll only be a minute. Excuse me, what were you saying?"

"I said, I'm going out tonight."

"You're going out?"

"Yes."

"Ah. With the American?"

By the constriction of his voice, Mireille understood what it had cost him to ask.

"Look. I'll keep tomorrow evening open."

"Good. Then I'll come and pick you up. We'll eat out."

Saul's voice was dull; he avoided mentioning a lot of things that he would never bring himself to tell her. Mireille ached for him.

"I'll be very sensible, Saul. I'll come home early. I promise."

By the sound of the receiver hanging up, she sensed that he had hung up absent-mindedly, slowly, his thoughts elsewhere. She set the receiver down in its cradle, put the money for the call down on the desk, and, smiling sadly at Ivan, went out to join Frank.

Frank wiped his mouth and put his napkin down next to his plate. He had eaten abundantly, almost entirely in silence, and had just ordered coffee for them both.

"You don't eat very much," he commented.

He smothered a belch, stuffed his pipe and lit up. The accumulated silence lay between them like the leftover meat and salad on their plates. Mireille insisted that she had eaten her fill. The silence closed in again. Frank yawned, puffed on his pipe, exhaled and yawned again.

"It's part of the digestive process," he said.

"It's boredom," thought Mireille.

The waiter brought the coffee. Frank continued to smoke in silence as he stirred the sugar in his cup. He made a remark about American coffee, which he considered superior, then, once again, settled into muteness. Mireille sighed: "Ah!" Her lips were trembling with anger and disappointment. He despised her, it was clear. She was no longer pretty enough. He resented her for his own disillusionment. She had to make an effort not to throw her napkin down and run out of the restaurant, forcing herself to remain seated across from him, enduring the humiliation in which his contemptuous silence imprisoned her. She thought: "Say the food is awful, that you didn't sleep last night... but that it's not because of my shabby clothes or because my hair is limp from the humidity." The kitchen noises floated out to them from the little window where the waiters picked up their orders. Unable to bear it any longer, she cried:

"If I have a soporific effect on you, I can leave."

Frank started, sat up straight, and offered her a cigarette, which she politely refused.

"I'm shy," he said, with his strange, mocking smile.

"You weren't so shy yesterday."

"Oh, yesterday..."

He made an offhand gesture that had the effect of making them both seem ten years older. His eyelids contracted and he began to observe her in a manner that was just the opposite of shy.

Mireille fumbled for the handbag that was resting on her knees. Get out of here without saying another word to him. No. That would be too easy, playing right into his hand. Whether she stayed or left was a matter of total indifference to him. He despised her. Imagined that by treating her to dinner, he had earned the right to despise her. When would he stop looking at her as if she were a shop window display? A great void opened up in her heart; all her dreams collapsed. He was probably waiting for her to repay him. Saul was right: they think that all they have to do is flash their dollar bills, offer some chocolates or a bar of soap. Are you ever in for a surprise, my friend.

"I've changed my mind," she said. I'll take that cigarette, thank you."

The haste with which he offered it to her and gave her a light, disconcerted her. A glimmer of gratitude lit up his eyes. "He really is shy," she thought.

"You must have found Paris very changed."

"I don't know. Everything is so different when you're a soldier."

"You had a girlfriend."

"I had lots of girlfriends. You're not hard to please when you're a soldier."

"And when you're not a soldier?"

"You make do as best you can."

He looked at her with a sheepish expression.

"I realize I'm shocking you, but that's the sad reality of human nature."

"That's not true. You're a cynic."

"I am not a cynic. I'm a realist. I don't run after impossible dreams."

"But it's un-American to say that something is impossible."

"Maybe..."

He raised his hand impatiently.

"You think I'm too chatty?... that I talk too much?"

"No... but you *ask* questions all the time. Like a judge."

"And my questions bother you; that's it, right?"

"I am what I am."

He was pushing the matchbox around on the tablecloth as if it were the marker in a game of hopscotch. The silence settled in on them again. He hadn't touched his coffee. Mireille recoiled under the intensity of his gaze, which seemed to nestle on her sweater in the depression between her breasts, then on her hair, on her lips, with such insistence that he seemed to want to speak to them. Imagination, reflection of desire, color and shape of desire.

"Stop looking at me like that--it's embarassing," she said with a laugh.

But in the depths of her laugh, in an undercurrent beneath her laugh, her voice groaned miserably, as if uttering a cripple's joke told by a clown who was himself a cripple.

"Excuse me. I didn't realize..."

He turned his eyes away, emptied his pipe, filled it again and stuck it in his mouth without lighting it. When his gaze returned to Mireille, it was steel blue, a locked and bolted door to his spirit.

"You see, I can't say anything that doesn't rub you the wrong way."

Frank's gaze became even steelier.

"You're waiting for me to court you. You want compliments. You think there's something special between us because I kissed you in the metro. But people kiss each other all the time, talk to each other all the time. Talk, talk, talk, like chickens, each one wrapped up in its own chatter, *and it doesn't mean a thing!*

"Ah. So. You flat out insult me. Did I ask you for anything?"

Mireille had gotten up, her eyes clouded with anger. She was trying to slip into her coat.

"You feel like seeing me, you ask for a date; you feel like talking, you talk. And I? Where do I fit in? I serve as your echo. When you don't feel like talking any more, I keep quiet and look at you like a crockery dog."

He grabbed her hand and gently pulled her back down.

"Will you tell me what this is all about?"

He slipped his hands under hers and looked at them for a long time in silence, caressing the long nervous fingers that trembled at his touch.

"Your hands are beautiful," he said. "Like leaves, very beautiful."

"It runs in the family. Saul has the same hands, bigger of course. Your own hands are powerful. Does that also run in the family?

Their hands became strangers again. Illegitimate questions separated them from one another. They returned to their respective sides of the table and looked at each other like a couple of blind people.

"See that," he finally said, in a triumphantly indignant tone. "Always questions."

"I had no idea that the minutest details of your life were state secrets."

For the first time all evening, they both burst out laughing.

"What can you do? I suffer from the defect of curiosity."

"Too bad. I have nothing of interest to confess. Not even the *purple heart*. Never been in prison, no venereal disease, nothing. Shall we leave?"

She got up and he asked the waiter to bring the bill.

It was snowing when they got out of the cinema. Using the slippery pavement as an excuse, he put his arm around her shoulders. They both laughed as they tried to reconstruct the parts of the film that had been interrupted by their necking. It was rare and good to hear Frank laugh. People should always go to the movies in couples, wrap their arms around each other, lose themselves mouth to mouth, and never watch the film.

At the hotel door, the evening came to an end. They had fondled each other without restraint, and now, full of desire and passion, they slowed down so as to put off the moment of separation.

"Why do I have to leave?" he suddenly asked, tightening the embrace with which he held her close.

"Why indeed?' After all, she was all grown up and vaccinated, as Denise would say. She had always been in control of her body, but this evening, she was tired of struggling with it. Frank was there, she could feel his breath on her neck, and she could imagine that breath caressing her all over her nude body. With an effort, she said: "If you don't go right now, you're going to miss the last metro."

It had stopped snowing and in the pure crystalline night she could see Frank's face, tense with aching passion, without guile, raw male desire written all over him. They were no longer *Frank* and *Mireille,* but Man and Woman blocking each other's path and unable to proceed except in mutual union.

"If the concierge sees you, she'll make a fuss."

"She won't see me. I'll come up a few minutes after you, Mireille, just a quarter of an hour. I only want to kiss you without all these people around looking at us. Just a quarter of an hour. *I promise.* After that, I'll leave."

"Number 27. Don't go into the wrong door by mistake, now, whatever you do!"

When he had walked off, she went in. The corridor was somber and silent, with only the nightlight glowing faintly outside the concierge's lodge. She found her key and began walking upstairs. "Only a quarter of an hour," she told herself. "Nothing can happen in a quarter of an hour. After a quarter of an hour, I'll make him leave." But it was not to be. Frank had known this also, even as he promised. It was a tacit agreement, kind of sickening, which made everything seem sordid. Overwhelmed by desire, she would soon enough release him from his promise.

Chapter 12

Settled into the back room of "Chez Gaston," Saul watched the door of the hotel. On every other evening, he had left without evidence, reassured. This time he had caught her; his eyes clouded up: she had brought the American back to her hotel. They were conspiring against him, making a mockery of his supervision. How helpless he felt! His fingers tightened, and the coat button with which he had been fidgeting for the past few minutes popped up and fell back down into the hollow of his hand.

"Lovers!" exclaimed Gaston who, having slipped in behind him, was watching the show over his shoulder. "You voyeur! You must have a lot of time on your hands."

Saul didn't have time to tell him to go jump in the lake. He was out of breath. The American was so close to Mireille. He was going to kiss her, follow her into her room... Saul was paralyzed with pain. He was like a cataleptic, seeing everything, hearing everything, who endures torture and is unable to move. But, no, the American was not touching her. He was walking away. Mireille was going in alone, safe for one more night. It wasn't too late. It could all be stopped. The course of events could be changed; he could still save her. Money. He needed money, lots of money.

In the space of a moment, Saul decided. All his scruples evaporated. Despite his revulsion, he would go see Bébert and beg pardon. The two of them had been buddies during the period when they worked together—Bébert as driver, Saul as guide--for the Paris-by-Night Tour. Maybe he wouldn't even remember any more, that one night in the garage, Saul had punched him in the face; a reflexive reaction to Bébert's big meaty hand deliberately smoothing the surface of his fly. In a year's time, people forget lots of things. Saul repressed a feeling of revulsion: a fugitive vision of Bébert, fat and dirty, with enormous buttocks shaking softly in the seat of his pants. He knew where to find him. At the "*Mât de Cocagne*" where he would be busy, as usual, looking for a lazy little boy with buttocks firm and taught as a drum who had nowhere to sleep. Saddled with such an expensive passion, Bébert had become ingenuity personified. There was no racket into which he had not dipped his hand and pulled it back up clutching a small fortune. Back then, he had regularly offered to help Saul out by means of his many useful connections. Maybe he would still be well disposed to help him. He had to find Bébert.

Collar pulled up, shoulders hunched over, Saul set out. He would find Bébert and rivers of money would flow into his pockets. He would buy an apartment: *the apartment!* Mireille would come and move in with him and they would be happy as they had been before. Oh! To be able to sit in front of her window and hide the horrors of the universe from her. To tuck her in, turn out the light, and contemplate her skin, rippling in the dark with its own light. To pat her head as he did when, as a little girl, she trotted along behind him everywhere he went. She wore short dresses then, and cotton stockings which, unselfconsciously, she would remove in his presence, playfully tugging at the garters to make them snap. It had begun to snow again. It was very cold.

The dome of the Sacre Coeur, draped with snow, rose up in the night like the breast of a female giant arching up toward the sky. Frank turned back toward the hotel. Any other night would have found him returning to his hotel on the Left Bank, lingering in solitude on the Pont Saint-Michel or on one of the *quais* to contemplate the blinking lights of a barge at anchor in the black water strewn with glimmering points of red and green light. He felt agitated, simultaneously full of hope and doubt, knowing and yet not knowing what would take place in Mireille's room.

The nearer he got to the hotel, the greater was his

desire. He slowed down. Would he know how to behave like a man, after having allowed himself for so long to act like a beast? There had been the daughter of the Bedouin chief who had been offered to him for five dollars with a formal bill of sale, whom he had sent back to her tribe at dawn. The girl from Lille who gave herself free rein because she saw her mother doing the same in the next bed. The taxi-bordellos in London. And that Roman woman who didn't charge because she believed it would purify her of German filth. And all the others, in New York, New Orleans, Anvers, Casablanca, from all over, all the time, and who left a bitter longing for unattainable peace at the bottom of his soul. And now, Mireille, whose eyes, even as she gave him the nod, were full of shame, fright and fire. An hour, even a quarter of an hour of humanity, so as to find himself, remake himself, recognize himself.

He went into the hotel and closed the door cautiously. All his fears, all his doubts went away. Lighting a match, feverishly, he looked for number 27. He waited until his heart stopped beating so fast and so hard. Beyond that door, he would penetrate into an unknown temple and accomplish a rite, without trying to understand its meaning, that would bind him forever and establish an essential claim on him. He knocked at the door.

The bells of some church were ringing the half hour. Under the portal, a hobo was sleeping, his feet wrapped up in newspaper. Saul stopped and leaned against the wall like a drunkard. With every step he took, a needle of pain plunged into his lungs and ransacked them. Inundated with sweat, he was shivering. Soon, the sulfa drugs he had stolen from the hospital and with which he had been stuffing himself, would go into effect and he would feel better. In the meantime, the "*Mât de Cocagne*" was still only a mirage, at the end of the earth, at the end of eternity. A year earlier, everything would have been so simple, so easy, within arm's reach. If only he had known! But then he was still trying to preserve the principles he had been taught. Bébert would laugh at him: "Well look at that, my pet, here you are, crawling back, just like all the rest." That was just it, actually. He needed to consider himself different from the others, to steal with a clear conscience, nibble around here and there and in the act of doing so, go through the doorway that makes everything normal and inevitable: the butcher and his meat, hacked and hanging in an old shed, the baker, selling today the ration coupons for flour without which, tomorrow, he will refuse to sell you his bread, the shoemaker, the coal merchant, the landlord—quiet, no receipt, you'll resell it for a profit. Everyone clutching him in a stranglehold and squeezing until the only air he could get to breathe was theirs. *Conscience is no longer allowed.* Who the hell does that guy think he is? You want to eat, avoid freezing to death? Into the arena with the others, buddy. We'll initiate you. Ideals? Tell it to your belly! Well, of course, we have ideals. Come by some evening. We'll show them to you: Museum of Mental Health, Hall of Ideals. Oh! And whose fault would that be? You know who? No? Well, it's plain to see. Adam said it was Eve. Eve blamed the serpent. The serpent pointed his finger at the apple. In no time at all, God made the apple mute. Aw, fuck that shit!

"Take off your shoes--they're wet; you'll catch cold. I'll set them to dry next to mine."

Frank took off his shoes and took them over to the little gas stove. Mireille laughed and moved them to one side. "You don't want them to cook," she said. "There, take the armchair. I'll warm up some wine."

There was a hole in her stocking and she curled up her toes in an effort to hide it. Frank thought: "How easy it would be to have some sent to her, stockings and shoes, warm clothes, everything she needs, things that people throw away without a second thought back home."

They looked at each other, smiling timidly, knowing that time was passing and hoping that if they pretended not to notice, propriety would be preserved. Mireille didn't say anything. Was she afraid all of a sudden? He would have to be very still, as in the presence of a wild bird, be careful not to frighten her, subdue the waves of heat that overwhelmed him when his eyes rested on her body. Ignore the heaviness of his lips swelling with desire. Not betray her trust, her unaccustomed hospitality. Ah! Yet, no, words and promises notwithstanding, she must have known what to expect when she agreed to let him come in.

"It's very hot. Be careful not to burn yourself," she said, finally, offering him a big mustard jar full of steaming wine.

Frank put the glass down on the arm of the chair. Was it the personality of the people who lived in them that gave hotel rooms that sad, gloomy aspect, or was it the other way around? Since his arrival, a radical change had taken place in Mireille: courteous yet reserved, hospitable yet distant, endearing but with her guard up, she had become an integral part of the room. One moment of uneasiness was all it took for the big mustard jar to become a teacup, for the wine to turn into tea laced with milk, for the scene of the nightmare to unfold; he was once again in New York, trying to make himself listen to the insipid prattle of that schoolteacher who seemed never to have suspected that making love could be a source of pleasure.

"Drink up," said Mireille. "It'll get cold."

She stared at him with an intense fixity, over the top of her glass, then turned her eyes away, giving him to understand that she had forgotten nothing, that that was the source of their silence and embarrassment.

The "*Mât de Cocagne*," twice closed down by the police, nevertheless did a booming business. The walls were adorned with frescoes depicting greasy poles laden with sausages and giant Dutch cheeses being stampeded by young callipygian gods.

With his frying-pan face, the two piggybank slots of

his eyes, and all his fat, which, by some miracle was held together in one piece, Bébert had not changed. He was seated at a table across from an elegant old man with silky white hair, almost drunk and rather lacking in dignity.

It was the hour when entertainments were scheduled, and Saul had to wait until the first number was over before he could cross the floor. A young mulatto, equipped with rubber breasts and a raffia skirt under which he was wearing nothing but a kind of a harness which flattened his sexual member out to the point of eliminating it, was standing still in the middle of the floor positioned with arms outstretched in an attitude of self-offering. This was the signal. Several bills flew up in the air and landed at his feet. Then, accompanied by a muted orchestra, his supple, copper-colored body began a sinuous swaying back-and-forth which gained in rapidity and rhythmic emphasis to the degree that the bills flew faster, piling up on the floor. Maddened and intoxicated at the sight of them, the dancer wriggled, smooth and shiny as an eel, his raffia skirt bouncing up so as to reveal nude flesh jumping with agitation. Slipping among the tables, he alternately offered and refused himself to the hands that lay in wait to grab him as he passed by; he caressed and revelled in his beautiful, half-negro skin. The bills kept coming, some of them folded in the form of arrows and carefully aimed at choice parts of his body, prompting, as they landed, cries almost as enthusiastic as those provoked by the dance itself. Members of the audience stamped around him, groaned, reached out, irresistibly attracted. Secret rites took place beneath the tables, in the shelter of damask tablecloths. Hands reached out to touch him, gliding over him as they might reach for a saint, or a religious relic; hands of the tortured and of the tormenting, hands of the shipwrecked and lost; brutal hands, delicate white hands, hands covered with jewels, hands chapped and peeling, hands of actors, financiers, businessmen, hand-picked members of society, hotel managers, poets, taxi drivers, unskilled laborers, beggars.

When the applause died down and the bills had been swept up with the aid of a broom and dust pan, Saul made his way over to Bébert. The latter raised a couple of glassy eyes that seemed to give no sign of recognition; then a wicked oily smile spread over his features.

"Well, what d' ya know, it's Lover Boy Sweetlips. Sit yourself down, Precious, I'll introduce you. You really do look like hell, little doll face. Sit down, you little slut, Coco here is treating to champagne. Say it isn't so, Coco, and I'll bite your prick. You make nice and sit, I tell you."

Reluctant to contradict him, Saul pulled up a chair and sat down.

"Don't be an idiot, Bébert," he whispered, grabbing the lapels of his jacket, "I've come to ask for a favor. If you don't want to help, say so right off. Those connections you mentioned last year, are they still available?" In between the folds of fat, Bébert's eyes lit up with cunning.

"Have something to drink, Sweet Lips," he said, pushing his glass over to Saul, "it's good for your health."

He turned toward the old man, who watched them, drooling.

"You see what a success your Bébert is. Who is it they come looking for when they're in a pickle? Why, Bébert, the cat burglar."

He turned to Saul. "Drink, Sweet Lips, it'll put some juice in your battery--that delicious little battery."

Somebody had set his hand down lightly on Saul's shoulder. From behind him, a childish voice lisped: "Tell me, you naughty thing, are you going to let me have a dance? Just a little dance?"

Saul reached out for the hand, which he twisted with a sharp, cruel jerk. There was an audible moan, then the voice rang out again, this time in admiration:

"Such vigor! If your song is as good as your plumage..."

He was a big ginger-haired fellow with finicky features and long hands, soft as leeks.

"Get out of here, you old fag," said Bébert. "this is a restricted area."

Saul got up, slipped his hands under Bébert's sweat-soaked armpits and pulled him up to a standing position.

"Come out into the street with me, dirt-bag. It's impossible to talk in here."

Bébert swayed on his legs. His enormous thighs wobbled like calves foot jelly. He leaned over to Saul.

"Are we gonna cuddle, now, Sweet Lips? Oh, those connections... Yeah... I've got lots of connections..."

He latched onto Saul and started drooling on him. The old man was gazing at them with the look of a gluttonous toothless old woman.

"Dirty bastard!" shouted Saul, exasperated; "You wouldn't lift your little finger if I were about to croak. I know your connections! That filthy money you get by fucking old faggots in the ass."

Saul gave him a shove, and Bébert plopped down on the chair like a slug.

"Evidently war is a little bit like a mirror," said Mireille.

She swirled the wine around in her glass as if she were decanting memories.

"There are people who will never be able to look at themselves in the mirror again. Before, they used to consider themselves courageous, loyal. Now their neighbors turn away from them; that means they are traitors and cowards. They didn't know it before. They would never have found out if it hadn't been for the war..."

Frank made an effort to follow her. His wit and his senses were all mixed up together in the shadow of desire. More than anything, he wanted to turn out the light, take Mireille in his arms and undress her. It wasn't that she was beautiful: her features were drawn with fatigue, the pallor made her freckles stand out all the more, and she was skinny;

but her eyes, lost in the distance, burned with an overwhelming intensity that lit up her entire face. The fire, Frank sensed, that animated and heated her blood, spurred and tightened his muscles. He had never desired a woman so passionately.

"It's one o'clock in the morning," she announced, suddenly, her face betraying no emotion.

She got up and extended her hand to him. "Come, I'll turn out the light. We can watch the snow falling."

The entire world was there in the darkness: he and she, Man and Woman, their power multiplied by the number of stars in the sky. Yet she was afraid, feeling his arms wrapped around her waist, his body pressed close against hers as if to burrow into it. She thought: "I should ask him to leave." But the moment exercised the fascination of centuries and they were both spellbound as if lost among towering precipices. Outside, the snow continued to fall, covering everything with its white petals. In the purity of such a moment, one could hardly do anything bad. Everything was perfect, immaculate, pious, calm. She sighed. Behind her, Frank's breathing became louder, his fingers tensed, pressing into her flesh, seeking her out. Even the pain was right; the pain of a vision whose absence would make you weep. Hand in hand, she let herself be led over to the bed and sat silently next to him in the dark. The dark was good for learning things by heart, by hearing and by touch, the sense more trustworthy than sight, the sense that guesses at truth, and cannot be deceived.

"I feel stupid," Frank suddenly said, "I don't know how to talk to women. I don't know poetic words."

She guessed at his exasperation. What did beautiful words matter? Gérard had known them; the gray of sadness, the blood red of contempt, the green of the unknown... the violent mauve of desire. Frank's strong arms squeezed her savagely. She struggled. In the dark, Frank's retreating motion seemed surly.

"*God damn it,* do you want to or don't you? If you want to play cat and mouse, find another partner." Then he was quiet.

"I know, I know," He continued in a tone that was softer but not resigned, "conventions destroy everything. You can't prevent yourself from thinking what you think..."

"You think... you think... but you can't help what you're thinking..."

"Think me."

Mireille wondered if she had heard him right, if he hadn't said, "Think about me." Actually, she liked "Think me" even better. She focused on that one thought: "Frank." She thought the eyes, the mouth, the entire person that was Frank; she thought his heart, his veins, his penis, and suddenly realized that in thinking him, she had integrated him into herself and filled him up with herself, making him her own creation. The danger was watching her, flowing in her through all the openings of her being. A phosphorescent dial warned her, but her entire being was drawn toward the revelation: to think a being. It was terrifying.

"Turn on the light!" she cried, "Turn on the light! What's the point of hiding in the dark as if we didn't want to know what we're doing?"

She heard him groping in the dark.

"Over near the door," she said.

At that very moment, the room was flooded with light. Dazzled, eyes blinking, she guessed where he was before she could see him, his face drawn, his mouth sour, his eyes red with blood. He was taking his coat down from the hook.

"I didn't ask you to leave," she said in an agitated tone. "I don't want you to leave," she added in a dryer tone, hoping to conceal her fears. "Hang your coat back up and don't act like a baby, Frank... don't leave me all alone." Her voice broke. Only her modesty prevented her from running after him and grabbing his hands to make him stay.

He hung his coat back up, came back to sit beside her

and ran his hand through his hair in an expression of bewilderment. Suddenly, he grabbed her arm just above the elbow and began to shake her violently.

"What do you want? Do you know what it is you want?"

"Stay. Oh, just stay!"

"I'm a man. I act like a man. If that's not what you want, I have to leave."

Confronted with the threat of seeing him leave, Mireille didn't answer. Then, she burst into violent sobs that racked her entire being, while he put his arms around her, held her close against his body, so strong, so powerful, so warm. Suddenly, she had an upside down vision of her room. Despair was pinching its nails of shame and anguish into her heart, and in the capsized room, with walls ready to crumble and topple over on her, burying her forever in their locked and bolted solitude, Frank's pleading voice became the only living sound that could reach her. The cries of refusal on her lips were smothered under Frank's trembling mouth. Torn between fear and desire, she clung to him, kissing his hair savagely. She struggled against his hands insistently searching for her nude body under her clothing, at the same time stretching her body out toward him in an arc, painful, hungry, offering herself up to this male power which would put an end to all suffering. Her eyes met his and in his pleading glance, she saw her own reflection.

"You can't ask me to leave now," he groaned, burying his head between her breasts.

"No, Frank," she said, hardly hearing the sound of her own words.

She thought his name again, focusing hard, for herself alone, recreating it, reassuring herself as to the thought that was he, forgetting her anguish, seeking out the man's gaze filtering into her, flowing, spreading even into the secret place that palpitated and struggled like a butterfly caught in a net. The room, the present moment, all vanished into the darkness.

The odor and breath of the man so absorbed her that she sank into an annihilation until now unknown; she sensed in herself a fertility as of wild flowers soaking up the river of life which would burst from him, unfolding to accept and absorb him into herself. Lips taut with the death-life cry, she went limp in his arms, without strength, like a flower that has been culled.

With a well-directed jerk of his elbow, Saul pushed away the prostitute hanging onto his sleeve and continued on his way to Pigalle. After Bébert, it was the only solution. Maybe in one of those cafés, a sudden change of destiny was waiting for him. In front of him, an Arab, bent beneath his carpets, clambered painfully up the hill, dragging his babouches in the snow. The Arab, at least, had an idea where he stood, with his carpets and his babouches. As for Saul, he felt completely lost, wandering between the darkness and the light, despair and hope. At this moment, he would like nothing better than Marcel's company, to listen to his stories about pieces of ass, about his family, the sorrows of the poor fellow for whom life is all planned out in advance, and to forget all the rest. Forget Bébert, the little whore with the face of a jailbird, Mireille and her American standing so close to each other in front of the hotel. In the last analysis, to forget himself; become another who might, like everybody else, see the world the way it is and make do with it.

He went into a café, ordered a cup of bouillon at the counter and went over to the phone booth. There, he hesitated, tossing the token up in the air a few times as he reflected. And what would he say to Marcel when he got him on the line? "I know, old buddy, this is not a good time to be waking people up, but I'm really sick and tired of being alone. Wouldn't you like to shoot the breeze for a few minutes?" It was completely idiotic. He put the token back in his pocket and went to drink the bouillon that was steaming on the counter. Despite the late hour, the café was quite lively. The proprietor was walking around, jumping like a squirrel in his eagerness to see that everybody was happy.

"No, this must be the thousandth time I've told you, no checks. It brings bad luck."

Pronounced in a muted tone, with a marseillais accent, the phrase reached Saul's ears in its entirety. Behind him, with his elbows resting on the pinball machine, stood a tall man with a dark complexion, black pomaded hair, very dark cold eyes and a kid who looked as if he had grown up too quickly, wearing a short leather jacket. Saul could see them in the mirror behind the counter. He kept on listening with his eyes fixed on the mirror. But he couldn't hear the kid, whose back was turned to him.

"As you like," resumed the Marseillais, "but if you want some advice, you won't buy any more of them. Only travelers checks or greenbacks. The rest is of no interest to me."

The kid shrugged his shoulders and went off to peddle his goods elsewhere.

Saul threw the money for his bouillon on the counter and, as he turned around, bumped into the machine. The Marseillais shot him a dark inquisitive glance.

"Like to play?" Saul asked casually, sticking a coin in the slot.

"If you like."

In the offhand tone of the Marseillais, there was a hint of something that said: "Let's see what you have up your sleeve."

The match began. At first, they both made a point of seeming to be interested in the game, parrying the ball with the full range of players, repelling it with dexterity, leaning avidly over the glass, then, little by little, the match, as if by mutual consent, slowed down. The ball got stuck in a corner for a few seconds without either of them bothering to dislodge it.

"Travelers' checks happen to be just my line," Saul observed, in a detached tone.

The Marseillais didn't say anything. Giving the

machine a knock, he dislodged the ball and the match resumed.

"Three to zero," he announced, quietly scoring a goal.

Saul felt himself shrinking up under that look that seemed to be memorizing him inside and out.

"With seven balls left, I can still catch up," he managed to answer.

The fourth ball bounced in between the rows of players.

"What's your price?" asked the Marseillais without letting his little men miss a beat.

"You know very well that depends on the market."

"For today? Four to zero."

"I have nothing left."

"Hey! You're doing OK all on your own."

He smiled indulgently and added: "A margin of five francs is enough for me. Unlimited quantity. Only, I'm warning you, if you work with me, you don't work with anybody else."

"I ask for nothing better," said Saul, forcing himself to endure that look that, like a bad omen, filled him with fear.

Anyway, you couldn't be in this business and remain a choir boy. You had to have sharp sensibilities, a brutal desire to live. This brutal desire was paramount in the Marseillais' face. He would see to it that anything constituting danger or even the hint of danger that got in his way would be cut down. Saul knew already that he would never forget that face. He thought: "All I have to do is keep my guard up, avoid playing dirty tricks on people, and when I've put together what I need, I'll close shop."

"Not so fast. Just slow down a bit. First of all, you need somebody to vouch for you."

"How about me?" asked a familiar voice.

Whirling around, Saul found himself face to face with Denise, who was standing behind him, for how long, he had no idea.

"Is this one of your regulars?" asked the Marseillais.

"Just trust me. I know him."

The way Denise deferred respectfully to the Marseillais had the effect of undermining what little confidence Saul had managed to muster. At this point, he could still get out if he wanted to, but the thirst for money and all that depended on it had him in its clutches.

"I didn't know you were here," he said, addressing her familiarly in the hope of persuading the Marseillais that they had known each other for a long time.

"I was busy when you came in, but I wasn't going to let you get away without saying hello."

Saul smiled at her, wondering why he had always detested her. Deep down, she was really a good kid. She didn't even hold a grudge. She had pulled the Marseillais aside and was having a lively conversation with him, trying to convince him. The Marseillais listened with interest, nodding his head with an air of satisfaction.

"OK, you're in," he finally said, walking back over. "You'll deliver it in an ordinary envelope... Oh, and the boss here will explain the rest. In any case, you'll be dealing with him. As for me, you've never seen me."

With his thumb, he released the six balls remaining in the drop. He watched them scatter down and get wedged in among the players. "Good luck," he said. Then, with a nod to the bartender, he walked out.

"Come with me, Mr. Wise Guy," said Denise in a mocking tone as she took him by the arm. "Boy, are you lucky I'm here."

She called the boss over. "It's OK, Antoine. You can show him the ropes."

Giving him another sly look, she sauntered off slowly towards the back room.

"You really were lucky," said the bartender. "The Marseillais doesn't show up that often. Anyway, here's how it works. You'll get in here around five o'clock, just before time for the *apero*, when it's kind of quiet. You go into the phone booth and slip your envelope under the phone book, then you come out bellyaching that something's the matter with the phone and you lost your token. I go in after you to see what's up; while I'm at it, I get your envelope. Then I go into the rear to look for a screwdriver, to get your token out. I fool around with the phone for a minute, and tell you that it works now. You come back, make your call, and look under the phone book, where you'll find another envelope. In case of unexpected trouble, I'll say: 'Pull harder on the door, it doesn't close well'; you'll get it."

The system was ingenious and pleased Saul all the more because he really wouldn't have to deal with anybody. All transactions were between him and the phone booth. It was impersonal and, stretching things a bit, a little less dishonest.

"Now, get the hell out of here," added the bartender. "There's no point in your being seen around here any more than you have to."

Saul felt his eyes following him out the door. He decided to phone Marcel from another bistro.

Chapter 13

Frank stretched, ran his hand over the warm body lying at his side, and, his eyes still full of sleep, looked out at the snow piled up on the window ledge. Then he remembered. Lying on his back, hands crossed under the nape of his neck, he tried to reassemble the scattered debris of his thoughts. He stretched his hand out on Mireille's thigh and felt it tremble, in a reflex that was immediately controlled. In a muted voice, he called her name. She answered in a clear tone by which he knew that she had been awake for a while.

"You aren't asleep?" he asked.

"Now that's a ridiculous question."

He asked her if she wasn't sleepy, or cold, if she felt OK. She answered in monosyllables, a method he had often employed himself, in order to let people know that it was time to say good-bye. "She's ashamed," he thought.

"You mustn't be ashamed, Mireille."

In a flash, she turned over on her side and turned on the light. Her face was full of such contempt that he felt distraught.

"Oh, no, please, that will do," she told him. "If you want to play riddling games, we might as well quit now."

"I just thought... because of your brother. He'll never know..."

"And why should I care? What if he did know? He can't do anything about it, absolutely nothing. It's done. And to think, that it happened with you. A while ago, when you were sleeping, I was thinking of someone I used to know... You, you're strong, powerful; you move in on what you like and plant your flag... but you're not exactly a sensitive soul."

"I never said that I was."

Stricken by this answer, she ran her hand through his

hair in the way that you might caress a child whom you felt you had scolded unjustly, a child on whom you had imposed unrealistic expectations.

"That's true, she said. "I have no right to reproach you for that. It's not your fault. Deep down, you're not so different, it's just that you disguise yourself better than they. Deep down inside of you, there is nothing but the breath of life struggling to break out, as it also does in me, as it does in everyone... OK. I see that you don't understand half of what I say. If only I knew a little English. You know, if only I could see myself with your eyes and you could see yourself with my eyes, then maybe we could get somewhere."

Raising herself up on one elbow, she leaned over him and stared down into his eyes. Frank closed his eyes to shield himself against that gaze drilling into his soul. Cradled, lulled into a dream, he woke up now with the feeling that he was being slowly devoured by a giant black spider that was swinging over him at the end of a long thread, poised to ensnare him. He had been so impatient to have her that it hadn't occurred to him that afterwards, there would be accounts to be squared, that she would insist on figuring him out... she would call it an "act," she would project all responsibility for it onto him. If only he could hide, eradicate all memory of the event. The light was beginning to dawn. He pulled himself up into a sitting position. It was easy to explain: if he didn't leave now, he would be likely to run into the neighbors or be seen by the concierge...

"The gossips?" said Mireille. "If they can't find anything bad to say, they make it up. They never feel more virtuous than when they're dragging somebody else through the mud. Fortunately, they don't frighten me."

She sat up, taking care to wedge the end of the sheet up under her arms, her eyes insistently seeking him out.

"But that's not why you're in such a hurry to leave."

She lifted her arm to brush a lock of hair away from her forehead and the corner of the sheet slipped, revealing her breast, high on her chest, smooth, almost perfect, with a coral tip that seemed also to be staring at him. Frank pulled on the sheet and covered her breast back up, irritated at the accuracy with which she guessed at his thoughts. The sheet began to slip again, but this time, he didn't try to stop it. His heart beat all the more rapidly as desire was reawakened. He waited, in fascination, for the coral tip to reappear, remembering how it had felt, stiffening in the palm of his hand.

"Well, if you don't care about your reputation," he commented dryly.

Suddenly, all Mireille's modesty disappeared. Sitting nude on the edge of the bed, she was shivering, and he had no idea whether it was from anger or the cold.

"No," she cried. "Please, no gentlemanly gestures. Stop worrying about saving my honor. As far as I'm concerned, honor is located above the waist. Don't be rummaging for excuses. Leave, if you can't wait to get away. I'm not trying to keep you, but please, spare me your excuses, your lies--you're not very good at it. I thought we could dispense with falsehood and lies so as to carve out a new truth together. Easier to do when there are two of you. But for you, even the two of us, wouldn't be enough. You want the usual platitudes. They may nibble away at you, but you prefer to be sick in company than healthy with me alone. Get out. There is really nothing left for us to say to each other."

She lay back down on her belly, her cheek on the pillow, turned away from him as if she were sleeping.

This took Frank's breath away. For the first time ever, a woman had succeeded in making him feel ashamed. She even presumed to humiliate him by kicking him out. But to tell the truth, he wanted nothing more; she was just making things easier for him. He got to his feet without saying anything, shivering in the glacial air of the room, regretting the warmth of the bed, and began to put on his clothes. Dawn was shooting pink arrows of light across the dark sky. A bicycle bell rang out in the courtyard. Somebody was going off to work. Everything was going to be as it was before. He was still free.

He was adjusting the knot in his tie when, her voice smothered by the pillow, Mireille reminded him that he had left his shoes under the gas burner. Then she turned toward him, leaning on one elbow. "You'll get sick, leaving here in this cold on an empty stomach. If you'll wait a few minutes, I'll make you a cup of tea."

He sat down on the edge of the bed, right next to her. He wanted to take her in his arms, comfort her, but her look, contemptuous and consoling at the same time, kept him from it. It wasn't hard to guess what she was thinking: "It's your fault it's come to this." Suddenly, he realized that he no longer wanted to leave, but to get undressed, slip back under the warm sheets and forget to be afraid of happiness. To hold Mireille close, smother her resentment, restore her confidence and give her the pleasure she had every right to expect, and which, in his hurry to achieve his own, he had not been able to give her. The smell of her flesh pervading the room: the smell of love, the odor of desire and the fullness of life. He remembered the touch of her warm moist flesh sticking to him; but her arms were like those reeds that tie you up and break you with the very flexibility of their unsuspected strength; her eyes were like high seas agitated by maelstroms, a dizziness hidden in the dark that pulls you down into deep abysses and snuffs you out. He put on his shoes, without even lacing them up, and left, his overcoat slung under his arm.

Chapter 14

The metro was making a deafening racket. Even at the ticket booth, you could hear it. While waiting for the train to start moving, Marcel polished his fingernails on the lapel of his overcoat. Saul, who wanted an answer, watched him with mounting impatience. The train began to move.

"Are you going to lend it to me or not?" he finally asked.

"Suppose you decided to commit suicide," Marcel began, sententiously, "and if I loaned you a gun, it would be as if I had killed you. And if I lend you this money and you end up in the klink, who will you blame then, eh?"

"Not you, that's for sure."

"Not me... not me... that remains to be seen. And do you think I could have a clear conscience if you did?" He fixed his soft, hazelnut eyes on Saul with a mixture of fear and compassion.

"Look, you stupid idiot, for more than an hour I've been trying to tell you that there is no risk involved and there's big money to be made in this."

"All the same, there's a difference between making money and money to be made."

"If you start playing with words there'll be no end to it. And then, you're really not in a position to judge, are you?"

Marcel didn't flinch, but the reproach that he read in his friend's eyes filled Saul with remorse. "Well, it's true, isn't it?" he asked, covering his shame with rage. "Have you ever yet had to earn a single nickle?"

"How true," said Marcel. "I'm not really an attractive character. Everybody makes fun of me behind my back, even my parents, and sometimes, even to my face... Mind you, I don't give a fuck, because I don't care much for them either. I go to prostitutes, no, let me finish, and I drink as if I had a hollow leg; but between that and helping you throw yourself into the lion's mouth, there's a bit of a difference."

"So, the answer is no?"

"Look, buddy..."

"OK. Chicken out. But don't forget that yesterday, you promised."

Marcel leaned forward, his cheeks lit up. "What? What did I promise? Anyway, you extorted that promise from me. I would have promised to go to the gallows to get you to let me go back to bed. Three o'clock in the morning... I don't even remember a word of what you said to me last night."

"I see."

"What? What do you see?"

"Nothing. Never mind. I'll manage."

"Sure. You're much more likely to find people ready to help you do idiotic things than sensible ones. They enjoy it; not to mention that they often enough find it profitable to do so."

Saul was winning. Besides, he couldn't care less about Marcel's approval. Marcel's view of the world could be divided into two opposing columns: on one side was written: "Things to do" and on the other, "Things not to do" : but since he referred to the lists very rarely, he had never noticed how often the entries changed sides, depending on the circumstances.

"I didn't make such a big deal over principles when the time came to do you a favor," he said.

"Leave Simone out of this."

Marcel blanched, lips trembling, every trace of tenderness having disappeared from his eyes.

"OK. My mistake. Excuse me," said Saul sheepishly.

He really had a knack for screwing things up. You couldn't get anything out of Marcel when he was angry, couldn't make him budge a centimeter. Like a donkey, the more you pushed him, the more he resisted, feet firmly planted in the dirt. To distract him and get him back to the business at hand, Marcel took out a couple of newspaper clippings and showed them to Marcel.

"Here, look at this, judge for yourself, and then tell me it's not worth the trouble."

It was a listing of the Foreign Currency Exchange Rates. But Marcel, while examining the clippings with interest, didn't seem at all impressed by the yawning gap between the official and actual rates. At most, he nodded his head indulgently, his anger already forgotten.

"It could all fall apart in the blink of an eye, then you'd be up the creek."

"No danger. I've been studying this for three months. Every time it goes down five francs, it goes back up by fifteen."

"No wonder prices are rising."

"Go on. It's not my fault the purchasing power of the franc is sinking."

"Anyway, it's a shady business."

"Listen, Marcel: when you don't have good luck, you have to make your own luck. Try going up to a baker and telling him: 'I want a two-pound loaf of bread but I can't pay you because I'm an honest man.' You know what the baker'll do? He'll give you a fat kick in the ass and tell you that the world is full of honest people. It doesn't matter if it's true. That's beside the point. But plunk a bloody bank note down on his counter and he'll wipe the blood off on his nice white apron and then give you a smile. What the fuck does he care where your money comes from, as long as it winds up in his pocket? All the rest is hot air."

Marcel said nothing. He was scratching the side of his nose with a worried look.

Desperate, Saul continued: "A while ago you said that I was your only friend. Well, all right. Now's the time to show it. Me, I've never let you down when you asked me for a favor."

Marcel seemed not to have heard him. With a clean, well-filed fingernail, he continued to scratch the side of his nose.

"Very true," he said, finally, "very true! And then, I know you. Nothing will stop you. Who knows? Maybe you're right. But I'm not so flush as you think, and at the moment, I happen to be a bit short... I've only managed to scrape together eighteen thousand francs," he admitted, without realizing that he was thereby conceding defeat in advance. "The twelve thousand that I had set aside to go skiing, and what was left to cover ordinary expenses for the rest of the month. That leaves me flat broke."

"You've got it with you?"

Before Saul even knew what he was doing, his hand reached out to Marcel, palm extended in the gesture of a beggar. He lowered it casually, as if he had only been stretching. Marcel had taken out his wallet and pulled out a wad of bills from it that Saul slipped slowly into his pocket.

By way of a thank you, he simply said, "I knew that you wouldn't let me down."

"I hope I don't have occasion to regret it," said Marcel.

Some high school students ran up the steps, calling and shouting to each other.

"Will you walk with me for a way?" asked Saul.

"I'm already late for my date with Simone. I'll have to take a taxi."

"So it seems that things are going well with you two?"

"I'm not complaining."

Marcel was clearly on the defensive.

"So much the better. She's a good girl. She has a nice disposition."

"Drop it. You don't need to assume such an air of superiority because you had her first. For your information, that doesn't bother me in the least! I'm open-minded. Anyway, these days, she can't stand to hear your name."

"So much the better. Nothing could please me more."

"You don't believe me, do you? Could it possibly be that you're mistaken about your seductive powers? Well, you come along with me, and you'll see."

It took three failed attempts for Marcel to light his cigarette. The flint of his lighter kept slipping in his fingers.

"Deep down, you too despise me," he said, drawing

nervously on his cigarette. "Don't deny it. I'm neither clever nor proud. If necessary, I eat leftovers, but the leftovers are mine. I may as well admit it: I sometimes hated you. Yes, it's true. You were my friend, but I hated you. It was stronger than I was. It should even be worse now. But, no, I don't hate you any more. From the moment Simone and I got together, I no longer gave a damn about all the rest. I guess that amazes you."

"No," Saul answered softly.

Lucky Marcel. Marcel, the bon vivant. Marcel, quick to anger, but as easily appeased as a child. Marcel the enviable. The last person in the world that Saul would have expected to break out of his protective shell and reveal the nakedness of his vulnerable and wounded heart. Saul was disconcerted. It had never occurred to him that despite his brutal, sensual exterior, Marcel might be, deep down, completely without defenses. He realized that he was beginning to respect him.

"Come with me," Marcel insisted. "I want to see for myself."

Saul shrugged his shoulders and climbed the steps with him. When they got to the street, he extended his hand.

"You chickening out?" asked Marcel.

He was swaggering, but without conviction. It was as if he were afraid that his victory would prompt Saul to change his mind. He hunched his back.

"Yes, I'm chickening out."

Marcel stood up straight. His face lit up, serenity returned. He sighed as if somebody had just discharged him from a dangerous mission, self-imposed but nevertheless terrifying.

"I wanted to give her the opportunity," he explained, with an air of contrition.

"Go on, you prick."

Simone needed time. She was not one of those who wasted away because of an unhappy love affair, but on the contrary, one who knew how to bear her sorrows in mind so as to love better the next time, better every time. Like Marcel, she was sensual, her blood burned all by itself with no need to fan the flames. She lived for her appetite, by her appetite, with her appetite. She was magnificent, powerful, savage, a cannibal. All you had to do was leave her alone, not complicate her existence. It could have been like that from the beginning: Marcel and Simone, two beings from the same stock, created with the same needs, sharing the same bread. How he envied them.

"Buy her some roasted chestnuts," he said. "She adores them."

Chapter 15

The night threw a drapery of amethyst fog over the verdigris statues at the *Opera* as Saul made his way through the crowd streaming towards the metro entrances, heading for the American Express office, where, in front of the closed doors, he assumed his post. New at this game, he watched everybody go by, wondering if the others had made off at the first sign of danger or if they had just been luckier than he was. Beginning to despair of making a single transaction, he saw a couple that looked American stop, somewhat exasperated, in front of the American Express office. Despite the fact that the office was evidently closed, the man was stubbornly twisting the doorknob with his fist, his cigar clamped firmly between his teeth.

Saul pulled out the butt he had reserved especially for such occasions and asked for a light. He gave them a sympathetic look, explained that the office closed at four o'clock, and offered them his services. In any case, he was likely to do better than with the hotel porter who only gave three hundred and forty-six francs to the dollar, when he would go to three hundred and eighty. But the American was crafty. He held out for Saul to make him a better offer, reminding him the transaction was highly illegal. The woman had quickly wandered off, as if this negotiation, or perhaps all financial dealings, were repugnant to her. Saul pretended to think things over. Actually, he was prepared to go up to four hundred and twenty, but not unless he had to. The American wouldn't go along. He had gotten it into his head that he'd get four hundred francs to the dollar and he wasn't letting go of them for less. Saul bargained for the sake of form, but finally, with a resigned expression, said all right because it was getting late and he wanted to go home. With the American in his wake, he crossed the street and headed for the large shady corridor where they had arranged to meet. The woman waited for them outside a furrier's window display. The transaction was concluded agreeably, each one thinking he had gotten the best of the other. Saul told the American not to hesitate to come back if he should have occasion to require his services. The American told him he was leaving for Venice the next day and, after offering him a cigarette, walked back over to his wife.

Left alone in the corridor, Saul took out the Traveler's Checks that he had hastily stuffed in his pocket, smoothed them out, removed his cuff link, opened the cuff out flat and folded it back over the checks he had placed inside it. Once he had fastened the cuff back up, he gave a tug on the sleeves of his jacket and gabardine, wriggled his fist, stretched out his arm, bent it back, waved it in the air, all so as to make sure that, whatever movement he might be called upon to make, the checks would not slip out.

At this busy hour, the metro was crowded: not only with office workers, but also with the idle patrons of art-house cinemas and prosperous women who stroll around in department stores the way others do in museums. By dint of persistence, Saul managed to elbow his way into the train, got hit in the groin by the corner of a cardboard carton, squelched the insult which the pain brought to his lips, and converted it into an impersonal exclamation. With what he was carrying on his person, it would probably be best not to make a scene. Weighed down by all these passengers, the train seemed to go more slowly than usual. It crawled along, reeled forward on the rails, crawled along some more.

The train took forever, stopping at every station. Once it stopped, it seemed to take forever to take off again. The passengers were in no hurry to get off, to get in, to close the doors. They were doing it on purpose, to delay him. Good, now the doors were closed; what was this idiot of a conductor waiting for? Well, he had all the time in the world! What did it matter to him if others were in a hurry? And these fools who get off and then get back on, and can't seem to decide what they're doing. There they are, doing their best to make their way back inside the car, stopping to tell somebody off or get back at somebody for the accidental impact of a knee or an elbow. What a bunch of jerks, it's not as if you had to be a wizard to get on and off a train. We'll never get out of here. We'll be here until the cows come home. Seven stations to go. At this rate... Saul became enraged. Did they have any idea that he was walking around with seventy dollars tucked into his cuff? Full of anxiety, he kneaded his wrist, trying to feel the stiffness of the checks under the cloth. They were there, carefully hidden, safe and sure; the miraculous effects of a privileged and protected race.

Twenty-eight hundred francs profit; twenty-eight lessons with that brat Menard, twenty-eight hours less drudgery; after this, let them talk about purchasing power! A man in overalls, eyelids heavy with fatigue, was looking at the picture of a luxury car in a dog-eared magazine. Curious, listless, he looked as if he realized that this item was not for him, would never be for him. No spark of imagination lit up his dull pupils. Another one who would never understand, who would never search for the means, make the connections, who would never ask himself: "How do the others manage?" He would accept everything because he had been told that that's the way it was; "Anyway, what good did it do to eat yourself up?"

Suddenly, the doors opened, and, as the throng crowded in, the string of a package got caught on Saul's cufflink. Panicky, his fingers trembling as he tried to move too quickly, Saul struggled to disengage himself. The doors were about to close. The train would pull out before he could get off. In trying to undo the string, he pushed himself out toward the exit, but making his way through the crowd was like pushing a rubber wall. Finally, with the help of the person who owned the package, they managed to unhook the string. Panting, pushing forward, oblivious to the insults thrown his way, he got out to the platform, stumbling over a cane in the clutches of an old man who was forging a path through the crowd. The platform was just as crowded as the train from which he had just exited. He was beginning to think he would be pushed back into the car, when an employee saved the day by closing the doors and the train took off. The corridors were blocked and the passengers, worn out by their struggles in the train, seemed hardly able to stand up. They were slowing him down, he who was in such a hurry. Come on, get a move on, you snail! Let me by, you legless cripple! Monstrous insults rose to his lips and stopped there, stifled just in time.

He ran through the streets, bumping into pedestrians. He needed to slow down, walk like other people, avoid calling attention to himself. Upon patting his cuff, he all of a sudden felt faint. "Imbecile," he said to himself, "it's in the other one." The checks were right where he had put them, inert, indifferent. He stopped in front of a shop window to catch his breath. The sight of his taut features startled him. It was the face of a guilty person, a madman, a face likely to catch the attention of a cop. And if something should happen and they took him down to the station and searched him, how would he explain the seventy dollars? A million francs, you could explain away, but seventy dollars... how could you explain seventy dollars?

While he was trying to calm down, a new anxiety took hold of him. He couldn't find the café. He would have sworn that it was only a few meters away from where he was. Now, in his distraction, he had gone all the way to the Moulin Rouge, recalling that, the night before, he had seen its red lights gleaming in the distance. It must be closer to Pigalle. "That'll teach me to run around like a madman," he told himself.

He retraced his steps, walking slowly, examining every café along the way. He ought to have made note of some landmark. It was a café on the corner of a street, he was sure of that; yes, but was there an oyster stand outside? A sudden tranquility descended upon him. Through an open door, he had just caught a glimpse of Antoine, leaning with his elbows on the counter, chatting with a patron. Antoine shot an indifferent glance in his direction and turned back to his conversation.

In the rear of the room, there were two guys playing chess, a couple of lovers sitting on a bench, a few bourgeois quietly sipping their aperitifs. You would never have taken it for the same place, but it clearly was.

"If you want to use the telephone," Antoine called to him, "Go ahead. The booth's empty."

So Saul was given to understand that the coast was clear. He went into the booth, leaving the door open so as to remain in the dark while taking the cuff link out of his sleeve.

"Sit down, M. Saul, there's no charge," said Ivan, offering him a space on the folding cot that had been opened out and covered with an army blanket. "Mlle. Mireille will be down soon. Ten minutes. Bad times. Business not good."

"She's with Sarand?" asked Saul as he sat down.

Ivan smiled. It made him smile, the idiot. Saul, however, was not smiling. The thought of Sarand, drooling and smirking over Mireille, made him feel like going upstairs and smashing the guy's face. But he was also thinking of the money in his pocket, of the fabulous sum which he would soon get his hands on, so as to liberate Mireille from this miserable job.

After asking if it would bother him, Ivan turned the old gramophone on. "Good music," he said, tapping the record with his thumb to get it started, nodding his head, inclining his head to listen. The record was old and scratched, the needle was dull, but in spite of everything, Ivan glowed. *The Death of the Swan,* he announced, proud as if he had composed the music himself. "Ukrainian; I danced. Yes." He stared at the floor as if he could see the ghost of the past rising up out of the tomb, his attention focused on his feet. Then, as if he were afraid the fragile phantom of memory might be frightened away, he sat down next to Saul, folded his hands together and began to wag his head in time to the music, talking to himself, engaged in a strange deaf-mute dialogue with his feet.

On the wall, there was a large yellowing photograph, draped in black. It was recognizably Ivan, young at the time, tall and muscular, immobilized in a prodigious leap. And he? What about him? Had he not awakened one day to find this hole in his memory, big as a fist, through which all of his knowledge had been drained, like a lake emptying into an underground river that runs off into the Ocean? The horrible, hoarse, mutilated music finally stopped. Ivan carefully wrapped the record up in newsprint and returned it to its niche behind the gramophone.

"How's school, M. Saul?"

"It's OK, thanks."

"Much courage. Very difficult."

"What you really need is a good memory."

From upstairs, loud vibrations drifted downwards.

"Doesn't all that noise bother you?"

Ivan leaned forward, the better to listen. All this stamping had meaning for him. His face lit up. "Not noise. Listen. Work music. I remember... I remember."

His foot had begun to express itself again, remembering this strange language of the feet.

"One evening," he continued dreamily, "no more work. Leg dead. Like big stone."

Saul felt no pity. He just wished Ivan would be quiet. So what? Was he the only one who had a dead member? A part of his being so crippled that it no longer functioned without the crutches of memory? All it had taken was one bad move for Ivan, but the others? What about all the bad moves made by so many others, for which he, although blameless, must suffer the consequences? Who knows? He might have finished his studies, lived an uneventful life, never dreamed of resorting to such sordid dealings. He might never have asked for anything more than to be absorbed into the system if the system could have managed to absorb him.

Ivan offered him a cup of tea. Their eyes met; Saul looked away. But Ivan's inquisitive look followed him, penetrated him like a scalpel, dug around, turned over the hidden layers of his being until an almost physical pain was shooting in between his eyes. In order to hide from this look, at once tender and relentless, Saul got up and studied the metro map hanging on the wall. Ivan's gaze plunged into his back like a dagger. With the tip of his finger, Saul traced a path through the old Paris of his childhood.

Twelve years old, could it be so long ago and at the same time so recently? The mind seemed able to dispense with temporal limits and live in two periods at the same time, like two plays being performed on either side of a dividing curtain. All you had to do was raise the curtain and you could live, at one and the same time, in the past and present, on the very threshold of eternity. To pass over to the other side and succumb to the child of twelve, let him envelop you in his magic, his tranquility, his dreams; or reinforce the curtain with all your bodily strength and remain in the hard, cruel reality where the dream is out of reach. The tortured face of Moishe appeared before his eyes. Had he looked for him when he woke up, searching every face with diminishing hope, finally fixating on the empty wall like a drowned man on the shore? And what if the operation were a success and little Moishe were all set to prove that it's possible to go on living in spite of memories? Bah, it would take a miracle for the operation to succeed on that being soldered to the past by sickness. Only death would claim that wasted body as its due, not life, which had failed to keep its commitments.

"Here," he said to Ivan, putting his finger on a green spot, "that's where we used to live." Then he walked to the stairway, to wait for Mireille.

"That idiot Marcel has gone and bought two tickets for *Lohengrin*," he said, as he crossed to the edge of the sidewalk. "Mind you, he hates the opera. He just thought it would make

Simone happy, and come to find out, she also hates the opera."

Saul, who had prepared this lie ahead of time, thought, "If only that dimwit Denise hasn't told her anything."

"Oh!" she said, joyfully, "and he gave them to you?"

To tease her, he showed her the corner of the tickets sticking out of his wallet, delighted by her astonishment, warmed by her joy.

"What luck!" she said, grabbing his wallet, "orchestra seats, yet!"

"All right, give me back my wallet, before you lose something for me, Mireille!"

But she was teasing him back, grabbing the bills. Suddenly, hiding the wallet behind her back, she gave him a look in which curiosity was mixed with fear.

"What's all this money?"

"Don't be so curious. Marcel asked me to buy something for him. Come on, now, give me back my wallet, don't play with it. You can see it's stuffed with money. And especially since it's not my money."

She simply said, "You're lying."

"What do you mean, lying?"

"You're lying, Saul."

"Well, all right. I didn't want to say anything. It's supposed to be a surprise. That will have to do."

"Saul"--She was pulling at his sleeve—"You haven't gone and done something stupid?"

He burst into somewhat forced laughter.

"Do I look like a guy who would do something stupid? When the time comes, I'll tell you all about it."

They walked along in silence. It was clear that she didn't believe a word he had said. Yet, it wasn't all lies. He really was planning a surprise for her. Would she ever be astonished to know what he was cooking up; astonished and happy. He would have liked to tell her. "I'm superstitious," he thought, with amusement.

"You'll see," he said, slipping his arm under Mireille's,

"there are going to be some changes around here."

"Saul, you have to tell me. All that money... it frightens me. I can't help thinking the worst. Saul, it's not possible to come by that much money honestly overnight."

"Don't start that again. I get enough of it from Marcel. Yeah, yeah, I know the old fable about the reward of the old ploughman who engaged in honest labor all his life, but there's also: 'God helps those who help themselves.' Just look around at all these poor bastards!"

"Saul, don't shout so loud, people are looking at us."

"To hell with them."

"And the opera tickets?'

"What about the opera tickets? If you don't want to go, all you have to do is say so. Perhaps you'd prefer that I give your American friend a call and present the two of you with the tickets on a silver platter, my blessings upon you?"

"You're impossible. You always have to bring strangers into our quarrels. But while we're at it, may I ask what did he ever do to you?"

Saul had no answer. How could he tell her that because of this stranger, he had suddenly understood that he had to get rich quickly, whatever the cost? Furious, he pulled out the tickets and slapped them into her hand.

"There," he said, "I hope that your American likes Wagner, because he's going to get his fill."

Without a word, without his making the least effort to stop her, she tore the tickets to pieces and threw them into the gutter.

"Well that's seven hundred francs down the drain," he said, regretfully. "We could at least have given them to Marcel."

She watched the torn bits fluttering in the running water. Bitter tears rose up in her eyes. "A lot of good that's done for us," she said.

In the restaurant, during dinner, her eyes filled up with tears again and he knew that she was thinking of the tickets, cursing the impulse that had prompted her to destroy them. He told her stories, trying to cheer her up, even resorted to making silly faces. Nothing worked. Finally, at his wits' end, he suggested they go to the opera anyway; they'd surely be able to pick up a couple of tickets. But she shook her head, in some strange way bent on punishing herself. Suddenly she cried out: "Always these idiotic quarrels. You see what I wound up doing. I've had it. Enough, you hear! If every time we get together, we have to quarrel, then it's just not worth it."

She got up and left the restaurant, ordering him not to follow her. He followed her anyway.

Having drawn the curtains closed, Saul crouched down next to Mireille, who was sitting on the bed, unlacing her shoes. Gently, he pushed her hands away.

"Let me do it," he said, "'you're tired out. I can see it. You're pale as a ghost."

For a long time, he watched her face, so pale and drawn it made those big eyes, filled with sadness and discouragement, seem all the more somber. He unlaced her shoes and set them aside. Her feet were frozen. He began to rub them vigorously, feeling in his palms, the patches where the stockings had been mended, places where much walking had melded and hardened the darning threads and knots. How far away were those years when, in their innocence and solitude, she had cuddled in his arms all night. She no longer remembered how she had pressed against him full of fear, filling him up with renewed courage, the courage of those who cannot afford to be afraid. Suddenly, he felt Mireille's hand run through his hair. Would she finally remember and fall into his arms, begging him not to leave her: "What would become of me without you?"

"Saul..."

He lifted his eyes to her, in a look full of tenderness and expectation.

"Saul, promise not to get angry..."

He promised.

"Don't give up your studies. I don't need money, Saul. I manage very well. I don't need anything, Saul. Think of all the effort you've made, all the sacrifices... your studies are all we have left."

What did she know? How much had she guessed? Despite her innocent looks, her mind was as sharp as a blade.

"I know. Don't worry," he answered.

He was still crouching down, his knees hurting; but his gaze, reaching out across the room to that window on the darkness, said everything he would never confess to her in so many words. The wound in the depths of his being, the atrophy of his memory: this degenerate adolescence. It's gone, Mireille; my memory is gone; the accident of the past has mutilated it for good. It tries, it pushes up, but can never get over the wall. I spend hours looking at a single page and when I lift my eyes from the page, what I can remember of it would fit on a postage stamp. The practice of medicine requires love and I am full of hate. I can no longer remember love, Mireille, just airplanes spreading machinegun fire all over the roads in summertime, the pounding of boots on paving stones, the columns of smoke, black with human grease, rising upwards towards the sun and blackening the face of heaven. Our future is languishing in those shadows. Everything is all fucked up in advance. There's nothing worth saving, except you. He reached out his hand to touch her, to reassure himself that she, at least, was real.

"Let's go, little girl, to bed with you!" he said abruptly, his hand reaching nimbly under her skirt.

Mireille sprang back, terrified, against the wall.

"Mireille, my little one, don't look at me like that."

He dared not touch her again, for fear that she would let out a scream.

"I didn't mean to frighten you. I was only going to undo your garters and undress you as I used to when you were little. Surely you're not bashful with me, after all?"

Mireille didn't answer. She just kept on looking at him, her face pale, her enormous eyes set in a fixed stare, like that of an animal betrayed who would never trust anyone again. Suddenly dizzy, with aching legs, Saul got up. The room began to spin around; he was stifling. He staggered over to the window, opened it wide and breathed in the cold air. Then he leaned his feverish forehead on the window frame and closed his eyes on the giddily spinning world. "That's it, I'm going to have a relapse," he said to himself, hearing his own noisy breathing and feeling the sweat build up on his shivering flesh. But he didn't have time to be sick, or money either. There was Mireille, who took up all his time, all his means. He forced himself to open his eyes. The window was a loophole into the past and the future that would try to separate him from Mireille. Horror had thrown the two of them into the solitude of the night and from that horror of being alone with her had sprung the sweet comforting knowledge that he was not *alone* with her but *together* with her. The future was far away. She was nearby, a few feet away from him. He could hear her nervous, rapid movements as she got undressed. "Now," he thought, "she's uncovering her breasts." He had watched them blossom, night after night, while she lay sleeping. He spun around, but the cover, suddenly pulled up to her neck, hid her completely, all except for her eyes, which kept on staring at him in terror. Slowly, he approached, ready to freeze at the slightest signal.

"Mireille, you and I, we're the same. We always have been so. Give me your hand. Give it to me, Mireille, I beg you."

From under the cover, Mireille's hand appeared and fearfully slipped into his own.

"Look, see how they're alike: same pale skin, same slender fingers, such fragile joints... Who is this Karson, anyway? Nothing. He doesn't exist. You see? There has never been a Karson. It's always been you and I together. That's the way it's been from the beginning. It had to be so. I will always be here for you. Nobody will ever hurt you. That's why I was born first, so I'd be right there at your side, right away... My little one, we'll never ever quarrel again. I promise you."

Then he put Mireille's hand under the cover, tucked her in, folded the bedspread in two and spread it across her feet so she'd be warmer.

"Sleep now," he said, "I'm here."

After turning off the light, he sat down in the armchair. From there, he could contemplate her face and her nude shoulders, gleaming white in the dark. A ray of silver light fell at an angle on the bed. For a long time, she would lie awake, watching his every move, but, finally, overwhelmed by the peace that seemed to emanate from him, she fell asleep, her face turned toward him. Then, without making a sound, he got up and left. He was happy.

Chapter 16

A towel on her shoulders, a fine-toothed comb in her hand, Denise was examining herself, searching for lice, not finding any.

"Must be nerves," she said to Mireille, who was watching her. "Like with my rash. You should look around my waist. Appetizing, eh?

She opened her peignoir wide, exposing her large, round belly, the tuft of brown hair where her sumptuous thighs began. A rosary of pink spots wound its way around her waist.

"It's that filthy Pierre. Just thinking about him makes my blood curdle."

"Why don't you leave him?"

"It's not that I don't feel like it. Did you ever try to make a mad dog stop barking? If you yell at it, that doesn't stop it from jumping you. If you try to run away, it'll bite you in the leg. A lot of good for the trouble."

While talking, Denise had put on her girdle; now she was pulling up her stockings.

"Say, that *Amerlo* of yours, he wouldn't be a big blond guy who smokes a pipe?

"Yes, why?"

"No reason. Just that he's been prowling around the joint for the past few days. It just occurred to me that it could be the same guy."

"I doubt it," said Mireille, but now her heart was beating more quickly.

"In any case, it's not a cop, that's for sure, so it must be your fellow."

"I'm sure it's not Frank."

But what if it was? No, it was too much to hope for. He

wouldn't come back any more than Gérard had, or any of the others.

"He jilted you, eh?" Denise shook her head in disgust. "It's not as if I didn't warn you. That's the way it is with men. Either you treat them rotten or they'll treat you rotten. You've got to choose. You can give them little treats to make them sit up and beg, OK, but never let them have their fill."

"He didn't, as you say, jilt me. It was mutual."

"That's what they all say. But then, what the fuck should I care? All the same, you must have gone to bed with him, or he wouldn't have cleared out in such a hurry. Did he even so much as give you a pack of cigarettes?"

Mireille looked at her in disgust, ashamed. Suddenly, Denise had finally shown who she really was. There was no avoiding it. When all was said and done, Saul was right.

"It's not worth getting down in the dumps over it" exclaimed Denise, misreading Mireille's expression, "just count yourself lucky he didn't slap you around while he was at it.

How could she possibly tell her, how could she possibly explain what had taken place between her and Frank? How different it was from everything Denise had ever known! And what if Denise had gotten it right? What if she had just let herself be used? She banished the unbearably humiliating thought from her mind and decided to leave the room immediately and never talk to Denise again. But at that very moment, there was the sound of knocking at the door and a loud male voice ordering them to open up:

"Police!"

"Open up, Mademoiselle, it's the police," they heard Mme. Dufour exclaim, quite gleefully.

Mireille, terrified, looked at Denise. Her face had turned the color of clay. She was casting wild looks around her, and in a dull voice, begged Mireille not to leave her--as if there had been some other way out of that room. Suddenly, puffing out her chest and making the effort to speak in a somewhat natural tone, she shouted:

"OK, OK, hold on! Just a minute, please! You can't expect me to open the door in my birthday suit!"

In the brief respite that followed, she looked around, making sure that everything was in order, then, with her hand on her heart as if to muffle the sound of its pounding, she opened the door. Mireille immediately recognized the men standing at the threshold.

"Gentlemen," said Denise with a mocking air as she stood aside to let them in, slamming the door in Mme. Dufour's face as she was about to sneak in behind them.

"Are you Denise Rabaud?"

"If not, I don't know who else it would be," said Denise, facing them directly.

"And her?"

"I live next door," Mireille said hurriedly, making her way to the door. "I was about to leave. I just came in for a minute."

"Like she says, she's my neighbor. I don't care too much for solitude, if you don't mind."

"May I leave?" Mireille asked. To think that a minute later she would already have been home. Who knew what she would be mixed up in, now? The inspector shook his head, telling her to sit down and keep still.

"And if you act nice," said Denise, "the gentleman will give you a lollypop. Anyway, would you mind telling me what you guys want? Everything's above board here."

"Guess."

"You can't imagine how stupid I am at such games."

"And suppose we search your apartment? How would you like that?"

"Well, maybe if you show me your warrant, I'll think it over."

But she only asked to see it as a matter of form, not even bothering to look at the piece of paper Turin extended to her.

Mireille forced herself to remain calm, not to ask

again if she could leave. She hoped he wouldn't find anything, that it was all a mistake, that they'd leave and she'd get off with a scare.

"Look, are you going to cooperate and hand the goods over, or do we have to turn everything upside down?"

"What? What goods? Who me? I'm not in business."

"Look, it's time you stopped taking us for jerks. You know what this little game could cost you?"

"What you've got to put up with! But far be it from me..."

"Then let us put the dots on the "i"s for you. Thousand-franc bills--does that ring any bells for you?"

"Look, are you here to search the place or hold me up? It'd be nice to know, eh? Because if it's my stash you're after, you can just come back another time. Let me see your cards , so I can get a good look at them."

"Are you doing this on purpose? You know damn well what it's all about; pretty little counterfeit bills."

Denise gave them such an incredulous look that it seemed impossible to doubt her sincerity. She burst out laughing, striking herself on the thighs with resounding slaps.

"Counterfeit bills, like you read about in the paper? But really, do I look dumb enough to let people feed me counterfeit bills? You don't believe me? Conduct your search, gentlemen. Rummage to your hearts' content."

The inspectors looked at each other, confounded. Turin turned to Mireille, who, hoping that they had forgotten her, hiding in the corner, sat shaking with anxiety."

"And you, you probably have no idea that for months, there's been a steady flow of counterfeit thousand franc notes?"

"No," she said, timidly.

He grumbled and turned back to Denise.

"So, you insist?"

"I can't pull them out of thin air just to please you."

"Shall we, Turin?" said the other.

"OK," said Turin.

Mireille shrank up against the wall. She was expecting them to turn the room inside out, pull the stuffing out of the mattress, break up the drawers. But they proceeded methodically, inspecting the grooves in the seams in the floor with electric lamps, moving the wardrobe with the mirror on the door. They took down the photos hanging on the wall, found the crack under the sink and, with a triumphant air, pulled out the wad of bills.

"In the name of God, leave that alone! It's my stash!" cried Denise, charging at them like a fury and snatching the bills out of their hands.

"These are legitimate," conceded Turin, regretfully.

"Legitimate? You better believe it!" said Denise indignantly, opening up her peignoir with no sign of embarrassment, and stuffing the wad of bills into her girdle.

They lifted up the mattress, took the box spring apart, put everything back together again, emptied out the night table. At the moment when Turin lifted the basket of artificial flowers to make sure that the top of the night table could not be removed, Mireille saw Denise blanch, waver, nostrils trembling. But she regained her poise immediately. Just in time, Mireille swallowed an exclamation. The inspectors were there, doing their job. Maybe there was nothing in the basket after all.

Three quarters of an hour later, the two men wiped their foreheads, looking perplexed and disappointed. Denise crowed.

"So now that you've gone to all that trouble for nothing, are you guys satisfied? I told you nobody slips me any counterfeit bills."

"Who do you work with? asked Turin, with no trace of amusement.

"Me, I work on my own. I'm a big girl. I can take care of myself."

"All right. Don't waste your breath. We'll get you next

time around. And you, Miss, I would really advise you to change the company you keep."

"What nerve!" exclaimed Denise, pulling herself up in such a way as to poke her large breasts right under the inspector's nose. "Excuse me, but is this a free country or what?"

"Just bear in mind what I said. We'll get you next time around."

When they had gone, and she had locked the door back up, Denise glued her ear to the wall and listened in silence. Then she collapsed, exhausted, on the bed. She tried to make a joke of it, but her voice was trembling. She seemed to have turned to jelly, undergoing some kind of delayed reaction to the pressure she had been under. But Mireille could feel her looking out at her from under heavy, half-closed eyelids. No longer doubting that the police were on the right track, she went straight to the basket of flowers, pulled the moss off the top, and pulled out a pack of bills wrapped up in cellophane.

"Is this what they were looking for?" she asked.

In a flash, Denise was on her feet, her face white with rage and fear. Brutally, she pushed Mireille up against the wall and grabbed the packet out of her hands. In a hoarse, dull voice that Mireille would not have recognized as coming from Denise, she gasped: "So you've been spying on me, you little slut." A shrewd, cruel look gleamed in her eyes.

"OK. Now that you know about that, there's something else you need to know. You turn me in and you turn your brother in. Get it? You think I'm making this up, right? I'm not making anything up. He's in it--in hot water--and I mean up to his eyeballs. If I go down, he goes down with me. Get it? Yes, that's it; you're beginning to see the light. You can't get over it, but that's the way it is. So, now, you can just keep this to yourself. You see nothing; you say nothing. Because if your brother gets picked up, you won't see him again for a long time. Me, I hide them, but he palms them off.

"It's not true," groaned Mireille. "You're just saying

that to scare me off, so that I'll keep quiet. But surely you know that if I wanted to talk, I could have done it, just now, when they were here. The minute that guy touched the basket, I knew it was in there. I was looking at you. You almost fainted. I'm not a dimwit. I just knew it."

Deliberately, though with some difficulty, she loosened Denise's stiffly grasping fingers from around her arm.

"You know very well that you have nothing to fear from me. The police have done me so much harm that I'm not about to do them any favors. Today they're after you. During the war, they were after me. I'm not asking you for explanations, I don't want to know anything. But why would you drag my brother into this dirty business? Why would you make up such a lie? It's disgusting."

At the sound of the word "disgusting," Denise, who had, until that moment seemed more and more contrite, became herself again, mocking and full of defiance: "Disgusting! Just who is it that's disgusting? It really suits you to be so stuck up... as for me, I've attended services at St. Lazare, and if sweet Jesus himself came down from the cross to help me, he'd get a hernia, poor lamb. Well, OK! What? Why are you looking at me as if I had two heads? Disgusting! Everybody is disgusting; only the others wear perfume so you can't smell it. You think that mud won't stick to you. Just come down from the clouds. I'm not making this up. What I said about your brother is true. I swear it. He's passed hundreds of those things around."

"It's not true!" shouted Mireille. "You're lying. You're horrible. Saul would never do a thing like that. He has his entire future ahead of him. I'll go to the police. I'll tell them everything..."

She stopped, racked by sobs. That money, all that money, he hadn't wanted to tell her...

"Yes, Mimi, it's true."

There was no more malice in Denise's voice, only a calm tone of resignation tainted with sorrow that chilled

Mireille to the bone. Denise's eyes were no longer triumphant. They were a mournful gray, gray with pity. Then she pulled herself together, tore the cellophane off the package, scattered the bills over the sink and set fire to them. The printer's ink smoked a lot as it burned. She opened the window, took out a cigarette and lit it from one of the flaming bills.

"Look," she said, "quit sniveling and I'll tell you how it happened."

When she had finished telling her story, she washed out the sink in silence.

"You understand, your brother doesn't know they're counterfeit. Hell, we couldn't tell him that. That's why it's absolutely necessary to keep this quiet. If he suspected, he'd be capable of raising a rumpus and then he'd be dangerous. Mimi, you have to understand-- the Marseillais doesn't put up with dangerous people. Do you know what I mean?"

She shook Mireille by the shoulder.

"Say something. Do you hear what I'm saying?"

Mireille lowered her head. She had nothing more to say, no more reproaches for anyone. Everything was her fault. By saying nothing, without knowing it, she had been the one to betray Saul. Now, it was too late. Ah! She had thought she was so clever with her secrets, proud of her new independence, her misplaced suspicions. Nice work. If only she had listened to Saul, if only she had trusted him instead of complaining to Denise about him. And now, to avoid the worst, she would have to keep on betraying him. How would it be possible to go on living, knowing what she had done to him?

"Why? Why us?" she cried through her tears. "I never did anything to you. I even defended you..."

"Look Sweetheart, in this life, you have to know how to defend yourself. You can't allow yourself the luxury of counting on others. After your little trip down to the precinct, we had to do something. With your brother in the picture, we felt safe. And if you stop to think about it, it wasn't such a bad idea. When I explained it to the Marseillais, he leaped at it.

Besides, for some time now, your brother has been getting on my nerves with his holier-than-thou bullshit. Now, he's the same as me. He owes me. He can no longer look down his nose at me as if I were some kind of a bedbug. He's like me, same tribe, we're linked together as if by blood."

"You love him," stammered Mireille.

The anguish she had felt up to now was nothing compared with the feeling that hit her when she perceived the danger of being loved by a woman like Denise, who loved darkly, fiercely, savagely, and who would sooner take you down in a stranglehold than let go. In Denise's eyes, needles of ice gleamed brightly. She started to snicker, then lost her breath; she let out a howl, then fell, stock still from head to toe, flat on the ground. As Mireille rushed over to help her get back up, Denise went into convulsions, flopping up and down like a fish on a kitchen table. A pink foam formed at the corners of her lips. Afraid to leave her alone and not knowing what else to do, Mireille soaked a towel with cold water and put it on her forehead, then sat down on a chair and waited, her face leaning over Denise's. At the end of a minute or two, Denise came back to herself. With a distracted look, she lifted herself up and stared at Mireille for a long time, as if she had never seen her before. Then she stepped over to the sink and spat into it.

"Shit!" she said. "I bit my tongue. It's been a long time since I had a fit. I had them often when I was living at the orphanage. Also at the farm. They punished me by locking me up in the cellar all night. I howled. Of course, at that age, I was afraid. She rinsed out her mouth, lapping the water up out of her hand, from under the faucet.

Mireille couldn't wait any longer to ask the question that was burning her lips.

"Denise, what are you going to do about Saul?"

"Saul?" said Denise, astonished. "Oh, yes, Saul, well, I don't know... Say, did I really burn all that up? I didn't dream it? Three hundred thousand smackers? Criminey. Just think what you could do with three hundred thousand smackers."

She dreamed out loud about the *Cote d'Azur*, grand hotels, fur coats, cruises, and even starting some kind of business. Mireille thought: "It's all the same to her. She has no conscience. And I'll lock myself in my room, torment myself, remember, adding, subtracting, calculating..." If she didn't warn Saul, he was in danger of being arrested. If she did warn him, he was at risk of being killed. She should have thought of all this before, long ago. And it wouldn't do any good to reproach Denise.

"Denise, what are you going to do about Saul?" she repeated insistently.

"Don't worry. In any case, it's time to close up shop. As long as we didn't get caught, there's no more danger. Each of us will pull out with his own little stash. Anyway, he did all right for himself. So what's your beef? He needed a recommendation, I did him a favor, there ain't no law against that. Don't worry. I tell you it's over. We'll explain it all to him, of course. It'll all work out fine. There, you feeling better now?

Mireille shook her head. Overwhelmed, she opened the door.

"Don't ever say another word to me. If you do, I won't answer you," she said before she walked out.

Denise shrugged her shoulders. Leaning over the drain, toward the mirror, she was squeezing blackheads.

Chapter 17

Frank lent a distracted ear to what Pamela was saying. She was still excited about her recent trip to Florence. Descriptions of places, mixed up with funny stories about the frustrations of dealing with her mother, who liked to think of herself as a polyglot, came one after the other, without leaving time for her to catch her breath. She had cornered him in a hallway at the Sorbonne and he hadn't been able to get away. Not that he disliked Pamela's company, but today, as for the last few days, he preferred the peace and quiet of being able to ruminate on his unhappiness and misfortune in solitude. In a sense, he envied her. She had recently put an end to her grand love affair with Sita, and seemed none the worse for it. He was about to tell her so, when he noticed that, despite the cheerful tone of her voice, her eyes were melancholy, the whites yellow, the irises dull. "She's blustering," he said to himself. "Deep down, she's as miserable as a dog."

"But I talk about myself all the time," she said suddenly, "And you? What have you been up to?"

She chattered incessantly, as if fearing that if she stopped, she'd be overwhelmed by sorrows once again. Frank responded in monosyllables, then only with gestures, nodding his head to say yes, shaking it to say no, shrugging his shoulders when he didn't know. Pamela's company lent a cynical note to his thoughts about Mireille, since it had been thanks to her that he had met Mireille, with her brave declarations of honesty: "I thought we could dispense with all that's false and deceptive, together forging our own truth for ourselves."

"Truth." Such a pretty word, but what did it mean? A long time ago, a very long time ago, he had caught cold in the glacial atmosphere of his family, and ever since then, had remained fearful of open windows and doors. He needed to forget that name, Mireille, and allow himself to be guided by his own light. But it was impossible, all alone. All alone, he was swimming in the dark, always clinging to that name: Mireille; indecipherable to him. He was a dead man, lost, searching for his tomb in the fog, during a storm, and for whom that name, Mireille, was his only guide. He was stuck on an interminable route, like a horse wearing blinders who doesn't dare go forward or backwards. All that because, entirely satisfied with himself, he had run into Mireille and now, he could not accept her defiant insistence that he was not the essential solution to life's problems.

Outside, the sky was hanging low, heavy with clouds, too lazy to burst open. At Pamela's suggestion, they crossed the street, went into the Café Martel and went downstairs to the Aquarium. The light in the basement, diffused through the heavy ceiling of glass and fish tanks, filled the cellar with a dewy, restful mist. At the back of the room, a couple of young people, fingers interlaced on the table, were looking into each other's eyes, blessedly deaf to the racket emanating from other groups of students. The sight of this happy couple filled Frank with fury.

"These places are always full of people dying to fuck," he observed drily while Pamela was taking off her coat and sliding into the circular booth. "Why don't they just go to a hotel, instead of..."

"Are you jealous, Frank," Pamela gently asked..

He shrugged his shoulders and stared at the couple, eyes full of disdain. But the delicious satisfaction of contempt evaded him. Bitterness was sticking to his tongue like a rancid host that would neither peel off nor melt. To his surprise, he was thinking of Mireille again. She might have been here, instead of Pamela; he would have put his arm around her neck and they would have sat there, beatifically happy, trusting and warm. Suddenly, he detested Pamela. Her emerald-colored sweater not only emphasized the boniness of her chest but also the sharp angles of her features, her long ostrich-like neck and her typically neurotic gray complexion.

"Why don't you get your hair cut?" he asked dryly. "It's not as if it were curly."

"Because my mother likes it this way and it doesn't bother me. You know she's never given up on the idea of marrying me off. She thinks long hair is 'feminine.' You should see the guys she drags home for me to meet. But she's convinced she's being helpful... Do you know what I just learned today? Once, prompted by the desire to shock his friends, Baudelaire dyed his hair green. Can you imagine?"

"So when are you going to dye your hair blue? Baudelaire was crazy. Obviously not an ordinary madman, but crazy nonetheless!"

"Frank!"

This time Pamela was undeniably upset. "Frank, you don't know what you're saying. He wasn't crazy. He was wretched and his wretchedness made him the purest of poets. He transformed his profound *ennui* into, into..."

She couldn't find the right word; her eyes misted up with a kind of pagan adoration. "*Ennui* is the most magnificent gift to human life. It's what drives us to go beyond ourselves and achieve great things."

"All that means nothing to me. You've fallen in love with a dead man because it's easier that way. Obviously his uniqueness intrigues you, but that's no reason to make a god out of him."

"Now you're being cruel," she said with astonishment.

"Well, maybe..." he said wearily. "Please forgive me. I had no intention of hurting your feelings."

She excused herself on the pretext of freshening up and went to the bathroom. During her absence, he ordered a Raphael for himself and mineral water for her. Wasn't it bad enough that he was in a lousy mood? Was that any excuse to hurt Pamela? He groaned and called himself an imbecile. There had been a time when she was his entire kingdom, with her blond hair, her pale skin and her crooked baby teeth. He tried to recall the image reflected in the mirror when he was all dressed up in his idiotic new suit, transformed into a little Lord Fauntleroy, his neck squeezed and hurting in his starched collar. "I won't call you a sissy," she had said, setting her pale cheek next to his.

When Pamela came back, she had neatly combed her hair.

"Is that better, now?" she asked, without the slightest trace of coquetterie, not that she was really capable of any such thing.

"Very nice," he said without meaning a word of it.

"You really haven't changed. You still lie with the same disconcerting kindness."

"You snake! I should have put some poison in your drink while you were gone."

"Then you wouldn't have a single friend left," she smiled. She tried to gloss over it, but it was too late. Embarrassed, they both turned toward the aquarium where the fish were swimming in place in their glass cage.

The extent of their world: as big as a thimble. Their mouths stuck to the glass opened and closed, forming silent words while their fins cleaved the water. Frank listened. "Space... give me space," they said with their ghostly voices.

"Unlimited space is the symbol of freedom," he thought out loud. "Only the symbol. In actuality, freedom depends on our five senses, and these five senses are precisely what stands between us and freedom. Well obviously, there are also visionaries, but visions are like soap bubbles--as soon as you try to get into them, they pop open in your hand."

From the look on Pamela's face, it was clear that she was not following him.

"Well, yes," he said, with irritation. "The five senses are a cage for us."

"You're looking for excuses," Pamela said.

"Well, you're clearly above it all. You've found

yourself. You know where you stand. You know where you're going."

"We never find ourselves, Frank. We can never stop searching for ourselves. We become what we decide to become, to the extent and degree that we decide to do so. We are what we do and nothing *a priori.*"

"In that case, we would be responsible for what we are!"

"But Frank, liberty consists in doing, in acting, it's... (to hell with the world!) to be oneself for oneself."

"That's practical. A pretty little package, nicely tied up. Nothing gets in, nothing gets out, it's all in there. But everything has a definitive meaning, and the meanings are inherent in the beings. If beings are definitive, then so are their meanings."

"Only imbeciles and dead people are definitive. An intelligent living being knows himself to be free. He is constantly searching for a dimension beyond himself, as we reach out for the infinite, always approaching it, never quite getting to it. To get there would be to go backwards; it would be to die."

"Look who's talking!"

Only after he said it, as he watched the color drain out of Pamela's face, and her hands squeezing each other so hard that her knuckles whitened, did Frank understand how cruelly he had cut her. He had treated her like a monster, and she blamed him for it, without saying a word, having well understood the allusion. "There is a secret sorrow in each of us," he thought, "and the fear of reaching out to accept what's offered as if it were a trap, an invisible snare which would make hope disappear at the moment we set our hand on it. That's why we aren't free."

"We're all sick," he said.

He was going to add: "And love is a big man-eating plant on the path to freedom." But the image, too painful, evaporated.

A fish with golden scales fluttered in the water, like a petal of fire. It seemed to have fallen asleep. "No," Frank told himself, "he's at peace. He's figured out that it doesn't do any good to batter his head against the walls of that glass cage. He's stopped tormenting himself. He's accepted his fate."

Frank had also known peace. Lying in Mireille's arms, asleep and yet awake at the same time, wandering in dreams, his senses appeased, alone with her in the salutary darkness where nothing could get to him and pull him out of that plenitude that was not sleep and yet was dream. He had feared that glass cage. But if he was responsible, himself, for his actions, Mireille, on the other hand, was responsible for hers. Not bad at all, come to think of it!

"No!" he cried suddenly, "no. Is it his fault, I mean that fish, that they put him in a glass cage?"

Suddenly, Pamela exclaimed: "Why are you hiding behind that little fish? He felt her take hold of his arm and reacted by drawing away from her. He found her body repugnant and couldn't stand for her to touch him.

"Don't be silly... you see that fish. Suppose we took it out of there and threw it back in the ocean; I'm quite sure it would keep on swimming back and forth in a space twenty inches long and it would never even occur to it to think that it was out of its cage."

"But you are not a fish!" she exclaimed, with irritation.

They drank in silence for a few minutes. Pamela seemed preoccupied. Frank had often seen this expression on her face. It did not bode well. He could not bear the thought of spending another evening taking firearms apart and putting them back together with Pamela's father. Suddenly, while maintaining a certain caution — since she anticipated rejection —and without looking him in the eyes, she said: " I just bought a new copy of *Les Fleurs du Mal.*"

"No!" he said in an uncompromising tone.

"We'll be alone. Father has gone off on a trip. Mother

is dining out. Well, of course, if you have something better to do…"

But he didn't have anything to do. He might as well go have a drink with her, rave about her new Bible, to make her happy, her future full of dead things, the sketch of a face on a sheet of glazed paper. He said "yes" with a distracted air. He thought of the house the Pierce family had sub-let in Passy, and of the disagreeable memories it would awaken in him. He thought of Mrs. Pierce's paintings, Pamela's mother having belatedly discovered a remarkable talent in herself; he also thought of the opinions he would be obliged to express. He thought of the New York apartment to which, after the war, he had not wanted to return; with its oversized furniture upholstered in satin, enormous tapestries that absorbed all human sounds, transforming every room into a mausoleum.

The wood fire burning in the fireplace would have brightened up the room if it had not been electric. Frank accepted the Martini Mrs. Pierce offered him, and settled into a deep armchair across from her. She had put on weight but still had fine ankles and the fresh complexion of people to whom only good things happen.

"My, how nice it is to be among Americans," she said in a voice that was light and pleasant to the ear. "Don't think for a minute that I mean to criticize them, after all, I'm a guest here, but Europeans can be tiresome. They never stop complaining. When all is said and done, you just have to muster up some courage and strength of character, grit your teeth and not let yourself be ground down by bad luck. There's no sense wallowing in misery like this. You decide to get over it, you work hard and you get over it. Only you can't be lazy."

Her nose in the air, she waited for a note of approval that was not forthcoming.

"I don't think we're in any position to appreciate the precise dimensions of the situation," Frank finally ventured, so as to appease his conscience.

Mrs. Pierce shot him a scandalized look. She had just discovered a traitor, but, fully aware of the requirements of hospitality, she hastened to change the topic of conversation, undertaking to tell him all about her trip to Italy. Florence was a veritable museum. In Rome, Protestant though she was, she allowed herself to be blessed by the Pope. After all, a benediction could not do anybody any harm. As for Naples, she'd just as soon never hear about it again! In all her life, she had never seen so much grime!

Fortunately, Pamela came back, carrying in her arms, as if it were an object of adoration, a great volume, bound in red leather.

"Exactly as I feared," cried Pamela's mother. "You absolutely cannot show that book to Frank. The illustrations are revolting. Pamela!"

Not deigning to answer, Pamela knelt down near Frank, folding her feet under her body and opening up the book she had set down on her thighs. The aroma of leather intermingled with that of the Martini.

"Pamela!" Mrs. Pierce cried out again.

"Oh! Mother, let me be. Frank's not a child."

"The children of this generation don't show any respect for their elders," said Mrs. Pierce, making no effort to hide the chagrin that this realization caused her.

She was hardly ready to concede defeat. Raining examples down on them, she hauled out her entire entourage of grievances. Back in her day!... Pamela calmly turned the pages of the book, as if there had been an airplane droning overhead. She waited patiently for it to go away so she could take her turn at making herself heard. Thanks to an entirely personal series of associations, Mrs. Pierce had gotten around to the last summer she had spent at Bar Harbor. Back in her day, you could be sure what you were going to find there, but now you never knew what you were going to be exposing yourself to. It seemed that these days such places were accessible to anybody and everybody. She gave her opinion, opened up new questions, laid out the rules. Yak... yak... like a pepper mill, and each word, carefully chiseled, point sharpened, the better to penetrate and wound.

Pamela sighed with resignation. Frank saw himself, years ago, sitting at the great table, impeccably dressed, suffocating in his starched collar, not daring to lift his nose from his plate, thanking his stars for the basket of gladiolas sitting on the table in front of him in such a way as to hide him almost entirely from view. And what if, turning toward Mrs. Pierce, he suddenly said to her: "My dear madam, you are nothing but a big, fat, dead eel floating back and forth, back and forth, along the Gulf Stream from Bar Harbor to Miami." She would snap like a rotten cord. The enamel of her perfectly composed face would crumble; and the greenish decomposing flesh beneath would appear. When, out of breath, she had to stop for a minute, Pamela, who had been waiting patiently for this moment of respite, quickly began to speak before her mother changed her mind.

"It's mostly this passage that I would like to read to you," she said. "Listen, Frank. Then you can tell me if he's crazy--"

> *Homme libre, toujours tu chériras la mer!*
> *La mer est ton miroir; tu contemples ton âme*
> *Dans le déroulement infini de sa lame,*
> *Et ton esprit n'est pas un gouffre moins amer*

Pamela read well, with intelligence and sensitivity, her accent hardly discernible.

"Ah!" cried Mrs. Pierce. "Finally, some wholesome literature! Finally, an author who affirms the importance of cherishing his mother. Unlike our own literature, in which all mothers are described as witches! Nothing could be more natural than cherishing your mother. If only there were more writers like this one, the psychiatrists would not be up to their ears in work, as they are these days."

Without even smiling, staring fixedly, Pamela spontaneously translated the lines she knew by heart: "Free man, you will always cherish the sea!/ The sea is your mirror; you contemplate your soul/ In the infinite unrolling of its waves,/ And your spirit is a gulf no less bitter." Mrs. Pierce let out an irritated sigh.

"*Mer* and *mère*," she said. "They do sound so alike."

Then she drowned her confusion in a mouthful of Martini, a wave of embarrassment reddening her face. She got up, reminding Pamela that she would be dining out, asking Frank to please excuse her and be sure to come again soon, then slipped out.

"Peace, at last," said Pamela.

Legs folded beneath herself, with her thumb stuck in the pages of the book, she had not budged.

From one moment to the next, it was as if they had returned to the time when they regularly confided in each other, with all that implied about intimacy and recollections of the past. Frank let himself slip out of the armchair and lay down on the rug alongside Pamela.

"Do you remember that little French woman at Sita's?"

"Which one? The one whose brother is so strange?"

"He's not strange--he's crazy. What do you think of her?"

"You know, I had problems of my own. Her brother was acting so weird that I couldn't help noticing him, but that's all."

She shrugged her shoulders and opened the book back up to the place she had marked with her thumb.

"She was a virgin," said Frank.

"But she isn't any more, eh?" Pamela remarked indifferently.

"Is that all you have to say to me?"

"You make an announcement like that in cold blood and you want me to get upset over it?"

"I know, there's no such thing as telling half a secret. You have to explain it all. But it's so confusing. Love is, after all, women's business," he said, avoiding her eyes.

"I would not have believed you could be so mean-spirited as to say such a thing," Pamela said, with acid in her voice. "You know very well that love is everybody's business. What do you want me to say? This is about you, about your life. When you get to the end of it, it won't be what I said that counts... but what you did."

These words made something inside him snap. Although he had sort of expected them, when they fell from Pamela's lips, drained of blood, like a death-knell calling out to him in the night, he recoiled.

"Damn it! Can't you answer a simple question without cramming a philosophy lesson into me? Is it so difficult to answer a simple question?"

"Listen, Frank, let's not lose our sense of proportion. You're not asking a question, you're asking me to decide for you. You're asking me to solve your problem for you. In the last analysis, you're asking me nothing less than to assume the burden of your freedom."

She lowered her head as if she were going to bury herself in the book again, but Frank was not finished. He put his hand on the page to stop her from reading. She raised her head and he could see, from the shadows under her eyes, that she had suddenly become very weary.

"You see," she said in a resigned tone, "what you want is to be able to tell yourself, no matter what happens, 'It wasn't my doing. I was in a cage when it happened, just like the fish.' No, Frank, that's not the way it works." She leaned over her dead man's book.

Frank got up. Mrs. Pierce's home was a house of the dead: he would never set foot in it again.

Chapter 18

Sweet friend, dearest Mireille,

It's a mistake to think you can consume your passion for life under the African sun. Our life is a rosary of acts, and in trying to destroy a single one of them, by refusing to remember it, we break the equilibrium, and the one-way direction of our existence becomes illogical. In vain do we keep our eyes wide open on this life: we no longer recognize ourselves except in the squat shadows projected on the path at noon. Thus, I have forgotten nothing of what is "you," nor the harm that we did to each other.

At the intersection of two starry roads, they got me by the scruff of the neck. Drafted, I no longer exist. As a soldier, having become clairvoyant, I foresee the face and the form of my death as she will give birth to my cadaver. Yet it's too soon to die, to become immortal. Immortality has no face and honor is a curious buffoon who wears many masks.

I must quickly put my possessions in order: as a well-known poet would say, "two fingers to pull the trigger, a thought at the back of your head, a shoulder of veal and thirty-six stars." Whether it's in front of an execution squad or a haystack, a pile of manure in a bloody little village, what good will it do me to remember the promises Mankind held out to me? Heroes are a thing of the past. Monuments attest to the fact. There's no way they could inscribe, for example: "Here lies a poor dumb fuck"... etc., etc. "It's as plain as the nose on your face," they will say, wiping away a tear and rinsing their gullets with drink. Woe to those with convictions! The time of the

Legions has come and gone; long live the herd!

Solutions are like stars; distant guides that disappear in the daylight. We can't spare ourselves anything, Mireille, or erase anything, or ever begin from scratch; only make provisional reparations, the way people reconstruct things in between wars; thus the child with his feet bathed in foam rebuilds the castle that the cunning wave will wash away in the sand. Rice? Rubber? Banknotes and portfolios for government ministers.

I am writing to you from a railway restaurant. I bid you good-by, recalling that I loved you and realizing that that was much more important than I thought it was.

Gérard

Mireille folded the letter back up and put it in her pocket. She thought: "Maybe he'll get through it." Her heart ached but her eyes were dry. A sharp sound made her jump. In groping his way along, the blind piano tuner had banged one of the keys on the end of the keyboard.

"Not bad news, I hope," he said, focusing his cloudy wide-open eyes on her. He had heard the rustling of the paper and with the terrible sensibility of the blind, intuited the rest.

"I'm afraid so. One of my friends has just been shipped off to Asia."

"We won't see those guys again anytime soon."

He tightened a chord, played a "C," then sounded a chord.

"You need to replace the pads. They're all worn out. A bunch of guys are going to be fucked over there, much good it'll do anybody."

He shook his head as he rummaged around in the exposed chest of the piano.

"What a goddamn shame!"

Suddenly, he stopped fingering the insides of the

piano and stood up.

"It's noon," he announced. "Say, if you're going out, would you be so kind as to pick me up a half a pound of dates for my lunch. I'm nowhere near finished here."

"Noon!"

Once again, Saul would reproach her for being late. What could be so urgent that it couldn't wait until this evening?

He was waiting for her at the metro exit. He must be very impatient to have come all the way upstairs. However, despite the fact that his face was too pale and his eyes too shiny, he displayed no anger. He simply brushed her cheek with his lips and hailed a taxi. While she objected to the pointless expense, he was talking about surprises, telling her to be quiet and wait. When they finally got into the taxi, he managed to give the driver the address in such a way that she couldn't hear it, and then urged her to close her eyes and not open them again until he told her to.

"Five minutes," he told her. "Less than five minutes. Close your eyes and whatever you do, don't cheat. You'll ruin it for me."

When the taxi stopped, she blinked, but, right away, Saul covered her eyes with his hand.

"Not yet," he whispered, and did not take his hand away until she promised not to try and peek, to let herself be guided like a blind man.

He led her carefully along. She climbed up some steps that seemed high and narrow, vaguely familiar. The odor of the corridor also seemed to evoke memories that were both sweet and sorrowful. All of a sudden, she realized that she was walking upstairs alone, eyes closed, that a vague instinct was guiding her familiarly through the darkness. She pushed Saul's arm away and went up a few more steps. Then she stopped, prey to a vague mixture of anguish and anticipation. Suddenly, she knew that Saul was leading her right into no good. It was too late to run away. A door opened up.

"You can open your eyes now," said Saul.

But now it was her turn to want to keep them closed. Blindly, she felt her way, brushing the walls with the tips of her fingers, smelling and recalling the place; the years had bequeathed to her memory the feel of these walls. A trembling agitated her body. She opened her eyes and wanted to flee, but Saul had taken her hands and pulled her forward.

"So, is it a surprise?" he asked her. "Admit it. You never expected any such thing. Well! Come on. This is our home. We're home, Mireille."

The triumph in his voice was obsessive.

"A week from today, everything will be just the way it used to be. I'll buy back the same furniture, the same curtains. It will be as if we had never left. Everything will be just as it was before. Just as it was before. Come see, remember, touch, breathe. We'll put your piano back over there, I saw a splendid one the other day..."

But Mireille didn't budge from the doorway. It seemed to her that if she took another step, the ghosts of her parents, grey with terror, as they must have appeared to the Germans who came for them, would appear out of nowhere. Saul's steps echoed in the adjoining rooms. Suddenly, the door behind her opened and the face of Mme. Chalard, the concierge, somewhat aged, as ruddy as ever, appeared in the yawning entryway.

"My little Mireille!" she cried warmly, clasping her hands together. "We thought you were lost, you and your brother. You have no idea what a surprise it was to see him again! As if I were seeing a dead man... How big you both are! How happy your parents would be to see you! Ah, poor souls, if you had only seen them! Your father could hardly stand up, he was so ashamed, it was miserable to see him... Your mother, she didn't want to go. They dragged her out, all the way downstairs. She held on to the bars on the stairway, she called out to me... I can hear her still... and when I went upstairs afterwards, oh! Everywhere you looked! What a shambles! It had to be seen to be believed. They didn't leave anything right side up, those turds! There was a sack of flour and a sack of coal-dust, both ripped open with a knife; all strewn together over the kitchen floor... Would you believe, they even popped out the strips of wood over the wiring. Of course, we had them replaced, but... What an idiot I am, these are not things I should be telling you."

With his lips sealed tightly, Saul walked toward the concierge with a threatening demeanor. He grabbed her by the arm and threw her out.

"Get the hell out of here," he began to shout, "You're all as guilty as they are, all of you."

Then he closed the door and leaned up against it.

A ray of sunlight beamed a floury patch onto the floor. Mireille walked over to the patch. At her feet, her mother, a scrub brush in her hands; beside her, a bucket of soapy water; Hairpins falling down from her red chignon. Maybe they had dragged her downstairs by her chignon...

"I can never live here again," she said.

"Sure you can," Saul said, firmly.

"No. I can't do it. I can't. At night, every time I hear a step, I'll think they're still alive and the Nazis have come to get them."

"Nah, you'll see."

"Saul, listen to me!"

She shouted these words, grabbing him by his arms and shaking him so that he would listen to her, so that he would understand.

"Listen to me! Every night, do you hear me! Every night, I'll relive their..."

She could not pronounce the word that, so torturously piercing, was tearing her apart.

"It's because it's empty it has that effect on you. But after we get it furnished, you'll see. You'll remember the years that were full of sweetness and warmth. It'll all come back to you." He gave her nose a flick of his finger.

"And, anyway, who's in charge here? Eh!..."

Saul's hands were weighing on her shoulders.

"On Monday, I pay the key money and sign the lease, and then we'll be home again here."

"You're not going to get me to live off of that money!"

At the look that he shot through her, she understood that it had hit him that she knew. She had to tell him the entire truth. When he paid that key money, he would be making a fatal error. It would be necessary to justify the possession of such a sum. But Denise's secret and Saul's life were bound together behind her sealed lips. In telling what she knew about one of them, she would be throwing the other to the wolves. Dilemma of the damned. Seized by an obscure illogical ray of hope, she held Gérard's letter out to Saul. He looked it over, then began to read it more slowly, absent-mindedly taking a cigarette and some matches out of his pocket. The moment when, with that same absent expression, he struck the match, she tore the letter out of his hands.

"You're afraid I'll set fire to it, eh? I did think of it."

"Very clever of you."

"OK. I read it. So what? Is that my fault?"

Discouraged, Mireille shook her head. What could she say?

"Don't you see that we're all headed straight for trouble? And you most of all! Saul, pretty soon there will be no way out. You're trampling your future underfoot and, with it, the hopes of who knows how many others. You'll destroy us all, Saul."

It was just the thing she could not say to him.

"Is that my fault?" he repeated.

"That's what other people said, five years ago. We are all responsible, you, me, everybody. You said just that to Mme. Chalard a little while ago. You were right. Every time a man dies before his time, it's everybody's fault... It's also, a little bit, everybody's death... Saul, remember, we were standing right there, across the street."

She took him by the arm and took him over to the window and pointed with her finger at Marcel's old apartment.

"That day," she continued, "your hair turned gray."

Saul didn't take his eyes off the window. He was thinking.

"I never talked to you about Moishe," he said, his eyes riveted on the window. He was a sweet little guy; poor kid! They operated on him. If he didn't pull through, it would be no worse, and if he did, they might be able to learn something from his case... What could have prompted him to undergo that operation? The suffering, evidently... Well, after all, maybe he was lucky and never made it off the operating table."

"You mean you don't know?" By the bewildered look he gave her, Mireille suddenly understood that he didn't even know if the young man was still alive or not. Intending to console him, she said: "Well, maybe the operation was a success."

"A miracle! No, you don't get it. Birth is a miracle. After that, there are no more miracles. From the time you're born, you've been had. And then, there's no way to go back. Life is the reversal of the miracle, the devil's dead leaves. It's all so subtle and so fine, all that: a masterstroke!"

The reflection of the conflict taking place inside him stiffened his features, widened his feverish eyes. He ran his fingers through his hair without seeming to be aware of what he was doing. It seemed to Mireille that she could hear the pounding of his heart, wild as waves that break against the cliffs in a ferocious urge to annihilate: and that noise had the effect of drowning her thoughts and her resentment. She no longer had a thought for anything but to stifle the sound of that heart, for fear that it would break, for fear that there would be one last monstrous rending beat and afterwards, silence."

"Saul," she called, softly, not daring to touch him, as if he had been walking in his sleep. "Saul... Saul..."

Startled, he looked at her in a daze.

"What? What, Saul?"

The sound of his own voice seemed to pull him out of the abyss into which he had almost plummeted. He took her hands in his and put them on his chest.

"You're going to come live here with me," he said in a weary tone. "You'll have everything you need. You will be happy, sheltered. I'll be at peace."

His look had become piercing again, his voice getting louder, he promised her everything she wanted, he was dreaming out loud, he shouted, moving forward by just so much as, to hide her terror from him, she backed up against the door.

"But I don't need anything, Saul. I have... I have everything I need."

He was still holding her hands and she didn't know how to get them away from him without provoking a crisis. Suddenly, she broke free.

"Go on!" he shouted, full of hatred. "Go find your Gérards and your Karsons. You haven't see the last of your troubles with them. Go slinking around with that whore friend of yours. Pretty soon you'll be giving her lessons."

Without having fully registered what she was doing, Mireille slapped him right on the mouth. It was too late for regrets. The hatred, pain and astonishment in Saul's look overwhelmed her.

"You know, you slapped me too, one day, and yet I forgave you," she stammered.

Then, in a very weak, very low voice, as if she were talking to herself, she added: "Why must you force me to despise you?"

He opened the door with such rage that it flew back against the wardrobe, and, seizing Mireille by the neck, threw her out. The door slammed between them and, immediately afterward, resounded with the impact of Saul's fists, as he tried to bang down that barrier which, much less than his deed, separated them from each other.

Holding onto the banister, her knees wobbling, she hurried downstairs, trying not to hear Saul's large body bruising and punishing itself against that door, knowing that, if she stopped, even for a second, the recollection of that face, convulsed, sorrowful, mad, would pull her back upstairs.

In the street, she found her way mechanically and bought a package of dates at the corner near the metro station.

Chapter 19

Recollecting that room in his imagination, Frank had forgotten none of the details which made it so much a reflection of Mireille herself. The branch of mimosa in the toothbrush glass, the worn-out slippers on the bedside rug, the big mustard glasses in which she had served him warm wine, the sheets which, in slipping away, had uncovered the coral colored tip of her breast.

Wearing her coat, Mireille waited suspiciously and impatiently for him to get to the point of his visit.

"What brings you here?" she asked in an imperious tone.

He had told himself that he would be able to overcome all obstacles; now, imagination failed him and he found himself standing there stupidly. Sheepishly, he asked if he could take off his coat and sit down. Mireille nodded her head with that same imperious air. She didn't seem all that happy to see him and he told her so.

"If you wanted a brass band, you should have given me fair warning."

"You would have told me not to come."

"That's true," she said, more gently.

She accepted one of his Camels, but refused the lighter he extended, lighting her cigarette with a big wooden kitchen match.

"I was in the neighborhood, so I just thought..."

"How touching!"

One hand behind her back, she stood with her back against the door and contemplated him with an ironic smile. She clearly had no intention of making things easy for him. Not finding the right words, he pleaded with his eyes. But she misread his silence and turned pale.

"Oh, so that's it! You have your nerve. But you've wasted your time, my friend. There'll be none of that."

"You're crazy!" He cried, as her meaning dawned on him. "I don't want anything from you. I only came to explain..."

"What? What do you have to explain to me? The damage is done. Your explanations won't change anything. And anyway, have I blamed you for anything? What happened was what I allowed to happen."

"That's not true," he stammered.

"Your vanity is astonishing."

She turned everything he said against him. Just for fun, she made him lose the train of his thoughts, and made him look ridiculous.

"Be quiet!" he shouted. "Let me speak, let me explain myself. You're turning everything I say upside down! You do it on purpose!"

"OK," she said calmly. "You have five minutes. After that, I have to make supper."

She sat on the edge of the bed and glanced pointedly at her watch.

All the pretty phrases he had prepared, what had happened to them? Did they get lost between floors on the way up? Had the draft blown them outside when Mireille slammed the door? Without those pretty phrases, he was like a nearsighted person without glasses, a cripple without his crutch. Mireille kept on smiling that scornful smile. When she looked at her watch again and announced "One minute," he almost hit her.

"Look, my dear Frank, if I don't help you, you'll never get around to saying anything and your time will be up. I am not pregnant. Does that put your mind at ease? There, you see, now you can leave with a clear conscience."

The game was becoming too cruel for Frank not to understand. Wounded pride must have its revenge, have its turn at humiliating somebody.

"Mireille, let's be friends."

He immediately perceived the enormity of his plea. She burst out laughing. But he had resolved to ignore her sarcasm.

"Mireille..."

"No!"

She got up abruptly, went over to the window, and turned her back to him. He recalled her trembling in his arms, high spirited as a pony escaped from the corral, feeling alive for the first time. It had been through him that she had become conscious of herself for the first time.

"No," she repeated, firmly. "Everything is quite simple. We tried to pull the wool over each other's eyes. For a few hours we let ourselves be taken in by our own games, and we were so happy, thinking we had fooled each other, a little like allies. That's why it was all so easy. Don't you understand?"

There was a hole big as your fist in this pretty line of reasoning, but he couldn't quite put his finger on it.

"Have you finished playing this tragedy?" he asked, irritated.

"Tragedy!" she said, fiercely, turning around. "I only wish. Then we could applaud, cry bravo, and go away, our minds at peace. But the game is over. What did you expect to gain by coming here? That we could glue the pieces back together? Start again? Then, every time you find your solitude unbearable, you'll come back and look for me, the good, the sweet, the agreeable Mireille, so you can unload your burden and go away smelling as sweet as a flower? And what about me? What if I've had enough of being the sweet, the good, the agreeable Mireille? It's no use looking at me like that. It's true, buried in every person, there's a little child, still intact in all his fears and his ferocity; a little child capable of cheating, of betraying, yes, of *betraying.* Well, all right! What, then? You don't know what it is to betray?

Her eyes had slowly filled with tears. When Frank grabbed her and held her in his arms, she fell against his chest, like a frail little old lady. He held her against himself for a long time, without speaking, without moving. For the moment, that was enough. He was savoring his happiness, feeling himself come back to life in that sweet maternal aroma that emanated from her. He no longer feared his vulnerability. Oh, to have the courage of a god and the heart of a man! Softly, cautiously, he turned her toward the window. Outside, the calm of the evening heralded the arrival of spring. There was no longer anything phantasmagorical in the vaulted and angular shadows of the old houses where, shut up behind the shades, the daily business of life went on without asking questions. It wasn't even desire that prompted him. He was happy, relaxed. There would be time, a long time, for love. Yet eternity is nothing but the fleeting moment caught in mid flight, imprisoned, separated from its temporality. Like all dreams, this one shattered on the stumbling block of reality when, with an abrupt movement, Mireille detached herself from him.

"You're still mad at me?" he asked, discouraged.

But she shook her head with a sad, weary motion and he sensed that she was prey to some intense anguish.

"Your brother?" he asked timidly.

"You wouldn't understand."

Why wouldn't he be able to understand? He wanted to understand. He wanted to help her. She would have to at least let him help her.

"Just what's the matter with all of you? There you are, one of you pulling me by the arm, another by the leg. You're determined to help me even if you have to tear me apart while you're at it."

She smiled the way people do when they want to demonstrate strength they don't have, revive the remains of courage and pride, muster a kind of ruined nobility. Suddenly, she pulled his hair backwards and gazed at him fiercely.

"You listen to me without saying anything," she said. "You think I can't see what's what, that I dream about what we were for centuries: a race of kings and patriarchs. You think that all I have left is what you're willing to offer me; you come to me arms outstretched, hands full, thinking I'm a poor madwoman to close them back up on what they're holding and you're the only one who could put my house back in order. You're full of good intentions, but I'm the only one who knows where the shoe pinches. Everybody has to clean up his own mess. If I left it to anybody else to do, I'd be completely lost."

An unanticipated tenacity emanated from her, manifesting itself in the sharp, impersonal expression on her face, the air of one suffering from gangrene and determined to endure the amputation that will save her life. She was no longer the little girl whom he need only enfold in his arms for her to become just like him. He needed to find a weak spot, take her by surprise, since she had become too audacious to be attacked head on. Was Saul no longer a threat, then? This well planned blow made her lose her neat equilibrium. She wavered on the taut slippery thread of her new courage, but caught her balance.

"I don't know," she said, crushing her cigarette out in the sink. "In any case, I'm on my way. I've fooled myself long enough without changing anything, but now, change is indispensable. I had lost the habit of thinking for myself, with all of you who were more than willing to think for me, and it's always hard to reestablish a good habit once you've lost it. You say to yourself, let it be, it'll all work out. But nothing works out by itself. It just goes from bad to worse."

She raised her head and looked at him, her eyes lost, looking for the reflection of her newborn self, so fragile that it would take very little to destroy it.

"Mireille, if you don't break away from your brother, you'll destroy yourself along with him."

He had spoken sincerely, logically, and he had no idea why she was looking at him with such hatred. Her face turned pale, her eyes, piercing and narrow. There was nothing left in those features but the old atavistic hatred of the defeated.

"You speak with such smug self-assurance," she said in a low, biting tone. "You who sow well-being all along your path. No, don't interrupt me. You think you have nothing to do with all of that? Didn't you make him feel ashamed of his threadbare clothes? With your indifference, your way of ignoring him, and worse, your contempt, did you not let him know that he would never be master again in his own house? Go away."

These last words were shouted in a rage that disfigured her.

"When a man is killing himself, don't you think that we should at least wonder what we did to him? Go away. The show is over. Change of program."

The sobs which, helplessly, he had heard rising in Mireille's throat, burst forth. Blinded by her tears, she yanked at his overcoat. There was a dry ripping sound. He pushed her away, roughly, and unhooked it himself. The entire lining of the sleeve had come apart.

"If I leave now, I'm never coming back," he told her.

Her only answer was to open the door wide. Disconcerted, humiliated, he grabbed her fists and pulled her to him, despite her resistance.

"*I'm going, you little bitch. But you'll regret it,*" he hissed in her face.

"Good riddance," she shouted, slamming the door behind him.

Chapter 20

The door shook beneath Saul's pounding fists, but it did not open and there was no answer from inside.

"Can't you see she's not there, Smarty?"

Recognizing Denise's voice, he turned around to see her standing in her doorway, framed in a funnel of light, staring at him with a mocking expression.

"Where did she go?"

"She didn't bother to tell me."

She was getting her revenge, the slut. She knew perfectly well where Mireille had gone and was enjoying keeping him on tenterhooks.

"Would you mind going to see if she's in the bathroom?"

"Maybe you'd also like me to go up on the roof to see if she's feeding the stray cats? I'm telling you she's not here. Maybe she went to the movies. She sure could use some entertainment, the poor kid."

"The movies! I didn't think of that. Yes, she must have gone to the movies."

"See that? No need to get upset, is there now? Why don't you come in and wait for her here? There are drafts in the corridor. You can hear everything from inside here. You'll hear her come in, don't worry."

Denise's offer was hardly tempting, but the show at the cinema wouldn't be over before midnight, and he had an entire hour ahead of him. He resigned himself to spending it in Denise's room. After all, deep down, she wasn't so bad as all that.

'How do you like my little nest? Now don't go out of your way to be agreeable. You could sprain your tongue."

"Be quiet."

Straining his ears, Saul listened for the least sound coming from the corridor. There was nothing but silence. After only two minutes, Denise extended her pack of Gauloises to him, but he shook his head, rolled himself a cigarette of his own, lit it, and crushed the match out on the floor without offering Denise a light.

"Look, Professor, do you act like this with everybody or is it a special sign of affection for me? Thanks a lot," she said, catching the box of matches Saul threw her in mid-flight.

"Look, Denise, let's get things straight. I'm not a client, so there's no sense in knocking yourself out. Be quiet, Relax. It'll do you good."

"Gee whiz! If they were all like you, I'd be eating in the Soup Kitchen. Never mind. OK. I'll keep my mouth shut."

Saul settled into the armchair and smoked in silence, ears straining towards the door. Everything was quiet. Sitting on her bed, Denise rustled her peignoir and he started at the sound.

"How do you expect me to hear anything with all the noise you're making. Are you sure she went to the movies?"

"Look, I'm no fortune teller. I just said: maybe."

In Saul's feverish mind, anxiety reigned. Speculating wildly, he imagined Mireille lying in an alley somewhere, a dagger in her back, strangled, raped, or struggling with all her strength, getting weaker by the moment, calling on him for help. He closed his eyes and rubbed his face to chase the nightmares away. "She's with the American," he told himself. Never would he have believed himself capable of such hatred. He inhaled a big puff of smoke that cut into his chest like a blade and made him choke. A dry cough shook his frame. Denise perked up her ears as if responding to a familiar voice.

"You got TB?" she asked quietly.

"Why not the pox as well," he answered, strangling. "I just swallowed the wrong way."

"Do you want me to hit you on the back?"

Leaning over, almost doubled up, his handkerchief

swiftly pulled out of his pocket and held tight over his mouth, Saul was unable to answer. The fit came to an end. He rolled his handkerchief up in a ball and stuck it back in his pocket.

"It's nothing. A bit of bronchitis. I really shouldn't smoke."

"That don't sound like bronchitis," said Denise, with the air of one who knew.

"You would know better than..."

He began to cough again; smothering, his voice sounded strangled as if emerging between spasms of vomiting. His handkerchief was already soaked. Denise didn't take her eyes off him. He would have liked to be able to tell her to turn away, not to watch while he was suffering helplessly at the mercy of whomever, of whatever. But the cough gave him no respite. He was flooded with cold sweat; he trembled with chills. He was as weak as a newborn child. When he finally managed to calm down and lie back in the chair, he saw the red spots in his handkerchief. "Must have come from my nose," he said to himself, not really believing it for a minute. "It's nerves. I'm at my wits' end, anxiety, lack of sleep." He didn't resist when Denise took his cigarette away and crushed it out on the floor. He even accepted the glass of alcohol she offered him and drank it slowly. The warmth returned to his body, and with the warmth, a bit of energy. He told her brutally:

"I didn't ask you for anything; don't expect any thank yous from me."

Denise shrugged her shoulders and coughed in turn, a thick, moist cough.

"That," she said, with evident satisfaction, "is bronchitis."

Then, she took a magazine that was lying open on the table, stretched out on the bed, her chin settled into the hollow of her hand.

"It's a quarter after," said Saul, suddenly.

"Can't be. We didn't hear any bells ringing."

A few minutes later, the bells of the church rang the

quarter hour. Denise raised her head, smiled triumphantly, and went back to her reading. That is to say, she pretended she was reading so as to be able to observe Saul without being noticed. He was gnawing on his cuticles, grinding them the way one might grind an aching tooth, in order to avenge oneself. Denise thought: "It's incredible how interested he is in me. There he goes, ruining his beautiful hands, so fragile, so smooth, his fingers so delicate and so strong that you might imagine they had steel casings, a little flat on the ends from so much tapping on the backs of patients, telling them: "take a deep breath and let it out slowly." As for her, it would not be with his ear flat on her back that he would listen to her breathing, but ear, cheek and corners of his lips, no towel, right on her skin, resting, trembling on her large warm breast. Touching her, his fingers would be trapped in the snare of her flesh, electrified, palpitating... He was so close; so close that it would be a sin if nothing happened. How beautiful he must be in the nude! Her lips trembled with desire to kiss his nudity. Crossing her legs, she squeezed her thighs hard so as to savor the sweet sensation evoked by her imagination, then closed her eyes and remained motionless. Her peignoir slipped open, uncovering her Amazonian thighs. Roughly, Saul woke her up, pulling her out of the dream which didn't even cost him a thing, intimating that she should cover herself up.

"Why," she asked innocently, "It's not Friday."

He wasn't fooling her with his insistence on never touching her; she was no dupe. Little hypocrite, he had no need to see women's thighs; he could smell them, breathe them, guess at them, he knew them well enough. She closed the magazine and stretched, watching him from underneath her long eyelashes, wondering if he had not at least noticed how long and silky they were.

"You're not very talkative, for a scholar," she said, suddenly. "Suppose we drink something to pass the time?"

Saul agreed. Judging by the effect of the first, another glass of alcohol would do him good. They drank separately, without clinking glasses. As soon as the glasses were empty, Denise filled them up. The bottle seemed inexhaustible. The bells rang the half hour. Now they were drinking undiluted alcohol, belting it down fiercely, consulting each other with casual glances, nodding agreement. Denise's features had softened. When she kept quiet, she was even kind of sympathetic, and then, he really owed her a little something for having helped him close the deal with the Marseillais. When they got to the next round, he didn't refuse to clink glasses. He was beginning to acquire a taste for the armagnac. It warmed him up. Maybe a bit too much. The alcohol whipped up his blood, made his skin tingle. He took off his overcoat and folded it over the back of his chair, loosened the knot in his tie; but the light was too bright; it burned his eyes, or was it the heat?

"What a pain to have to wait so long," he said, wondering if his voice was really as thick as it sounded.

"You're telling me! I spend my life waiting," said Denise, filling his glass again.

Denise's voice seemed to come from far away.

He closed his eyes to give them a rest. When he opened them again, the room was spinning around. Denise's hair was dazzling, rippling with light, like a spotlight. Just trying to move took a great deal of effort. Even raising his arm seemed a task way beyond him.

The tightening of her elbows to keep herself from quivering was the only motion that might have given Denise away when she heard Mirieille come home. She glanced at Saul to see if he had also heard. His features muddy, he listened, his entire body leaning tensely to one side.

"Shall we have another drink, eh?" she asked in a loud voice.

"Shh!" whispered Saul.

He was listening with eyes wide open. To distract him, she gave him a little kick with the tip of her slipper and laughed noisily: "There you go! Are you hearing voices, or what?"

"Shh!" he whispered again.

Something actually was going on in the other room. The sound of a mouse, a nibbling inside the walls. Denise began to sing at the top of her voice.

"Shut your trap!" roared Saul.

"No, I won't. I'll sing if I want to. This is my place. You don't mind draining my bottle, but when it comes to keeping me company, chatting a bit, zip. What's the problem? I'm not made of straw. You could talk to me nicely. Oh, but the gentleman wouldn't care to debase himself. Look at me! Do I disgust you? The fact is, if I had been born in a different age, I could have been a Pompadour, a Dubarry. Absolutely true--you would have come begging, on bended knees yet. Go ahead, laugh, go on..."

In fact, Saul was laughing, laughing in spite of himself, because laughter tickled his chest and put him at risk of having another coughing fit. "To each his own ideal," he thought, "it only makes sense that a whore would have a whore's dreams." Exasperated by his laughter, Denise, spat all the insults she knew in his face.

"Dirty kike!"

Saul's laugh died in his chest. Gripping the edge of the table, he hoisted himself up. Denise moved back. Everything moved aside before the fog that rose up inside of him and smothered him. His feet were leaden. Denise stood between him and the doorway, whining and saying that he had pushed her into saying things that she didn't mean.

"Get out of the way," he said with a weary voice. "If I touch you, I'll kill you."

She clung to the lapels of his jacket, begging: "Don't go, Love, do whatever you like but don't go."

With a shove that ought to have knocked her down, he pushed her away. But his motions had the slow ineffectuality of motions made in nightmares.

"You can't leave now, you have to wait for Mireille. Sit

down, Love, you can hardly stand up straight any more. I'll keep watch for you. I'll tell you when she comes back. I have the ears of a cat. I'd even hear a pin drop. Saul, don't go."

It was the first time she had called him by his name, and doing so destroyed something very fragile, very sorrowful in herself. She was hanging on to him, swaying with him, bringing her face up close to his, their breaths, heavy with alcohol, mixed together, her eyes searching his, drinking in his hallucinatory gaze. Suddenly he gave her a blow with his elbow that hit her in the breast. She moaned and let go.

"You stink like fish," he shouted.

"That's not true," she roared, "I'm clean. You just smell me, smell me and dare tell me that I stink. Don't push me away! I'm not an animal! Here, drink, drink, empty the bottle, I'll go get more; only don't go."

Her voice died in her throat. Everything was blurry as in a bad photograph. She couldn't hold her tears back anymore. They ran, salty, into her mouth, between lips deformed by begging, and the salt of her tears was bitterness and weakness, hatred and desire, rancor and repression, despair and the thousand ablutions in the bidet, and the slaps in the mouth, and the terror and the revulsions, the splattering of gallons of sperm on her face, the shit from their bellies streaming down her throat... and she was emptying out: a hole filled with salty water was forming in her guts, emptying her, draining her: a hole in her guts that all the kindness, all the charity in the world could never fill up.

She grabbed Saul's head and seized greedily on his mouth. This time, when he swung, the blow hit home and she went stumbling against the bed. The revulsion with which Saul spat on the floor filled her with shame. She grabbed onto his tie, wiping her eyes.

"Don't push me away, Saul. You need me, even if you don't know it. I don't want to hurt you, Saul. Far from it, I want to help you, work for you. You'll be a great doctor, you'll invent magical stuff that'll cure people without causing pain. I'll wash floors, Saul, I'll give you all my money; don't laugh, Saul. You'll need it. Because all the money you have is worthless. Not a penny, Saul, It's counterfeit. Try to pass a single one and you're done for, like a rat in a trap."

Saul grabbed her with his fist and held her at arm's length.

"What are you saying?"

"It's true. I swear it. Now you're like me, from the same stamp. If you squeal, the Marseillais'll buckle your mouth for good: so go ahead and call me a slut again! You have nothing more to say, now! You thought you had it made, you were rich, no one would ever know? A regular choir boy! Really! Well, you don't pick up money in the streets without stooping down."

She started to snicker as she watched him take out his wallet.

"Yes, really, take a look. All the same. Not a bad imitation, the work of a real artist, wouldn't you say?"

Saul gazed at his wallet. So that was why they were all so clean, hardly even wrinkled. And to think, he had never suspected a thing. But he had passed out hundreds of them! Fortunately, they couldn't be traced. But if he had laid out the key money for the apartment... he was bathed in cold sweat from his head to his feet. Then they would have traced them. All his dreams crumbled. Two hundred thousand francs and he was as poor as the most wretched laborer reading ads for luxury cars in the metro during rush hour.

Bent over double, Denise was contorted with laughter. He had to put an end to that laughter. He saw her backing away from him, her eyes popping out of her head, groping for the wall in behind her. She wasn't laughing any more. She was stammering.

"It was so we'd be alike, Saul, just alike..."

With a full fisted punch, as if to hit a man, he struck her right in the chest, so that she collapsed against the bed.

"What did you tell my sister?"

"Right. Let's talk about that!"

Denise tried to get up, but he kept her nailed to the floor.

"That little whore, the entire American army has passed through there. That's a good one! A pretty little whore, that sister of yours!"

She groaned and squirmed to get away from him. He grabbed her hair, and pulled her up to standing position. Then a slap landed full strength on her mouth and made her lower lip burst open. A sensation of *déjà vu* dazed him for a moment, but Denise continued to howl, throwing out obscenities in the same breath with Mireille's name. Then, to make her shut up, grabbing a handful of her hair, he pulled her head back, back, farther back. Words came out of her mouth in a gargling sound.

"She's just like me, only me, at least I'm honest about it. I don't hide..."

With a great swing of the head, she let out the cry of the tormented. She had managed to free herself, and Saul found himself standing there, his hand clutching a big fistfull of blond hair that hung limply from between his fingers.

"She's like me," Denise continued to bellow, holding her head between her fists, "you're all like me! Bet she's over there now with her Yank. He's probably slipping her some cigarettes. American ones. No sense doing without when the supply's at hand."

Saul's fists pommelled that swollen face, those bleeding lips, that limp body, without being able to stifle that voice hammering on his brain. The room spun around like a merry-go-round operated by a joyful drunk. In a minute, she'd lift herself up like a wound-up top, only to fall back down, splashing into a well full of ink. Denise's voice, begging now, reached him as if through a mountain of cotton wadding.

"Don't go over there, Saul. You'll do something you'll regret. It's not true. I was lying when I said that a while ago. I always lie. Beat me, kill me... but don't go over there..."

Words no longer had any sense. They swam, they

floated between these walls that were spreading out, stretching out, crumbling. Sounds reverberated in endless echoes. He pounced on that body standing between him and the door. The sounds stopped. Stepping over it without a backward glance, he threw himself out into the hall and onto the door of Mireille's room.

Standing up in the dark at the head of her bed, Mireille listened to the door rattling on its hinges. Trembling, freezing, she was twisting the shoulder straps of her nightgown. Saul's voice, hoarse, dull, broken, howled from behind the door. Lights were beginning to go on in the windows down in the courtyard. Her worst fear, reasonably enough, was that they would call the police. Knocking against the corner of the table, she ran to open up for him. Pushing her back with all his might, he charged into the room and took it in with the single sweeping glance of a madman.

"It isn't true," he said, his voice broken in sobs of relief. "That slut! I knew it! It's not true, you see?"

His arms dangling, suddenly dizzy, he began to laugh softly. Then his blood-shot eyes began to rummage around in the room, cruel, piercing, hungry, in search of prey on which to leap so as to strangle and beat it to death. He was drooling and he stank of sweat.

"Bitch!" he growled, turning around toward Mireille, accusing her with a hate-filled look, "Where were you?"

Mireille stammered: "Saul, lie down, I'll go and make you some coffee..."

Saul's fingers wrapped themselves around her arm and squeezed until it seemed about to break. He didn't hear her groaning, he didn't see the tears prompted by the pain, he didn't see her squirming to get away from him, he didn't feel her nails tearing into his skin to make him let go. He kept on shaking her, howling:

"Where were you? Where were you?"

The ceiling lamp went on and off, disappearing and

flashing back on like the search light on a ship caught in a storm.

"Are you going to tell me where you were? Bitch! Little slut! Say it isn't so. Say you haven't slept with him..."

They were waking up in the courtyard. A child began to whimper.

"Say it. Say it isn't so."

Hiccupping, gasping, blind with pain, Mireille was biting and scratching to make those fingers of steel, rigid as if rusted permanently in place, let go of her. Saul himself was looking at them with a distracted air, as if he couldn't make them do what he wanted. Then, as if in response to the dictates of some vague, obscure acquaintance with the human heart, the words surged up and burst forth:

"Yes, it's true, it's true. I'm even going away with him. It doesn't matter where, as long as it's far away from you. Drunkard! Madman! Let go of me..."

Disarmed, Saul let go.

"You want to know where I was? Imbecile! I was making love with him. You drunkard!"

Mireille's face was burning beneath the smacks he gave her with the back of his hand. "Madman, you're insane, they should lock you up, they'll put you in a straight jacket!"

Taking hold of her fists, Saul pulled her to him, so close that his breath, heavy with alcohol, filled her with disgust.

"Liar. You're lying. It's not true. Say it isn't true..."

"Yes, it is true. It's true. It's true."

Biting his hands, she carved red words into his flesh. She managed to free one fist and began, blindly, to pound him with blows. He wavered, hardly able to stay on his feet. Feeling his way with his free hand, he wrapped it around Mireille's arm again, in the same place that was already hurting so much she almost fainted.

"It's not true," he stammered in a pleading voice. "They told you to tell me that just to hurt me. But it's not true.

Is it? Say it isn't true."

One merciful moment and he would have fallen kneeling at her feet.

"Madman," she whispered hatefully, "they'll lock you up..."

"It isn't true. I know it isn't true..." He pushed her, tottering unsteadily, and though she braced herself, she lost her footing. The edge of the bed forced her knees to bend and she fell down backwards, dragging Saul with her, his hands wedged under hers.

"It isn't true," he repeated, his voice nearly gone.

His eyes, two cloudy glass marbles, stared at her without seeing. "Mireille, my little Mireille, my own little..."

His breath came in fits and starts. In his bloodless, twisted face, not a muscle stirred. He suddenly had the face of an old man to go with his gray hair and that terrified Mireille more than the sweat pouring off of his cheeks, more than those eyes staring at her, more than the heat of his burning fever sinking into her, more than those lips that crushed themselves against hers. Even her cries died before breaking out, sucked up by Saul's lips, smothered and consumed by Saul's madness.

In a last burst of fear, gathering together all that was left of her strength, she succeeded in getting her hands loose; but those same hands with which she had been pushing Saul away from her, suddenly wound around him, pulling him to her, drawing his face close to hers and, without fathoming the darkness gathering inside her, without wishing to understand the sudden change taking place in her heart as it opened up, drunken and mad, she was filled with love for him, no longer felt anything but passion for him, who, shadow with no face, had followed her since the first rays of light had dawned. She squeezed him savagely, expecting the arrival of death to reunite them just as the arrival of life had separated them. She closed her eyes so as no longer to see that face, troubled by hallucinations, twisted with suffering, those maddened eyes rolling around under copper-colored eyelids, sensing Saul sliding weakly down to the floor, shaking with sobs, like a child.

Agitated by the tremors this sudden revelation provoked, Mireille sat up and focused on him, without shame, but with such an overwhelming tenderness that it hurt. This man overwhelmed and appalled by the act he had almost committed, exhausted by the effort it cost him to avoid it, was Saul, the head of the family, the patriarch. Kneeling next to him, she took his head in her arms and held it against her breast. They could never look at each other again. His shoulders heaved spasmodically as a dry cough rattled his chest.

"Let me go," he finally said, gently pushing her away.

Then he pulled himself up on one knee, declining her help with a silent gesture and, leaning on the edge of the bed, hoisted himself up to a standing position.

He stood like that for a moment, gathering strength, then went over to the door and left. Not once did he look back.

Leaning over the stairwell, she followed his pale hand along the banister.

"Saul," she cried out, in a choking voice, "come back. We'll forget everything. Come back... Saul, you don't have your coat... you're sick..." The only answer was the sound of the door in the entryway as it closed.

She waited on the landing, unable to move, just staring into space; she knew he would never come back.

The courtyard, once again plunged in darkness, was quiet. Mireille picked up a slip that was lying on the floor and dropped it back in its place. Her entire body ached, especially her arm. She let herself fall down on the bed in a sitting position, stammering distractedly: "Is this possible? How is it possible?" One day after another slipped by, and suddenly time stood still and you looked each other in the face. That day, the past became the future. She had imagined it would be different, the way, hopefully, you examine postcards from distant magical countries, knowing very well that you will never go off on adventures of your own. Gérard and Frank were such countries. Now, having unlocked the secret and gazed at that which it is forbidden to know of men's hearts, Mireille knew that she was damned. The secret would live with her, only leaving her at the end to plunge back into the shadows. The secret: the being that exists in the depths of being, utterly unsuspected, the whip that silently prompts the actions of the clown whose reflection we see in the mirror, the reason for the petrified gaze transmuted into the agonized stare of those to whom it has been given to discover, before they die, who they really are. Once you had discovered the secret, you were obliged to accept your shackles and live chained to it. It was in this place that she had uncovered it, eyelids heavy, copper-colored, sorrowful, lips silent with despair.

Mireille turned over on the bed and lay there, transfixed, as the secret, like a drill, dug deeper and deeper, sinking in and completing her. The time of the chrysalis had come to an end.

When he got to the Gare du Nord, Saul just couldn't go on. Some of the travelers sitting in the railway restaurant held their noses when they saw him flop down on a chair. Looking down on him contemptuously, they thought, "Another drunk." Saul was too tired to be bothered. Even if he died there, on the spot, it would be a matter of indifference to him. He saw himself, split in two, falling, his head on the false marble slab, his skull fractured by the impact. He thought, looking at the figure with the hidden face lying there, "That's me, that dead man." From his wallet, fallen on the floor, the fake thousand-franc notes were scattering out. Around the cadaver, people were whispering, and he thought: "That's me, that cadaver." To die, yes, obviously. But first, he had to know. You did not have the right to go away like that, just a cadaver, without knowing.

In the panel of a mirror, he saw a reflection of himself, automatically smoothing back his hair. He grimaced and looked back at it, his eyes shining with fever. Lifting a pitcher of water from a table, he drank right out of the spout. Then, leaving the station, he hailed a taxi and had it take him to the Rue Vivienne, where Professor Leret lived.

He was finally going to find out. For that second before Leret said "yes" or "no," the meaning of his life would be in the balance. Then he would know.

In front of the double doors with well-polished copper knobs, Saul lost his nerve. It had not seemed such a strange thing to show up on Leret's doorstep at two in the morning. After all, he's a doctor. He must have to get up often enough in the middle of the night. But now it seemed preposterous. Everybody assumed he was crazy. Maybe he really was? Yet never in his life had he felt so lucid. With a precision that did not fail to astound him, he saw everything--everything he had done, everything that he still needed to do so as to restore the balance. "So what if he gets mad at me?" he thought, as he pressed on the bell. The steps approaching the door were heavy and slow, those of a man who has just gotten up out of bed and is dragging along, struggling against sleepiness. "He's going to slam the door in my face and tell me to come back tomorrow," thought Saul. But there won't be a tomorrow. What difference did it make? He would force his way in. He pushed his foot against the narrow strip of light; tense, he waited, listening to the metallic sound of the safety chain being unhooked. Then Professor Leret was there, surprised, standing in the yawning doorway, giving Saul a piercing look through his lorgnon.

"I know you," he exclaimed with wonder.

He was wearing a three-piece suit, and Saul was relieved to see that he had not gotten him out of bed.

"Goldine, fourth year," he said so as to refresh his memory.

"Why yes."

The professor's face lit up.

"Well, come on in, Goldine. Better late than never." He was alluding to the visit that Saul had owed him for months. So he never forgot anything, this old man.

"I don't keep money or valuables at home," he said, replacing the safety chain, "but still, I feel more secure this way; all the more so since there's always the closet where I keep the narcotics. Do you like my Vlaminck?" he asked, raising his head towards a tormented landscape hanging over a small round table in the waiting room. "It's only a copy; I accepted it as an honorarium. Poor fellow. He didn't have a penny... I would have preferred to take something of his to make him happy, but... I like my copy better."

He was chatting with animation, delighted to have somebody to listen to him.

"You'll pardon me if I suggest that we go talk in the kitchen? I was just warming up some milk soup for myself. It helps me fall asleep."

Saul followed him into the corridor, watching that weary, relaxed figure toddling along ahead of him with muffled steps, chattering cheerfully away.

"You see," he said, "I live alone. So I send the maid away after my office hours. I don't really need her because I take my meals at my sister's... She has a son your age who's studying at the *Polytechnique*. One hell of a guy in every respect, but *Polytechnique,* of all things! Five generations of medical doctors... *Polytechnique,* when he could be studying medicine!"

His severity seemed to have completely disappeared, making way for this affability which seemed so natural that Saul reproached himself for not having been able to discern his basic benevolence any sooner.

The kitchen, a large, well-lit room, was at the end of an L-shaped corridor. On the gas stove, in a little aluminum saucepan, the soup was simmering.

"Have a seat, Goldine. Would you like some? There's enough for both of us. If not, I'll have it for my breakfast tomorrow morning."

Saul shook his head. He wasn't there to eat soup. The night was slipping away and the day belonged to others. As

Leret sat down across from him, Saul prepared his questions, watching him eat, his white bowl in front of him, an elbow on the table, like a dreamy schoolboy who's forgotten his assignment and stares back at the teacher, expecting to be harrassed.

"You're not going to ask what brings me here at this hour of the morning?"

"What for? When a man comes looking for you in the middle of the night, it's because there's something urgent on his mind. He'll get around to telling you about it without your having to pester him."

He suppressed a yawn.

"I keep telling my patients to get enough rest, but I'm not at all opposed to skimping on sleep for myself. When you get to my age, sleep becomes a luxury you no longer have time to allow yourself. There are too many things left to do."

He leaned forward and pulled the lower lid of Saul's left eye down. "You know, you look awful. Have you been whooping it up?"

Saul shrugged his shoulders.

"You've been walking around with that for months. Is that why you've been absent for so long?"

Harassment notwithstanding, there emanated from those eyes enflamed by lack of sleep, a penetrating light, illuminating as an opthalmoscope, penetrating into him as if intent on examining even his soul.

"I'm through with school," said Saul, turning his eyes away.

"What?"

Leret swallowed two spoonfuls of soup, one after the other, and remarked with an absent air that it was getting cold.

"Oh well! Then I guess it doesn't matter any more..."

"What? What were you going to say? Like you give a damn!"

"Well, I certainly didn't ask you to come here so we could have a game of chess. Although..." Leret's eyes gleamed with unaccustomed light.

"When a man is on the verge of destroying himself, somebody should at least extend him a helping hand."

He crossed his arms and leaned his elbows on the table.

"Your hands have always intrigued me. Their movements are firm and precise, yet, your wrist has the lightness and freedom... of a musician's. It doesn't take a magician to write a thesis. And it takes more than a diploma to make a physician. What's really needed is that sensibility at the tips of your fingers, that intuition that leads to the cradle of pain, and that--that's something that can't be taught. That is the art of medicine. I thought I saw in you a man who would never compromise with pain, who would never give up the fight. It was because of that, I told myself, that you deserved to be closely watched, to be helped, and most of all, that we should never be too indulgent with you. And now you come here with this childishness: that you're abandoning your studies!"

"I'm confessing that I'm defeated. Is that childishness?"

"Because you know what it is: to be defeated?"

Leaning against the table, Leret got up.

"To admit that you're defeated, is to die, for God's sake! And to win, do you know what that is? That's also a possibility."

He slipped naturally enough into familiarity, and Saul sensed the great tenderness hidden behind the old man's gruff words. But that also arrived too late. A sense of sorrow full of visions of the future clutched at his heart. He gazed at the professor who, very tired, had just sat back down, this man, too old, too lost in thought to notice that he had just spilled some of the warm milk-soaked bread on his jacket, this man, whose lachrymal secretions streamed down his nose without his seeming to care, and whose cutting tone was capable, on occasion, of inspiring terror. This man, who, on the point of passing gently into the night, was passionately looking for a son to whom he could bequeath the fruit of his laborious apprenticeship. Saul could no longer bear the reproach in his eyes.

"Well, I was also full of ideals."

"Party-pooper ideals that you found easy enough to strangle."

"Ideals which, under scrutiny, proved to be lacking substance. Pretty little traps for imbeciles."

"You're the one who's an imbecile!"

The air snapped, as if at the crack of a whip.

"You imagine that the ideal is at your service; that it's supposed to warm your bed in the winter and see to it that your cupboard is always full. A currency that's worthless once it's no longer circulating. Goldine, do you want to be one of those men who, once he's lying on his bier, you look at his face and think: he lived for nothing? I'm warning you--you don't get out of that little game in one piece. But you're not listening to me."

The wave of despair that passed over the professor's face upset Saul. Still, it was a game. Each of them played the role that most suited him. It was important not to let yourself be taken in. You had to remember the stiff comportment of the *chief of staff* making his rounds with his starched, impersonal, impassive air, his revolting way of telling everybody off, of making witticisms at everybody else's expense, of terrifying patients when they disobeyed him. You had to remember him setting himself up as *God.* But the image Saul evoked was made of cardboard; the real Leret was this wizened old man with warm bread and milk around the corners of his mouth who was pleading with him even as he bawled him out.

"All that's very fine," said Saul, "but wake up and look at me. What am I? Where do I belong?"

"So finally, here we are," said Leret, very wearily. "You wish you had inherited a fortune. A business establishment, maybe. My poor child! No, I'm not making fun of you. I have the right to call you my poor child... The only heritage to which you are entitled is the fertilized egg you grew out of, and all that the men who came before you have done, whether good or bad, matters little. It's up to you to clean up and put things in order. In this life you can never stop struggling, never turn aside for a single minute if you don't want to lose your footing, founder, never come back up to the surface. Goldine, if you're looking for an ideal, it's what you're made of!"

He seemed to want to say something more, but resigned himself to a gesture of extreme lassitude, extreme discouragement.

"And little Moishe?" asked Saul, triumphantly. Wasn't this the proof that he, Saul, was right. He expected a gesture of impotence on Leret's part, a concession. But the professor lifted his head, and at the ray of light that suddenly spread over his face, Saul's chest tightened with apprehension.

"Just so. OK. Let's take the case of little Moishe; a perfect example. He fought like a lion; you had to see him! He's in the best tradition of his race, that fellow. He's not about to be done in. He shouts: 'When I'm good and ready, not a minute sooner!' We thought he was done for, didn't we? But that little guy, he wasn't ready. It's fellows like him who keep the world from falling apart. Two years at Royan, and he'll be as good as new. Hey! What's the matter?"

Leret had gotten up abruptly. Despite the anguish that he was barely able to conceal, he was once again, the master, the *chief* who gave the orders and expected to be obeyed. He grabbed Saul's fist."

"Idiot!" He cried. "What have you done to yourself? Take off your jacket..."

With his skillful old hands, he tried to help him.

"Let me go," ordered Saul, regaining the upper hand.

The old doctor let his hands fall back down at his sides.

"As you wish," he said.

"It's nothing. Malnutrition and lack of sleep."

"You don't say!"

Saul no longer saw the old man bent over him full of concern. He saw Moishe stretched out in the sun, smiling at the sea, building his future without bitterness; and that vision was more atrocious to him than his own failure. It was unfair!

"Let me go," he shouted, with strength renewed by rage. "It's too late!"

"Yes," said Leret. "I'm afraid it really is too late."

On his face, there was the profound sorrow of resignation.

"And how many are there like you for every little Moishe who manages to hold on? Alas, we forget that man is not a god and we cannot crucify him without engendering his hatred. We bind him with promises that apply only to him. We cheat from the very beginning. But he insists on a return for those promises."

He muttered to himself as he walked Saul back out to the door. He walked ahead, as usual, but no longer upright and sure of himself. His curved back projected a deformed shadow onto the wall.

"And you're out without an overcoat... and I can't even lend you mine, you wouldn't get into it... Goldine," he cried in the doorway, "Goldine, listen to me..."

But Saul wasn't listening any more. He didn't hear anything but the noise of his steps in the stairway.

A new day. He was still alive. The war is over. The morning heralds a new life.

"On that day, I'll put an end to your slavery."

Too many promises. One more promise had changed the face of the world. The face of the world is in ashes.

"The daughters of Lot made their father drink wine and one by one entered into his tent so that his race might be preserved."

Thus thought Saul as he walked straight ahead,

shivering with cold in the humid dawn, no particular destination in mind.

Trucks full of produce rolled along the boulevard. A pack of newspapers, thrown out by a cyclist, hit the sidewalk. On the first page: so-and-so found... searching for such-and-such... no more Saul; finished, disappeared. Torpor and fever forced him to slow down. There was no hurry. When you're done for, you have all the time in the world. Done for, more's the pity.

In the luminous dawn sky, a great day, full of new events, changes, beginnings; people would air out closets full to bursting with memories and trot out the Moishes, all cleaned up, whitewashed, bursting with life. It bode well for Marcel and Simone, looking beatifically into each other's eyes; not for Denise lying in her room, her skull caved in on the corner of the iron bedstead; not for Professor Leret who would be keeping office hours from two until four, and who had just discovered a secret chamber. But for the American, ever prospecting for advantageous friendships, for Mireille, free at last, the morning was off to a good start. New corpses, new lives. And for everyone, at the proper time, the fulfillment of that contract signed at birth, six feet of earth. The present closing in on itself, dying as it was born, fucked up ahead of time.

At the end of the street, there arose the sound of clattering iron works, a cackling of poultry, the hubbub of les Halles at five o'clock in the morning. In the stalls, rabbits freshly killed, gleaming with blood, lay like newborn children on sheets, pigs' heads coiffed with parsley, red radishes stuck in their mouths. At the corner, a bistro called *Aux Déchargeurs* offered a warm retreat where a person could recover his strength.

Moving easily around behind the counter despite his considerable girth, the boss was making a gruyère sandwich, distributing paper cones full of fries, pouring out glasses of white wine. Four *déchargeurs*, or porters, probably out of work, were sitting at the counter, near the entryway. They squeezed in a bit so Saul could get by, and followed him with curious looks to where he stopped, at the end of the counter.

It didn't take Saul long to figure out the meaning of those looks, which became narrower and sharper as they settled on him. His well-cut suit of fine wool, his new gold chronometer caught their attention, hypnotized them, especially the chronometer.

"They're wondering what the fuck I'm doing here," thought Saul, sensing their looks, shorn of benevolence, focused on him. He ought to have left right then, gone elsewhere or nowhere, just left. Except he didn't have the strength to move. What energy he still had was quickly burning up. He held onto the zinc countertop, realizing that if he let go, he'd fall. "A glass of port will pick me up," he thought, and, trying to sound steady but only managing to reduce the trembling of his voice, he ordered the port and a paper cone of fries. The toughs didn't take their eyes off him. His hands were too white, his fingers too tapered, his skin too tender. Their hands were square, knotted, hairy, covered with calluses and scars.

"Port? And fries?" repeated the café keeper with an incredulous expression.

At the end of the counter, they were snickering and elbowing each other.

"Are the fries to take out?" continued the café keeper.

Shrugging his shoulders with the air of a man who's seen it all, the boss called in the order of fries. Then he poured the glass of port and set the glass down in a puddle of red wine.

"Would you mind cleaning the counter?" asked Saul, as he moved his glass.

"If you don't like my counter, nothing's stopping you from taking your business elsewhere."

"Monsieur thinks he's at the Maxeville," said one of the workmen in a falsetto voice. Monsieur is slumming."

Saul ignored these sarcasms as if they hadn't been

addressed to him personally. He thought: "Would they think they were so clever if they knew that I'm done for?"

"As for the puddle, wipe it up yourself, your majesty."

Saul raised his head and looked into the bitter, hateful eyes fixed on him. He took out his handkerchief and wiped up the wine. Then emptied the glass of port. Now there was nothing left to do except pay and leave. But he didn't budge. These insults gave him some kind of perverse pleasure.

"The same," he said, sliding his empty glass over.

The proprietor poured, not saying a word. With an anxious eye, he watched the muttering porters.

"Look, these guys don't like the looks of you," he confided, leaning Saul's way.

"It's OK. I don't like theirs either. We're even," replied Saul.

A new surge of sweat soaked him from head to foot. A wave of dizziness swept over him and he held tenaciously onto the edge of the counter. When he opened his eyes again, he met the gaze of the café-keeper, who, as he wiped his glasses, was watching him with a hostile expression. Silence prevailed in the little over-heated café. All eyes were leveled on Saul. "There you have it," thought Saul, terrified, "I'm going to croak, right here in front of them." Another wave of dizziness blinded him. Everything began to spin around. He thought he was going to collapse but, thanks to an effort of pure will, got hold of himself, hoisted his elbow up on the counter and held on by dint of sheer desperation.

"You remember that little snot who came in here the other night with his chick?"

"The one we had to scrape off the floor with a shovel?"

They were trying to frighten him with their wisecracks. Saul felt like laughing. Toughs who would shit their pants at the sight of a syringe in the frail white hand of a medical student. Yet, the steely muscles that rippled under their tee-shirts could break a man in two with hardly any effort. If you pushed them too far, they would be capable of anything. Saul felt a perverse fear seep through him, less at the sight of those muscles than at the thought that was taking shape inside of him. Here was the answer he was looking for. As the hatred in their eyes became sharper, the answer became more acceptable. As long as he didn't let them get the upper hand... But then, he had to let them get the upper hand. It was more than an answer, more than a solution--it was an inspiration!

The proprietor shot uneasy looks from one end of the counter to the other. His instinct for danger seemed to tell him all he needed to know about the mute negotiations being conducted by means of furtive glances between Saul and the porters.

"Listen, buddy," he murmured, leaning toward Saul, "This is no place for you. Shove off, OK, before things get ugly."

"Pour me another glass of port," said Saul.

"It's for your sake that I'm saying this. It's your skin they're after."

"Hey, your lordship!" called out one of the porters, "I suppose you don't give a damn about the unemployed, or you'd buy us all a drink!"

Saul slipped his hand toward his wallet, but hesitated. To pull it out in front of all those hungry eyes, stuffed with bills—talk about inspiration! Cheating to the very end with counterfeit bills. For a moment, he savored the idea that flight might still be possible; then he pulled out his wallet. He had placed his bet.

"Give them what they want," he said, setting his wallet on the counter, in plain view, resting his hand carelessly on top of it.

"Now that's a real buddy!"

The ringing voice cut through the air like a death knell. Saul knew that his bet was covered. Only the cards were marked. In this game, there would be no winners. He put his wallet back in the inside pocket of his jacket.

"Drinks all around," he said to the café tender, who, evidently furious, was giving him his change. Although he pretended to be following the motions of the boss as he filled the glasses, it was really the four men at the end of the counter that Saul was watching, beneath his lowered eyelids. They were elbowing each other, talking to each other in lowered voices, but their eyes were riveted on the spot where, inside his jacket, Saul had stashed the fat billfold, filled with the stuff of their dreams. They had hands like wing-nuts that could squeeze the brains out of a man's skull as easily as you would squeeze a blackhead. Saul suddenly realized that he was examining the instruments of his death with the eyes of an executioner, not a victim.

Finally, one of them left. A few minutes later, another followed. They'd wait outside for him to leave, the jerk with the pretty clothes and the sumptuous gold chronometer, strolling around with a wallet full of bread, shoes, blankets and love. The game was about to begin. No. The game was almost over. Only a trump card could change the outcome: he could make a hasty exit, lose himself in the crowd milling around in *les Halles*, get the cop on the beat to take him down to the station. But Saul preferred his first inspiration. He could stand outside himself and speculate on the details of his demise. He examined and chose with care, from the perspective of both executioner and victim, the mechanism of his death. Their big stubby fingers, covered with scars that flattened and whitened around their glasses. They were waiting. One of them, afflicted with emphysema, was breathing heavily, mouth open

With the slow, lazy gestures of a gambler, Saul took out his billfold again and pulled out another bill. He had in mind some nebulous idea of something else he had to do and that his hands were accomplishing, to his relief. Now, he only had to be sure their eyes were still on him, their hungry eyes like unsheathed claws ready to close over his hands.

A market vendor who had just come in and was sipping from a glass of black coffee let out a whistle.

"Well, aren't you a brave soul!" she exclaimed, watching as he put his wallet away. There you go, wandering around with all that dough, and the guy who collects for the gas company just got his brains beat out not two days ago."

"Allow me to buy you a drink, ma'am. You can drink to my health."

"You're too kind. Boss, a brandy. Up to the top."

The smell of dairy hovered around her. She wore a big white apron over her navy blue coat. She was a vendor of cheese and eggs. Saul could just see her tomorrow, in this very spot, shaking her head. "To think that I had just drunk a brandy to his health, the poor kid. What a dirty shame!... A nice likable little fellow like that."

There was no sound to be heard except the wheezing of the guy with emphysema at the end of the counter. The café keeper seemed petrified. The kind vendor cautiously poured her brandy into her coffee.

"All right, Boss, pour us a drink. It's my birthday."

In the thick silence, the words echoed with such an impact that Saul was startled by the sound of his own voice. The café keeper did not pour any drinks. He scratched his ear, looking perplexed.

"Listen, mister," he finally said, in an anguished voice, "I don't want any trouble in here. I'm in business, I can't afford any trouble."

"There won't be any trouble."

Saul was exhausted. There was no longer any reason to wait around. Everything was ready; each of them knew his part and was only waiting for his cue. Soon all scores would be evened, all errors rectified. Everything would fall into place. Summoning up all the strength he could still muster, Saul dragged himself over to the door.

The cheese seller caught him by the hem of his jacket.

"Is something the matter, young man?" she asked.

He would have liked to disengage himself and straighten up with a neat turn of the shoulder, but he no longer even had enough strength to do so convincingly. With the movements of a dying man, more a wish than a gesture, he pushed her hand away.

"I'm OK," he said, as he left.

The cold lashed Saul in the face and braced him up a bit. On the sidewalk to his left, strewn with crushed vegetables and the heads of poultry, one of the porters, waiting for him, was pretending to tie his shoelace. The other one would not be far away. To the right, the entry to the Etienne-Marcel metro station, warm and protective, was filling up with sellers carrying crates, among whom it would have been so easy to lose himself. To the left, where the crowd was thinning out, some narrow stinking streets opened up, streets where large families crowded together in one-room apartments, streets haunted by impoverished old whores and two-bit pimps. A blind old man was selling shoelaces, shaking a tin cup and asking in a plaintive voice: "black or white?" The words took on a strange significance for Saul: last chance before *no man's land?*

Everything was ready and plotted out ahead of time. Saul walked into a narrow, silent street. The shutters were still closed, the inhabitants sleeping. Saul dragged himself along with difficulty, brushing the wall with his hand, listening for sounds coming up from in back of him; quick, confused steps getting louder and more distinct. He forced himself to take a few more steps but he felt so weak, so tired, he was shivering so, with blood flowing out of all the wounds in his soul. A gray sky was hanging down like a dirty sheet between the rooftops. He had been mistaken; this last new day would not be a beautiful one. The angry footsteps, steps of the hungry, echoed in behind him. He stumbled over a paving stone sticking out above the others and stopped, out of breath, leaning against a wall. It would have been tempting to say: "Saul Goldine, wake up, you're going to miss your class." You might have proved to him that it was all nothing but an absurd dream, and that life did, after all, make sense. But he was beyond the dream. His body was about to collapse, bent over double on itself like a flat inner tube. Six legs, or maybe ten, or a thousand, were rapidly bearing down on him; in behind him there was a mass of men with hate-filled faces and the hands of stranglers, because he was their hunger and the hatred of hunger and the cold in their souls.

Confronted with immediate danger, his legs were energized by a wave of strength. If he could make it through another hundred meters, the *rue Saint-Denis* would absorb him into its animation, its crowds of people, would snatch him from the hands of these hunger-driven killers. But the real test of will consisted in not moving, in simply standing and waiting. The steps came to a halt. During an eternity of expectation, nothing happened. He clamped his jaws together to stop the chattering of his teeth. Then, provoked, encouraged by his immobility, the steps resumed their forward momentum; the hammering was close by... Somewhere in the sky a mountain crumbled, the stones poured down on his head, his shoulders, his chest, his back. The stubby fingers rummaged through him, penetrated into him. A hairy arm strangled him, bending his head back until the sky turned upside down. A clipped blow to the chin made him bite his tongue and taste the warm bitterness of his own blood. The kick of a steel-tipped shoe in his lower belly forced a suffocated cry from him and he toppled over in a limp pile, his head on the edge of the sidewalk. With a bloody look that stained the gray sky with red, he saw the buildings wobbling and closed his eyes. From far away, the muffled din of life from the great market reached him. In a last spasm of agony, he saw himself, dressed in white, bending over the bloody thighs of a woman in labor, turning the shoulder of the infant to help it out into the world; then holding it suspended by the ankles, gleaming with his mother's gift, waiting for the first cry of birth and pain to be heard, for the child to take his first breath of the air men breathe; waiting to be himself as well, delivered by this cry, signaling the responsible accomplishment of this human task. The newborn howled as, simultaneously, a groan escaped from Saul's lips: "Mireille..."

And night covered the sky.